Spin
Doctor

By Leslie Carroll

SPIN DOCTOR
PLAY DATES
TEMPORARY INSANITY

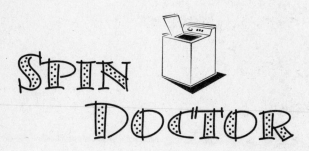

SPIN DOCTOR

Leslie Carroll

AVON
TRADE

An Imprint of HarperCollins*Publishers*

HarperCollins books may be purchased for educational, business, or sales promotional use. For information please write: Special Markets Department, HarperCollins Publishers Inc., 10 East 53rd Street, New York, NY 10022.

FIRST EDITION

Interior text designed by Elizabeth M. Glover

Library of Congress Cataloging-in-Publication Data

Carroll, Leslie Sara.
  Spin doctor / by Leslie Carroll.—1st ed.
    p. cm.
ISBN-13: 978-0-06-059613-2
ISBN-10: 0-06-059613-9
1. Women psychotherapists—Fiction. 2. Female friendship—Fiction. 3. Apartment houses—Fiction. 4. New York (N.Y.)—Fiction. I. Title.

PS3603.A77458S67 2005
813'.6—dc22   2005016564

06 07 08 09 10 JTC/RRD 10 9 8 7 6 5 4 3 2 1

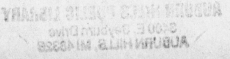

Acknowledgments

Spin Doctor would not have been spun without the encouragement, as always, of my wonderful editor Lucia Macro and my indefatigable agent Irene Goodman. Thanks are due to Rebecca Scarpati and my cousin Laurie Weinberg, for providing "shrinky" info during the novel's early gestation—any errors are my own; to Jan Leslie Harding, for so generously discussing the international adoption process with me; to my tarot guru Brian Vinero, for his inspirational guidance and for vetting my fictional "readings"; to d.f, for making me think way out of the box on this one; and to my apartment building's laundry room, for providing inspiration. Maybe one day all the washing machines will work.

WHITES

1

ME, SUSAN

My husband Eli didn't get home until two A.M. He never bothered to call, and only muttered something— just before he crawled into bed without showering— about a deadline. He writes graphic novels: comic books for adults. I suppose his deadline was more important than our nineteenth wedding anniversary. And if it did finally dawn on him, *No biggie*, I'm sure he figured, *after all, it's not like it's the twentieth*. I stopped sticking "countdown to our anni" post-notes on the bathroom mirror years ago, because Eli said they were an insult to our love. He didn't need the tacky reminders, he insisted. How could he forget the annual celebration of the happiest day of his life? And until last night, I have to admit that was true . . . although I have a sneaking suspicion that the placement of the post-notes earlier in our marriage acted as a positive reinforcement.

Yuck! The dog must have peed on our new sisal. God damnit! I stepped in the acrid puddle on the way to brush my teeth because I was bleary-eyed, having had only four hours of sleep, since I was worried sick about Eli until I heard his key in the door. I think he's become incontinent. The dog, not Eli. Eli's just somewhat immature. That might explain why he's still into comic books. Can a man be in his second childhood at age forty-five? I should know the answer to this: I'm a psychotherapist. I guess it's time to brush up on arrested development.

Our sixteen-year-old daughter Molly came home yesterday with a piercing in what I hope she still considers an obscure location. I regard myself as a fairly liberal mom, but I can only hope that the technician, or whatever they call them, was a woman. Is there such a thing as statutory piercing? Ian, our son, is my only hope for normalcy in this family, although I'm not sure that an eleven-year-old boy who already has a thriving career in musical theatre falls into what the red states would define as "normal." So, thank God, we live in New York City, where his jaded classmates are more jealous than weirded out when he gets to leave school early on Wednesdays to sing and dance on Broadway.

Our apartment is an unholy mess because everyone, including the dog, thinks it's someone else's job to pick up after them and I've always refused to become their full-time cleaning lady. The dog's the only one who's actually got a valid argument. My entire day is devoted to helping other people sort out their messy lives; when I get home, spent and exhausted from internalizing and absorbing the neuroses of a dozen different clients, the last thing I want to do is housekeeping! Gee, it sure would be swell to be able to kick back, have someone else fix dinner, and watch a couple of hours of mindless crap on TV while my children happily do their homework on their own. Is a bit of nurturing for the professional nurturer too much to ask? Complete disavowal of responsibility for a few hours every evening? Bliss! But I am definitely in denial for even entertaining the remotest possibility that this fantasy will ever come true.

It's now six A.M. In an hour it will be time to descend to our building's laundry room to begin the pro bono segment of my workday, helping my clients face, and hopefully resolve, their emotional crises. Believe me, I appreciate the irony.

FAITH

"I slept on Ben's side of the bed last night!"

"Whoa, sister!" This was quite a revelation coming from my seven A.M. appointment, the usually reticent Faith Nesbit. She's been one of my laundry room clients for a few years now, and it's been an arduous uphill climb to get her to finally become comfortable discussing her most deeply personal and intimate details. There were times when I felt like I'd earned my Ph.D. all over again. And after all that, Faith still shies away from bringing up anything that bears even the slightest whiff of S-E-X.

"At the risk of invoking the biggest cliché in shrinkdom, how did that make you feel?" Clichés aside, it was the question I needed to ask, as Faith exhibits a classic, virtually stereotypical WASP tendency to talk around her emotions, rather than about them.

Faith was perched on the edge of the couch as though she might take flight at any moment and soar clear through the gap in the ventilation screen behind the washers, while I cleaned out the lint traps, dumping their individual contents into a ratty white plastic bag. "I'm listening to you, Faith," I assured her. "I just want to get this done before everybody starts coming down here." Even during these early morning sessions—which a California colleague of mine refers to as "kinda therapy," meaning the variation commonly offered to acquaintances, friends, and relatives, as opposed to the more conventional variety conducted with those who are official patients—I find myself cleaning up other people's messes in more ways than one.

"*You* really don't need to go to all that fuss and bother with the lint traps, Susan," Faith chided, her patrician cadences still reminiscent of her Back Bay upbringing, even though she's lived in New York City for decades. "It's Stevo's responsibility." Stevo Badescu is our building's superintendent, and is notorious for slacking off whenever possible. "Whenever you need the man, he's positively nowhere to be found. It must be the Gypsy in him," she continued, as tart as a freshly harvested cranberry.

"I've been living in this building for forty-nine years, you realize, almost a decade before you were born! Ben and I moved in right after we were married in September of 1957—it was our first and only apartment—and I would swear on my mother's Bible that the supers have gotten steadily lazier over the years." Faith studied her wedding ring for a moment. "You know, I have a feeling that Ben—wherever he is," she added, glancing up at the grungy ceiling, "is planning a wonderful surprise for what would have been our fiftieth."

Ben Nesbit had passed away just a few weeks after he and Faith had celebrated their forty-fifth wedding anniversary. They lived down the hall from me at the opposite end of the building. Every once in a while I'd be in the hallway when the Nesbits' door would open and Ben would emerge with a waste basket in hand; Faith would stand at the doorsill, looking at him adoringly. He would give her a gentle peck on the lips before heading the fifteen steps or so to the little closet that conceals the trash chute, while Faith watched his every movement, brimming with affection. Their little ritual always brought a smile to my lips. Eli was never that romantic, even when we were dating. He's never even liked to hold my hand.

I dumped the bag of lint into a metal trash can and smiled at my client's attempt to avoid discussing a difficult subject by changing the topic. Some theorists believe that a therapist is supposed to allow her clients to ramble on indefinitely, even if it results in an avoidance ad infinitum of the important, though frequently painful, issues at hand. They think it's our job to wait it out patiently until the client decides she's ready to confront the hard stuff. But clients are individuals, not theories. And Faith needs a gentle nudge back onto the rails because she's the type of person who feels the need to make demonstrable progress in every session. At least her tangent concerning Stevo had been short-lived. Not too long ago Faith would have remained on the subject of the super's indolence for ten minutes. She was making progress. Progress is good.

"This is really exciting, Faith! I want to hear all about your stretching out like a queen on the king-size," I said, washing my hands and seating myself on the chair beside the couch.

Faith caressed the arm of the sofa, tapping at a stain on the faded floral upholstery with a lacquered nail. "You know, I enjoy working with you Susan because I don't *feel* like I'm getting my head shrunk. It feels more like we're just dishing the dirt down here. I couldn't walk into a therapist's *office*. This setup is much better. No receptionists who are reading their novels behind the front desk and secretly thinking 'that woman who dresses in purple all the time is crazy; no wonder she needs counseling,' no ferns in the corner or modern art on the walls. No fancy diplomas reminding the clients how well educated you are. No credenza displaying third-world artifacts to subtly demonstrate your open-mindedness. But I'm never sure how I feel about having a therapy session on my own couch," she added, reminding me that some years ago, when Ben had finally convinced her that it was time to get a new sofa, she donated this one to the laundry room so the tenants could have a pleasant place to sit while they did their wash.

"You know my tendency for parsimony," she chuckled. "I'm a classic New England tightwad. And I just couldn't bear the idea of spending all that money on a new piece of furniture when I could have had my girl run up a set of perfectly lovely slipcovers. But Ben was right as usual." She gazed lovingly at the mauve and aqua calla lily motif. "I loved the pattern—I still do—but it never quite fit our decor. It really belongs in a Miami Beach condominium."

"You're avoiding again, Faith," I reminded her, noticing that she never appeared to stint financially when it came to her wardrobe. Her pieces were all perennials from the top designers, always in various shades of purple: from lilac to plum, from lavender to violet. "Are you sure you've never cheated on your income tax, because, damn, you can be the queen of evasion."

"Well, you know, my generation never much went in for psychotherapy. We think that it's an admission that you're cuckoo in the head and need fixing, or else it's a silly luxury for silly, idle women; so it takes some getting used to for this old bird."

"Old bird, my ass. You're so active you put us middle-aged slackers to shame." We didn't have too many more minutes left in Faith's session so I had to nudge her again. "Faith, you've been in therapy with me for four years already. You know the drill by now. We can still do some good work before I have to unlock the door." Like a scolded child, she stopped fussing with the arm of the sofa and, much chastened, primly folded her pale, graceful hands in her lap. "You dropped one shoe; it's time to let go of the other. So spill," I prodded jovially. "Last night was the first time that you slept on Ben's side of the bed . . . in . . ."

"Four years," Faith admitted sheepishly, the color rushing into her already rouged cheeks. "I feel rather foolish about it all.

Making such a fuss over it, I mean. A real tempest in a teapot."
She took a breath, then exhaled very slowly before speaking
again. "I have continued to sleep on my own side of the bed—
the left side as you face it, so I can answer the alarm clock as
soon as the damn thing rings—since the day Ben died. I'm
seventy-two years old, Susan. And I've never been very good at
adjusting to change."

Finally, with five minutes to spare, we were talking about
something important. I leaned over and took Faith's hands in
mine. "There's no change without risk. And risks can be painful
because there's always the possibility of failure. Last night, you
took a risk to change old behavior patterns, and . . . guess what!
You survived to talk about it! So, it's not a tempest in a teapot,
in fact. We can get very lighthearted from time to time; that's
the way I like to work down here. But I'm not kidding around.
You took a really big step last night—even if you did it in your
sleep—and you should feel terrific about that."

"Well, I guess you're never too old to learn a new trick, despite the adage. My goodness, I'm chock full of them this morning. Adages. You know . . ." Faith chuckled at her own
unexpressed thought. "At first I felt very guilty—that perhaps
this meant that I was finally moving on."

"Why did progress make you feel guilty?" I asked gently.

Faith studied her wedding ring again. "Because I thought that
Ben, up on his celestial plane, was probably still thinking about
our upcoming anniversary, while here I am, suddenly hogging
our conjugal bed. But right now—at this moment—I must say
that I feel . . . a little bit selfish, but also somewhat *empowered*,
I suppose you could say, as though this is the first time in
decades that I've done something entirely for myself. Guilty,
yes, but like a guilty little pleasure—that's how it feels." Faith
grinned mischievously. "Like having a second helping of dessert

when no one is looking. For years I was Ben's part-time office receptionist and did it mostly because I hated to be alone all day. Separation anxiety, I suppose you'd call it. Ben was my world. I missed him every moment he was out of my sight. When he used to go golfing on Wednesdays, I worried myself sick if he was late in coming home. Then I cared for him after the stroke, even when he didn't seem to recognize me anymore, but I maintained that vigil until the day he died. And because I was never unhappy a day in my life, I didn't actively consider that there might be any alternatives to an existence spent almost exclusively in service of my husband's life and career. Naturally, I'm aware of the Womens' Movement; I read DeBeauvoir and Friedan and Steinem; I just didn't feel as though I were reading about myself. I'm not what you'd call a . . . militant person, Susan. If I'd grown up in Boston in the mid-eighteenth century instead of the mid-twentieth, I would more than likely have been perfectly content to pay the Stamp Tax." She checked her watch, an old Piaget that she thinks keeps far better time than the cheap clock above the door. She's probably right.

"Two more minutes." Faith rose, opened her dryer, and inspected her clothes for dampness. She tut-tutted and closed the door, inserting another quarter for an additional cycle of permanent press. "What the devil is that?" she asked me as I unloaded my washer, transferring an armload of colorful sodden garments to an empty dryer. "Those couldn't be yours, could they? You don't wear those sort of prints."

"Oh, God, no. Besides," I said, holding up a pair of hideously striped pants, "I don't think I could get *one* of my legs in here!" We both laughed at the folly of trying to squeeze myself into the tiny trousers. "No, they're not mine. They're Matilda's," I said.

"Who?"

"Matilda. The little homeless lady who likes to camp out in our vestibule." I raised my hand chest-high. "You know who I mean—she's about Ian's height," I said.

Faith clapped her hand to her mouth in shock. "Her? You're doing a homeless woman's laundry?" I nodded. "The woman who smells so much?" Faith wrinkled her well-powdered nose.

One of the reasons I became a therapist was to try to improve people's lives in some way. And I extend that self-imposed mandate beyond my clients to the world at large whenever I can. "Well, Matilda will smell considerably better with clean laundry," I said. I'm not sure whether Faith's snobbism is generational or cultural, but it does take a bit of getting used to for dyed-in-the-wool Upper West Side liberals like me.

"I always thought the phrase 'clean laundry' was an oxymoron," Faith mused. "Goodness, I shudder to wonder what Matilda's wearing now."

"Actually, she's wearing one of Molly's castoffs." My mother, bless her Eisenhower-era heart, always thinks that Molly should dress like a girly-girl, so she buys her all these cute print dresses, which my daughter would never be caught dead in. Molly's aversion to looking feminine is the least of my worries, however. I wouldn't care if she dressed like Darth Vader as long as she went to class. She's dangerously close to flunking out of high school, her SAT scores were in the toilet, and at this rate the only college she'll get into is the sort of two-year community program that is compelled to offer remedial classes to the incoming freshmen. My daughter is a very bright girl; it's just that at age sixteen she's still going through the terrible twos. I don't expect her to spend her adult life saying "Pass me the scalpel" or "My client pleads not guilty, your honor," but I really never considered that she might end up asking "Do you want fries with that" until it's time for her retirement. The fact that it's looking entirely likely that Molly will never use her inquisitive mind and her expensive education to make much of herself disturbs me greatly, no matter how permissive and progressive I like to believe I am.

Faith looked me in the eye. Her own were the watery gray of the Hudson River during a storm. "Is something the matter, Susan?" she inquired forthrightly. "I'm not one to pry," she continued, breezing past the irony, "after all, my mother was born when Victoria was still queen of England, and she taught me that it's impolite to poke one's nose into one's neighbor's business—but you look tired. Where's that wonderful husband of yours when you need him? And don't tell me he can't stop drawing his silly comic strips in time to come home for dinner." Faith had just hijacked the final seconds of her session; our roles had suddenly become switched and my client had begun to analyze *me*, a countertransference that's not entirely uncommon when both the counselor and the client feel open and comfortable enough to connect on a deeper level. "You tell that man you deserve to be pampered!" Faith exhorted. "That's what I told Ben from the day we were married, and he never gave me a bit of guff about it, no matter how tired he was from looking at his patients' G.I. tracts all day. You make sure Eli comes home at a civilized hour. He should offer you a foot massage and pour you a generous glass of whiskey to give you some zip, and then simmer a nice Scotch broth or a pot of good solid mushroom barley soup to give you some nourishment."

Perhaps unwittingly, Faith had touched a nerve; pushed one of *my* buttons. "Scotch broth? Faith, it's nearly July." Whenever someone is very nice to me, especially when I'm feeling particularly vulnerable, it always makes me cry. "I'm all right," I said, blinking rapidly. I turned my head away so I could regain my composure. "I'm so sorry about that. And unfortunately," I added, looking at the grime-covered clock above the doorway, "it's time to stop so we can let in the masses."

Faith opened her purse and removed a meticulously folded sheet of paper. "I keep forgetting to give you that pot roast recipe you requested. It was the mention of Scotch broth that jogged my memory. I've been carrying this around for weeks." With a conspiratorial whisper, she added, "A pint of good Madeira is my family secret." I glanced at the recipe and mentally tallied the number of fresh herbs I'd need to locate. For an older woman, Faith's penmanship is still remarkably steady, very elegant; very Seven Sisters. She loves to tell people that she attended Smith two years behind Sylvia Plath, so I suppose that she comes by those old-school affectations honestly.

I shoved the recipe in the pocket of my jumper and unlocked the door. Stevo lets me use the laundry room for my private sessions from seven to eight A.M., before it's officially available for the tenants' use. In fact, if I'm down here to open up for the day, it saves him the trouble. Theoretically, my ladies could see me in a more conventional capacity at the women's health center in lower Manhattan where I work on a part-time, sliding-scale basis three and a half days a week—that's the primary source of my bread and butter—but the building tenants are more comfortable here, and it sure as heck is a shorter commute! Also, given the proprietary restraints and code of ethics of the American Psychological Association, because these "clients" are also my neighbors and acquaintances—and they know one another as well—I can charge no fee for my laundry room sessions. As an active placebo, the decor in the laundry room is excruciatingly uninspiring—and, frankly, butt-ugly—but the comforting scents of detergent products—powder fresh, spring flowers, summer rain—have a cleansing connotation. The metaphorical aromatherapy is in fact conducive to my clients' progress. Down here, they're literally airing their dirty linen, washing away real dirt as well as the emotionally damaging detritus of their lives. Down here, there's an opportunity for a fresh start—goodness, isn't that actually the name of a detergent? There's hope of renewal. Besides, even if they did have to pay me for our gabfests, my ladies can't simultaneously do their laundry down on Fulton Street!

"At the risk of sounding 'shrinky'—but there's no growth without risk—you've really turned a corner this week," I told Faith. "You're beginning to recognize that you've been back-burnering or even ignoring things that you might have wanted for yourself over the years. Keep it up! It's okay for now to make things about *you* for a change. You've got a mission, should you choose to accept it. Actually," I amended, "I'm not giving you a choice in the matter. I want you to sit up and take notice—maybe even write it down in a journal—each time you have a moment—however insignificant, or even silly, you think it may be at the time—where you're focusing on your own needs and not your late husband's." I grinned. "I knew Ben too, don't forget. And we both know he would have wanted you to move on eventually. There's nothing wrong with mourning a death, but you mustn't let the grief prevent you from embracing life. Okay? It might seem scary at first because these are untested waters for you, but I promise you, if last night's behavior is any example, you'll rise to the challenge swimmingly!"

Faith graciously chuckled at my weak pun. "Well, Ben always was more progressive than I!" She leaned so far forward I thought her ramrod spine might crack, but she displayed the resilience of a willow. She was going to be just fine. "*My* distaff ancestors were proud members of the DAR. *His* mother was a *Socialist*, you know—and his father was a card-carrying *Commie!*"

TALIA

The following day my seven A.M. client was Talia Shaw. A few months ago, on the heels of an unpleasant divorce, *she'd* approached *me* for counseling, yet it's been like pulling teeth without anesthesia to get her to articulate what's bothering her.

Most clients fall somewhere in the middle of the spectrum when it comes to opening up during their sessions. At one end are the people I think of as the "reds." They're the ones who can talk incessantly; they are masters of volubility, but rarely say anything important for our work together. Their constant chatter without letting me get a comment in edgewise is an active avoidance of potential pain at hearing, or having to deal with, anything that might be unpleasant. At the far end of the spectrum are my "indigos": those who are excessively silent and frequently withdrawn. My questions to them are answered—finally—with barely verbal responses.

Talia is dark blue.

At Talia's sessions, usually I'm the one doing most of the talking. Most therapists rarely reveal something personal during a conventional session in a traditional setting (such as the fern-filled office envisioned by Faith), and even then employ self-disclosure only to further illuminate something directly related to the topic under discussion. But with my laundry room clients, I've found that when *I* open up, they do too. My methods of therapy down there are more unorthodox, more like sharing and dishing, which allows them to feel much more at ease than they'd be in a more classic form of psychoanalysis. With Talia, however, our discussions to date have been decidedly lopsided. While I still have learned very little about Talia's background, Talia knows all about *my* laughably ill-fated forays into modern dance at Bennington, and my own bouts with only child syndrome and bulimia. To look at me now, you'd never guess that I weighed ninety pounds all through college. Maybe my stressful, lifelong weight issues have something to do with the fact that I'd gone completely gray by the time I was thirty-five. Or not. Who knows? I stopped dyeing my hair two years ago and finally made my peace with being youngish and silvery.

"So, what's been up this week? You feel like sharing anything?" I asked finally, after Talia had spent the first ten minutes of her session seemingly absorbed with a bunion on her left big toe, leaving me to wonder whether she wouldn't have preferred seeing her podiatrist.

"Ye-es," she answered, as though speaking in slow motion. Several more moments elapsed during which I expected her to elucidate—or at least to be *somewhat* more verbal. I don't like to sit back and wait too long; though I have colleagues, including my mentoring psychologist Dr. Maris, who believe that the more we try to manage the sessions, pushing our clients into responding before they might be ready, the longer the client will continue their obstructive behavior. And the more control the therapist takes, the less the client assumes for her recovery and well-being. For me, personally, this view works better in theory than in practice.

"Okay." I waited a couple more beats. "I'm listening."

"Do you think I'm aloof?" Talia blurted, her question more or less coming out of left field, since we had started the session by returning to the subject of her divorce.

"It doesn't matter what I think," I replied. "You don't need my approval. Or my condemnation. Do *you* think you're aloof? 'Not that there's anything wrong with that,' as Seinfeld used to say. There's no value judgment connected to being aloof."

Talia cracked a tiny smile. "Because I'm not, y'know. Ballerinas in general get a bad rap that way. I'm . . . I don't know how to put this, exactly. Can I get up?" she asked me.

"Sure. You're not glued to the couch."

"I'm . . . I've just never been comfortable with words. It's one reason why I had to become a dancer. I never could have been anything else. I can only express myself through movement."

"Talia, this may be a horrifying reality to embrace, but unfortunately there will always be too many people out there who are ready to put you down because they can't deal with their own shit, so they're looking for someone to 'blame' for where they are; believe me, you don't need to do it yourself. So how about rephrasing what you just said so that you're not damning yourself?" Talia looked at me blankly. "Well, you could say that you feel that you express yourself *most confidently* through movement." She considered it, then gave me another weak smile.

"So, people think I'm aloof, y'know, because I feel so overwhelmed when they're yakking away about this and that, and all these words are zinging past like they've got wings, y'know, and I just can't join in. I can't think that fast in my head. I think in my feet. It's like I'm from another planet than them, y'know what I mean? So I don't say anything, and people think I'm aloof because of it. If I could, I don't know, *dance* my answers, I'd be . . ."

Talia settled back onto the couch. She'd been pirouetting all the way around the large table in the center of the room while she spoke. "So dance," I said. "Native healers all over the world use dance, chanting, prayer, song . . . whatever works. If dancing your answers works for you, it works for me. Do *tour jêtés*, if you need to. Just watch the fluorescents so you don't hit your head." Talia was visibly relieved.

"Let's pick up where we left off last time," I suggested, after another substantial pause during which Talia stretched her muscles. "We were talking about getting married. *I* was pretty young by today's standards. I was almost twenty-two—"

"Twenty-three for me," Talia said, jumping in as I'd hoped she might once I got the ball rolling. "And I'm twenty-six now. Almost twenty-seven. I was married for just about four years. We met in the Starbucks at Sixty-seventh and Columbus. Lance was a videotape editor across the street at ABC. And a few months ago he decided to leave *me* on the cutting room floor. He told me I was too self-absorbed. Which is pretty funny, y'know? Because if he could have put a mirror, y'know . . ." she opened her legs into a perfect split, "while he was . . . y'know, so he could watch himself . . . and people always say that a *dancer* can't pass a mirror without looking at themselves . . . well, I think he liked mirrors even more than I do." Her expression grew rueful and she returned her focus to the bunion. "When we first got married, he would like to experiment . . . with whipped cream, or honey, or chocolate sauce, y'know? And I thought that was pretty sexy because all the other guys I'd ever been with were more into vanilla sex. I don't mean the flavor—I mean, more . . . y'know?" She rose again and began to perform a sort of interpretive dance, facing the row of washing machines. "More . . . regular. Boring. Uninventive, or *uncreative*, I guess might be a good word. And then I started to realize at some point that Lance was doing all that desserty stuff down there because . . . because he really didn't much care for . . . I guess deep down, he really didn't like who I was. And that was his way of trying to change me."

With a sudden burst of vehemence she kicked her leg up on the top of one of the machines and began to plié with her other leg in second position. "And . . . here I am, not even twenty-seven years old and my life is almost over."

Some major abandonment issues here, perhaps? "That's harsh! So, okay, your first marriage didn't last. But you've got the whole rest of your life—decades—ahead of you, to either meet someone else and try again, or more than one someone else, if things turn out that way. And Lord knows there are plenty of *married* women who would admit that they're feeling unfulfilled— usually in more ways than one." *I suppose I'd fall into that category too, depending on the day of the week.* "You don't need to be married, or even in a relationship, to be *fulfilled* . . . y'know?" I added, parroting Talia's favorite phrase.

"I know that, deep down. That's not it," Talia said, switching legs. "I'm an aging bunhead. That's my problem. Like I told you, my life is almost over."

I regarded her immaculate skin, glossy dark hair, and zero percent body fat. "Why don't you tell me what you really mean by that," I said gently.

There was another long silence before Talia spoke. "Any professional dancer will tell you that Dance—with a capital D—is their life. From the time you're a little kid, you eat, sleep, and breathe it and dream that one day it'll be you up there under the lights. For little girls, the dream usually comes with the tiara and the tutu and the tights. It's your ticket to being a princess if you can just work hard enough. But a dancer—especially a ballet dancer—has a shelf life that's shorter than a quart of milk," she sighed, her voice full of resignation. "I came up through the SAB—the School of American Ballet—and was selected by Peter Martins, City Ballet's artistic director, to enter the corps when I was only sixteen. That's really young to be asked to join the company. So I thought I was going to be a star, y'know? Another Darci Kistler or Merrill Ashley. I was promoted to soloist at twenty. And since then . . . nothing. I've never advanced to principal."

I noticed that when the subject was Dance, Talia became un-characteristically eloquent. It was almost as though she'd re-hearsed the words, just in case she might be interviewed about her career someday. Absent was her hesitation, her self-consciousness about her verbal acuity, and her "y'know" tic.

Placing her hand on the top surface of the washing machine as though it were a ballet barre, Talia began to do *grand batte-ments*. "And y'know why?" She turned to me and waited for a response. "Because my head's too big."

"I'm not sure I understand why you think that has anything to do with it."

"I don't have a Balanchine body," Talia explained.

I held up my hand. "Wait a sec! Hasn't George Balanchine been dead for over twenty years?"

Talia nodded. "But the company body type remains true to his standard. Pinheads. You need a small head." She rapped her knuckles against her scalp the way people "knock wood" as a joke. "And my head's too big: pure and simple. I was good enough to become a soloist but not 'ideal' enough to get pro-moted to principal. So I'm destined to remain a soloist until I grow too old to perform the roles. I've got maybe two more good years—*tops*—before Peter starts looking at the younger dancers and putting me out to pasture. In fact, I think he's started to do that already."

Suddenly, Talia burst into tears. She returned to the couch as though she were approaching a shark tank.

"I'll survive my marriage breaking up, y'know?" she sobbed. "Even though I feel like a total failure. It's hard to deal with the fact that I've been married and divorced and I'm not even twenty-seven. But . . . dancing . . . it's all I've ever wanted to do. More than anything. More even than being married. If I couldn't dance anymore, I'd die. I can't even *do* anything else.

I've been dancing since I was three years old; it's all I know. I never had to have another job. I've never even drunk a Coke that wasn't diet!"

"You're not missing much on the Coke front, actually; I wouldn't fret over *that*. What about *teaching* ballet? I mean eventually."

"Never!" Talia snapped. Her narrowed eyes were filled with utter hatred and contempt. "You know that phrase 'those who can't do, teach'? Only failures end up teaching!"

"Oh, c'mon, you know that's not true. I'm sure there are people leading company class over at City Ballet who have been—and perhaps still are—luminaries." Talia begrudgingly conceded me that point, at least.

It was time to open the laundry room. "That's it for today," I told her, "so you can start focusing on what you want to dance about next week. And you've really got to stop dissing yourself all the time. Bite your tongue when you catch yourself doing that. There's a big difference between acting modest and being self-destructive. God knows I can relate, but I don't have your body or your skills. You're young, gifted, healthy, and beautiful; and bunions aside, you have a world of possibilities at those talented feet."

Talia nodded dutifully, clearly unconvinced. She retrieved her load of leotards, tights, and leg warmers from the washer and tossed them in a pink plastic basket about three times her body width. Balancing the huge tub in front of her, she resembled a pregnant duck, waddling over to the dryer with her ballerina's splayed gait. She loaded the machine and set it to permanent press. "Another thing—but I guess it can wait till next week," she said, studying her reflection in the dryer's porthole as her 100% cotton garments danced in clockwise circles behind the glass. "People seem to find me really vain."

2

ALICE

The first actual laundry-doer of the day was a young woman I rarely saw down in the basement. I think she used to be a nine-to-fiver during the weekdays. All I really know about Alice is that she's an actress, or an aspiring one, and that her grandmother Irene was a former showgirl who was always tickled to tell anyone who would listen that Alice took after her.

The poor girl was struggling to steer a collapsible shopping cart overflowing with garments through the narrow doorway. "Do you need some help with that?" I asked.

Alice knocked the front axle into the door frame. "Shit!"

A couple of polyester blouses slid from the summit of the pile onto the not-exactly-pristine floor and I realized that I should have swept up before I opened the room that morning.

"Yes, help would be good. Thanks," Alice said, tossing me a grateful look and glancing over at Talia. "My head isn't really on straight this morning. I guess I don't want to do this." She stared at the haphazard pile of clothes and her eyes and nose began to redden. "Sorry," she said, looking away, embarrassed to be caught by a stranger in a private emotional moment.

I relieved Alice of her unwieldy cart and rolled it over to the row of washing machines. "I knew your grandmother," I told her. "She was a wonderful woman—and very proud of you." My words released the floodgates; I felt terrible for making her cry again. Alice cast about helplessly for a tissue, and as she began to head toward the bathroom to unspool some toilet paper, I reached into my pocket and handed her a shrink-wrapped packet. "Keep it."

"Thanks." She tried to smile through her tears. "I'm going to need them. These are hers," she added, resting her hand atop the colorful pile of clothes. "Were hers, I mean. I couldn't bring myself to wash Gram's stuff until today. I'm still not sure I'm ready to handle it. But I . . . I have to clean everything before I donate it to the thrift shop. It's only right."

Without bothering to sort the garments, she started to load the laundry into an empty machine, but accidentally knocked her box of quarters to the floor, sending them rolling halfway across the room. "Shit!" Alice exclaimed again. She gripped the handle of the shopping cart and dissolved into sobs.

I draped my arm over her shoulder and helped her over to the sofa. "Why don't you sit there for a bit, okay? I'll take care of it," I assured her, chasing down the escaping change. "Just tell me what cycles you want everything to go on, and I'll load the clothes."

"I'm alone," Alice mumbled into one of the Kleenex. "Really alone. For the first time in my life. It's eight A.M. on Friday. It is Friday, right? Gram's been gone for twenty days, fifteen hours, and forty-nine minutes. Not that I'm counting or anything."

"Do you want to talk about it?" I asked her, and before I could add that I meant privately, Alice was off and running.

"If I weren't performing eight shows a week of this completely irreverent Off-Broadway comedy called *Grandma*

Finnegan's Wake—which is kind of a macabre experience in itself, since Gram's name was Irene Finnegan—I think I would truly go nuts. Every time I think about Gram, I start crying. Pretty unattractive, huh? I play an outrageously flamboyant former *Star Search* winner, so at least I can get away with wearing pounds of eye makeup to mask my swollen lids. When my mascara runs I probably look like Tammy Faye Baker." Alice loudly blew her nose. "I guess I should consider myself pretty lucky since I'm thirty-five years old and Gram's passing is my first real experience with death—other than the dissections I did in high school biology class—which I totally sucked at, by the way."

"It's okay. No one's judging you. Not even on the dissections; the statute of limitations expired years ago. Alice, everyone deals with death in their own way, and grieving is a process." I realized I hadn't introduced myself, in case she didn't know my name, despite the numerous times over the years we'd seen each other around the building. "I'm Susan Lederer," I said, offering Alice my hand.

She shoved her soggy tissue into the pocket of her jeans and apologized for giving me a damp handshake. "Hi, Susan, I'm Alice. But I guess you already knew that. You're the therapist, right?"

I nodded. "*My* grandmother—on my mom's side of the family—was my favorite relative. She was the only one who thought my teen angsty poetry didn't suck and I'll love her forever for it."

"Should I leave?" Talia asked; her discomfort at feeling like an eavesdropper was evident. "I mean I'm not really listening." She had been folding her clothes, but every now and then would stop to shuffle her feet a bit and waggle her hands, drawing little figures in the air. "Don't mind me; I'm just running the steps for *Agon* in my head."

"No, it's okay," Alice said, removing another tissue from the pack. "It's fine with me if you hear. Maybe you knew my grandmother too." Alice focused on the crumpled Kleenex in her hands. "She was my conscience in a lot of ways. Her bedroom's been kind of like a shrine for the past few weeks, because I haven't been able to bring myself to disturb anything. I've been trying very hard to convince myself that she's just on an extended vacation, rather than reunited with my Grandpa Danny up in Heaven, or wherever old hoofers go when they've executed their last shuffle off to Buffalo."

Alice was shredding the tissue into lint. "Gram's bedroom still has her smell—rosewater, AquaNet hairspray, lipstick, damp wool, and mothballs . . . and the scent of her skin too, even though she's not there. She wasn't in that room when she'd 'crossed over,' as Charlesy, her former cleaning lady used to say. My grandmother had a heart attack after a visit to the hairdresser."

"Talk about bad hair days," I joked gently.

"No kidding," Alice sniffled. "I like your sense of humor," she added, cracking a faint smile. "You're not maudlin. Maudlin makes me cry even more. I'm a sucker for sentiment. We're talking basket case. That's why doing *Grandma Finnegan's Wake* is really helping me get through all this. A few of my friends think it's in total bad taste under the circumstances. But I think Gram would have appreciated the irony. She was a real pistol, herself."

"Keeping your sense of humor is very important in times like this. And humor is often a very effective tool in therapy. It sounds to me like you're doing the right thing."

Alice nodded. "I hope so. But the moving on part is really hard."

"There's no timetable," I assured her. "I still cry every time I think about my granny, and she's been dead for fifteen years. My husband Eli still hasn't gotten past being an eyewitness to his dog getting hit by a car when he was ten. Eli, not the dog. The dog was forty-two—in dog years."

"It makes total sense to me," Alice commiserated. "Maybe the fact that I never really got to say good-bye to Gram has something to do with my inability to begin a thorough clearing-out of her possessions. Right after she died, I gave a few of her things to my friends Izzy and Dorian, who knew Gram well, but I didn't start tackling most of her stuff until yesterday. She had two closets and a dresser that were crammed with garments, shoes, and other accessories. And of course I also had to take the sheets off her bed and launder them."

Alice rose from the couch and walked over to the washers. "I guess the sheets should go in hot water, even though they're florals. I'm afraid there's so much stuff that I'm going to hog the machines."

"I'm done," chirped Talia, "so I think they're all yours. First come, first served, right?"

Alice was so deep into her grieving zone that I don't think she heard her. "When I opened the door to one of Gram's clothes closets this morning, I couldn't help falling apart all over again. There was this muted scent of camphor and Shalimar that was pure Gram." She lifted a Qiana blouse in an appalling faux Pucci print of camel, mulberry, and beige from the pile of clothes I was planning to wash on the delicate cycle. "This is really pretty vile, but I swear to God, for a few moments there I started to find it the most beautiful thing in the world . . . despite the unidentifiable stain just above the third button," she added, examining the mystery splotch. "Still . . . it's one thing of hers I'm never going to wear, no matter how much I want to honor her, so after I launder it, it's going to go straight to the thrift shop. She used to volunteer at the Second Chance store over on Columbus Avenue, doing intake. You know, the place that gives the proceeds from their sales to help rehabilitate crack-addicted teenage moms. She befriended the girls too; she took them to museums from time to time and she even taught a couple of them to tap-dance, which was her grand passion. I'm sure it helped to keep her feeling young; she was in her nineties when she died. I tried not to feel jealous whenever any one of those troubled kids who actually came into contact with Gram became kind of a surrogate granddaughter, but there were times when I'd get really annoyed with her because she so generously dispensed souvenirs from her former life as a Ziegfeld Follies girl: boas, gloves, tiaras—all that kind of stuff—as though they were Halloween candy. Anything someone admired, Gram would give to them.

"I think other people's donations fascinated her too. 'One person's trash is another's treasure,' she used to say. That Shakespeare knocker I've got mounted on the door to our apartment: that was one of her finds. She snatched it from someone's bag of donations, put a price tag on it, then immediately purchased it.

"Look at all this stuff!" exclaimed Alice, pointing to the various piles of clothes. "It's the story of a life well-lived, isn't it? Some of her things I can't even put in the washing machine. I'll have to take them somewhere special to be cleaned. In the very back of one of her closets I found a coffee-colored mink stole with Gram's initials embroidered into the lining. It's the wrap that she wore with white opera gloves every New Year's Eve during the 1940s—she looked beautiful in it. I came across a whole bunch of old photos of her wearing it. She looked like a movie star. And wouldn't you know, these stoles are suddenly back in fashion! I also unearthed one of those beaded twinsets from the fifties; two 1960s Marimekko A-line dresses; a red crocheted vest handmade by some friend of hers in the seventies, a heinous purple velvet Sergio Valenti warm-up suit—with shoulder pads—that was all the rage in the eighties—and they're coming back too, would you believe—as well as a couple of nightgowns and a peignoir I'd recently purchased for her. I think Gram's closets contained the fashion history of the twentieth century from the waning years of vaudeville right up through the Vietnam War and well beyond." Alice managed a chuckle. "I guess you could say that she was a bit of a pack rat."

I held up a housedress. "With a penchant for loud, geometric prints."

"God, that's really pretty awful, isn't it? I can't even imagine someone buying that from Goodwill!"

"Oh, I can think of someone who would just love it," I grinned.

"Oh! Yes! That smelly homeless lady who wears all that mascara. Matilda!" Alice burst out laughing. "It's all hers!" she said. "Everything that's louder and brighter than a three-ring circus? She can have it!"

"She'll think she hit the jackpot in Vegas," I agreed.

"Let's do it."

It was a good thing that Alice had brought down all her loads so early in the morning. The tenants get very cranky when they think that people are hogging the machines. In fact, anyone using more than two of the six washers at a time is accorded pariah status.

Over the years, I've observed the tenants' behavior down here, not without some amusement. They watch the little red light on the washers like it's the green flag at Daytona, and if you're not there to claim your clothes when it goes off, they make a mad dash to evict your load and insert their own. Actually, "in the interest of full disclosure," as they say, I confess to having done that myself on occasion. But naturally, I have a good excuse; I was in a hurry.

Given the lack of laundry room etiquette, I have a feeling that my patients tend to covet our private counseling sessions as much for a first crack at the machines as for any psychological enlightenment or epiphanies that might take place. Stevo doesn't unlock the door early enough for the nine-to-fivers to do a load or two before dashing off to work, and the room doesn't stay open late enough to accommodate their needs by the time they get home either. The room's also not open on Sundays, and I'm not allowed to unlock the door either or I lose my therapy privileges. I won't even chance any Sunday cheating, because there's always some wacko do-gooder tenant who will gleefully rat me out to the management.

"I think this is the first time I've ever been down here on a weekday," Alice said. "I was an office drone until just a couple of weeks ago. My grandmother did the laundry for both of us, even though I always promised her I'd get to it on a Saturday. After I got the *Grandma Finnegan's Wake* gig, I was finally able to ditch the insanity of an adult lifetime of temping. Not a moment too soon either. I thought if I had to work for one more two-faced, hypocritical asshole lawyer, I would hang myself."

Alice's disparaging remark about lawyers immediately made me think of one of the women I see at the health center down on Fulton Street every Tuesday at lunchtime. Carol Lerner is a Wall Streeter who exhibits several of the most negative stereotypical traits frequently associated with female attorneys: that they try to be men in order to compete in what is still very much a man's sphere in many respects; that they're tougher on their employees than their male counterparts are; that they're humorless; and that they dress like nuns, wouldn't know an attractive shoe if it was removed from their butt and shown to them, and that they display a nearly equal cluelessness when it comes to the application of cosmetics. I've been working with Carol to get her to acknowledge—and rejoice in—her womanhood, rather than attempt to live up to impossible expectations, several of which have been artificially imposed. Just because she's got a well-deserved and hard won reputation as a barracuda in the courtroom, she doesn't have to be so grimly aggressive and so aggressively grim in the other aspects of her life. She admits that she's a tough boss, and isn't just a tyrant in the office: Carol's teenage daughter Diandra, who is exactly the same age as my Molly, has tried to run away from home twice in the past year.

Unfortunately, Carol misinterpreted my suggestion to break old behavioral patterns and consciously seek appropriate times to soften her edges as an exhortation to become a one-woman Bacchanal. While she still acts like Medusa in public, behind the meticulously clipped shrubberies of her three-bedroom Westchester Tudor, Carol's become the Merry Widow, indulging in simultaneous affairs with two married men, both attorneys, one of whom is her law partner. Her other lover is the law partner's squash partner. Talk about bedroom communities!

I don't like to take *my* work home with me either, and my intrusive ruminations on Carol Lerner were exactly that. This was my much-needed mental "down time" between my laundry room sessions and my downtown ones. I was grateful for the unexpected appearance of Ian, my eleven-year-old wonder child. I have no idea how I ended up so blessed with this boy. He always slept through the night when he was an infant, never went through the terrible twos, cleans up his room without being prodded, has legible penmanship, and his teachers around the corner at Ethical Culture adore him: in short, Ian embodies all the things that are supposed to be lacking in the gender allegedly composed of snails and puppy dogs' tails . . . although he *was* eating Cheez Doodles for breakfast.

I assumed my voice of maternal authority. "Young man, those are not an adequate substitute for corn flakes."

"I know; they suck with milk," Ian said, folding the bag closed. All parenting should be this easy. "Mom, my agent called. You have to take me on an audition after school. It's a national commercial for McDonald's, and we can't be late."

"When are we ever late?"

"Last week, at the one for replacements for *Big River*."

"I'm an actor too," Alice said to Ian. "Although I really hate it when women refer to themselves that way. *Ess*. I'm an *actress*. I don't think it's un-PC or something to consider myself an act*ress*— as opposed to ac*tor*, I mean. It's a prettier word too."

"Oh, that's cool. Have you ever been on Broadway? I played Gavroche for eight months in *Les Miz*, and I was also in the national tour of *Peter Pan* with Mary Lou Retton. I did three national commercials and a local one for the Vision Center. It was their back-to-school commercial last year. And I did the print campaign for the Gap and a catalogue for Kids 'R' Us. Are you in something now?" Ian asked, finally pausing for breath. "Hey, Mom, there's a boggart in that machine!" he yelped, his attention diverted by the sudden violent shaking of one of the washing machines. It did in fact look like it was demonically possessed, or that some less-than-benign force was trapped inside.

"Well, sweetie, there's not much I can do about that now. If I open the machine, everything will stop like it's supposed to, but with these old washers, I'm afraid it might not start up again and our clothes will be too damp for the dryer to be effective."

"I'm in *Grandma Finnegan's Wake*," Alice told Ian. "I auditioned for it and got the part on the same day . . . the same day my grandmother died . . . and our last name is Finnegan. Can you believe it?" Alice began to choke up, and although I really don't know her, I decided she could use a hug. But that started her sobbing again, and in a matter of moments Alice's tears had completely saturated the shoulder of my Indian cotton blouse.

"What's a wake, Mom?"

Alice pulled away and I hesitated for a second before responding to Ian's question. "It's like a party for someone who died, honey. It's a big tradition among the Irish."

"Oh. How come *we* don't have parties for people when they die?"

"Because our name is Lederer. Jews don't have wakes."

"Can we go see Alice in the play?"

"Your father and I will certainly go support Alice's career."

"But what about me? Can't I go? You said it's like a *party*."

I looked at Alice, hoping she might confirm my suspicion that the interactive production, while billed as a "family comedy," was not quite appropriate for preteens. "From what I hear, it's far too risqué for you, honey. Too many double entendres."

"What's a double *entahnder*?"

"Dirty words."

Ian continued his campaign. "You let me watch other things with dirty words. Like *The Sopranos*."

"Your *father* lets you watch *The Sopranos*. And if you want my opinion on the subject, which I know you don't, I think he's far too permissive."

"Daddy's not permissive; he's *progressive*," Ian insisted.

"Daddy's" your classic Upper West Side Jewish liberal intellectual who lets our kids get away with far more than they should, completely devaluing my clout as an authority figure. "Yeah, Ian? Well, in one word: *fuhgedaboutit!*"

Talia, having folded the last of her all-natural fiber dancewear, finally got ready to leave the room, struggling under the weight of her basket. I slipped into my de facto role as laundry room "cruise director." "Alice, do you know Talia Shaw? She's a new tenant—and a performer too."

"A dancer, I presume," Alice said, eyeing the pristine pile of leotards.

Talia nodded. "I'm with City Ballet. They let me to do a season as a guest artist with the Martha Graham company last year, but it didn't work out. Got fired and served with divorce papers all within the same month." She gave a little shrug and the insouciant bounce of her dark ponytail seemed a sharp contrast to her crisp, unemotional tone of voice. "At least it was in my contract with City that they had to take me back."

"And you heard that Alice has just gone into *Grandma Finnegan's Wake*," I said.

Talia gave her a chilly little smile.

"I guess it's not exactly *Giselle*," Alice said, descending into embarrassed self-deprecation.

"I think it's wonderful that we have working performers in the building," I said cheerily, sensing the tension in the air. "It keeps the atmosphere vital." If my performer clients didn't have evening curtains to make, I'd give serious thought to conducting cocktail-hour therapy sessions down here instead. "By the way, Alice, have you ever read the book?"

"Which book?"

"Finnegan's Wake."

"At eight hundred and something pages? Gee, Susan, it's on my to-do list," she joked.

"You've never read it? Hmh! I spent an entire semester on it at Bennington."

Talia turned at the doorway to the laundry room. "I've never *read* it, but I think I *wore* it once." Ian, Alice, and I regarded her as though she were an alien. Suddenly she became tremendously self-conscious: the shy woman who had confessed her discomfort with being verbal. "Why are you guys looking at me like that? When I was about four years old, after I saw *The Nutcracker* on TV and told my mother I wanted to be a dancer, she laughed into her scotch glass and said that no klutz could grow up to be a ballerina. She said I had to learn balance and grace, and placed a hardcover copy of *Finnegan's Wake* on my head and told me to walk around the house like that. From my bedroom to the basement, y'know? When I could finally manage three flights of stairs—up *and* down—without dropping the book—she agreed to let me begin ballet lessons. 'Bye." She started once more to leave the room.

"You forgot your soap," Ian offered helpfully.

"Thanks." Talia fetched her soapbox—a brand of ecofriendly powder—from the table near the washers and balanced it on top of her basket of clothes. "Oops," she said, setting the basket on the floor and running into the tiny bathroom.

"What do you want to bet she's taking diuretics?" Alice whispered to me. "I mean the woman has absolutely no body fat." She regarded her own midriff, which was slender but far from skeletal. "I mean that should be illegal—the zero body fat, not the diuretics!"

I winced, recalling too well my own punishing bout with them, and how grateful I am to have recovered, physically and psychologically, from the devastation of an eating disorder.

A couple of minutes later Talia exited the water closet wearing a frown. "They took down the mirror over the sink."

Faith swanned into the laundry room. "I believe I left a knit top down here yesterday. This color," she said, indicating the orchid-colored scarf at her throat.

"I know you," Alice said to her. "You used to be a friend of my grandmother: Irene Finnegan."

"Yes, yes of course," Faith said. "And you have my deepest condolences. They don't make them like Irene anymore. We used to go to the opera together from time to time, after Ben— my husband—died. Irene was a very special lady. With a huge heart. After Ben passed away, it was your grandmother who taught me how to balance my checkbook. Can you imagine," she said with a throaty laugh, "I'd never paid a bill on my own!" Faith peered into each dryer, looking for her missing garment. "Ah, well, maybe I never even washed it to begin with," she sighed, heading out the door. "At my age, the mind tends to become a rather porous organ."

Ian, without being asked, was folding our dried clothes into piles based on which family member owned them.

"Is there such a thing as Stepford *children*?" Alice asked incredulously. "How old are you?"

"Eleven," Ian replied.

"He's a really good kid," I said, realizing that I couldn't make the same boastful claim about Molly, and counting my blessings that fifty percent of my children had turned out terrific.

"I've never gone for younger men, but I think in your case I might make an exception. Do you mind waiting until you've graduated from college so we can get married?"

Ian blushed and coyly turned his head away. "Mom, I have to go to school now."

I checked my watch. His first class started in twenty-one minutes. "Okay. I'll walk you over there."

"You're so *protective*. I can do it myself. It's only two blocks."

"I like to think of it as cautious. It's only two blocks but it's still Manhattan and you're only in sixth grade. Besides, there was an almost kidnapping on Sixty-fourth Street last week."

"An *almost* kidnapping, Mom. You worry too much."

"I'm a mother; it's part of the job description. If I didn't worry, you'd be taken away by Social Services. And I'd prefer that you got to school this morning safely, rather than *almost* got there. So suck it up: you're getting a chaperone."

I turned to Alice, who was watching the row of machines launder her grandmother's garments for the final time. Her face was a mask of sorrow. "Hey," I murmured, placing my hands gently on her shoulders, "if you want to make an appointment to talk to me, to set up some counseling sessions, I'm here. You shouldn't have to go through the grieving process alone."

"Thanks," Alice said, blinking back tears. "My parents are in Florida, I don't even have a boyfriend—although a while back I did meet a really cute guy who paid a house call to repair a piece of old furniture—and it's not right to dump on my two best friends all the time. They have enough of their own problems. But I'm not making a lot of money Off-Broadway, you know. 'Heigh-ho the glamorous life' and all that, but my paycheck doesn't leave me with much in the way of disposable income."

"I don't charge anything for my laundry room sessions. And they're very unintimidating; just think of them as a weekly fifty-minute gabfest with a girlfriend who happens to have a psych Ph.D. I hold private counseling sessions down here every morning except Sunday from seven to eight A.M., and I've got one day open, so if you feel that you need some help getting through this bump in your road, I'm here to listen."

"Wow." Alice blinked back a grateful tear and surveyed the row of aging washing machines. "Who knew I could come down here and shrink my clothes and my head at the same time!"

AMY

I can't remember when I've ever seen a young woman so angry. Amy walked in with such a chip on her shoulder that I admit I found it hard to like her—something I've never experienced with a laundry room client. In situations like that, I have to focus even harder so as not to betray my bias through my body language or nonverbal responses.

Amy was pissed off that she hadn't lost her baby weight six months after giving birth, particularly since her two older sisters had done so after only forty-five days postpartum; she was frustrated that her newly altered lifestyle often lacked the rosy optimistic glow of an infomercial for motherhood; she was perennially livid with her lawyer husband for never being around to help her with their new son, apart from holding him aloft right after his bris for the entire congregation of Temple Beth Israel to sigh approvingly over, and for retreating into their guest room for lengthy phone calls with colleagues and clients every time she asked for his assistance, even if it was only to hold a fretting Isaac while she took a bath.

"Is it right to want to strangle Eric every time I look at him?" she asked me. It was our first session and invective poured from her like lava. Obviously, we'd have our work cut out for us. "I'm only half kidding, you know." She looked down at her hands; her fingers were bent and tensed like claws. "I swear to God, there are days when I just want to put my hands around his throat and . . . *squeeze.*" Her pantomimed demonstration made me flinch. "But then again, he's never home long enough for me to grab him, so I guess you won't be reading about me in the papers anytime soon."

"I know what you mean. My husband hasn't been home for dinner in days. It sounds like a lot of your anger is stemming from the fact that you feel like you're doing everything yourself.

What I'm hearing is that you need someone to pick up the slack and look after Isaac so you can at least take that well-deserved bubble bath. Given his position, I would imagine that Eric's income would enable—" I began.

"Definitely," Amy interrupted. "He's a corporate lawyer." I thought about Carol Lerner again. What is it about that profession that morphs people who probably began life as mensches into monsters? "I was a lawyer too, until I was in my eighth month," Amy continued. "We both worked at Newter & Spade—well, Eric still does. He just made partner, so he's working harder than ever to prove he now *deserves* to be there—after seven years of slaving away just to get there in the first place."

"So . . . have you ever considered getting some help?" I asked Amy.

"Oh, we have a housekeeper. Meriel is a rock—I would never have gotten all our unpacking done after the move if it hadn't been for her, even though I don't think she likes dogs very much, and I'm certainly not about to get rid of Hector. My Chihuahua. I've had Hector since before I had Eric. But I would never have someone take care of my *child*. I even wash Isaacs's things myself. His onesies, his blankie . . . all that. Even his dirty didies. I won't put any plastic products anywhere near my baby's privates, so it's strictly cloth diapers for Isaac. Meriel cleans the house and walks Hector and does my laundry and Eric's, but I never understood why people have children just to foist them off on someone else. Besides, my mother won't hear of it. She says that particularly at the very youngest stages, a baby is so impressionable that it should never be left in the care of anyone other than a parent or a grandparent."

"Well, then, what about asking your mother to help you out? It sounds like you could really use some downtime."

Amy wrinkled her nose. "My mother hates the smell of poop."

Progress Notes

Faith Nesbit: Major breakthrough in accepting husband Ben's permanent absence by sleeping on "his side" of the conjugal bed. Encouraged her to continue to take steps—at her own pace—toward living for herself, rather than continuing (à la Queen Victoria) to live the existence she believes her late husband would have wished her to. Reminded client that Ben would have been pleased to see her treating herself well. While Faith characteristically tends to play it safe, rarely takes risks and typically resists change, she seemed open to the suggestion this time.

Talia Shaw: Breakthrough in her therapy when she serendipitously discovered that dancing during her session enabled her to open up in a way she'd never been able to do previous to this session. I took a leaf from Bradford Keeney's playbook and encouraged this creative, nontraditional approach, which I anticipated would be particularly effective with artists who thrive under that kind of stimulus. The effect on Talia was stunning and immediate. We need to work steadily on client's self-esteem issues, though, and explore abandonment issues as they relate to her recent divorce, termination from the Martha Graham company, and fear of losing her job at City Ballet. Must steer discussion toward mother's damaging negativity and help Talia recognize and accept that her mother lacks the tools in her bag of tricks to ever make Talia feel worthy, and to encourage client to accept that this is her *mother's* bundle of issues, not client's.

Amy Baum: New client. Needs to focus on letting go of her anger. Session helpful in that she acknowledged that she could use some domestic relief to help reduce the stress of caring for a newborn. I need to work with her on helping to find solutions to this dilemma, rather than looking to assign blame for her predicament.

Me: I should *speak* to Eli about his forgetting our anniversary instead of imploding about it. Ditto his increasing absence from the dinner table and two A.M. arrivals home. As much as I found Amy Baum's anger somewhat off-putting, I can relate to her situation perhaps more than I can to my other laundry room clients' presenting complaints, except perhaps for Talia, in that she's a dancer—enjoying a degree of success in the field I had to forego.

I empathize with the eating disorder issues as well. Last week a health center client asked me point-blank why I became a psychotherapist. While my first response had something to do with wanting to make the world a better place, my client actually challenged me and said, "No—*really.*" I told her about my experiences as a dance student in college, the related body image issues that led to my bulimia; and how, when I switched from a dance major into the psych program, I faced and overcame my fears of science classes—the frightening specters of courses like neurophysiology and biochem. I wanted to understand and then make sense of the emotional and psychological causes and effects of my illness.

But back to my issues with Eli: rather than dealing with the issue head-on, I'm stewing in resentment over his behavior and letting it affect my mood, my appetite, and my sleep, as well as my sessions on occasion (for example when there's an emotional trigger, such as when Faith came right out and said Eli should pamper me.)

Also must focus on better management of my time, so Ian doesn't arrive late to his auditions. That's potentially sabotaging my son. What's *that* about?

Consider taking dog to vet for incontinence problem. Or is he acting out too? While I'm an obvious proponent of psychotherapy, I think pet shrinks are as faddish as pet rocks. Perhaps Sigmund just needs a refresher course from the obedience trainer.

Consider sending *Molly* for obedience training if she doesn't stop cutting classes.

Progress? If progress is a measure of success, I'm not a very shining example these days. In fact, I feel more like a hamster on a wheel. Do hamsters ever wish they could actually *go* somewhere?

BRIGHT COLORS

MERIEL

"I don't like de sound of daht cold, Susie. A summah cold is a bad ting," Meriel said in the lilting Jamaican cadences that always make me crave a mai-tai. I adore the music of her voice. It has a way of relaxing and warming me like the sun on an early spring morning. "I studied nursing, you know, back in Jamaica, but sick people make me unhappy; too much for de emotions, you know. I don't have de tick skin you need to be a nurse. Did you try my remedy?"

"You mean the warmed rum, honey, and whole cloves?"

"Daht's de one," smiled Meriel proudly. "An old fahmily recipe. Guarantee to knock out anyting!"

"It knocked out *me!* " I told her. "I drank a cup of it at around nine P.M., and the next thing I knew Ian was telling me he needed a permission slip signed before he left for school that morning. And I've still got the cold."

"Ahhh . . . but when it knock you out, you get de rest you need, so you can get bettah!"

"But enough about me," I kidded. "Let's talk about what's bothering you today."

Meriel checked her watch. "Mrs. Amy always wonder why I stay down here with de wash instead of coming upstairs to do de dusting in the meantime. I tell her I worry someone else take her clothes out and leave them on de dirty table if I am not here when de light goes out." She rose from the couch. "I don't feel so bahd about sitting down here now and talking wit' you, now daht dere's one less machine. I have to watch more closely in case someone else want a machine dis early. She so busy wit' Isaac she don't remember de room's not open for business now."

There was some truth to Meriel's claims about the machines, though. We were now down to five from half a dozen. The washer with Ian's "boggart" in it had died the following day, but remained in the laundry room with a length of yellow tape stretched across it, as though the defunct unit were part of a crime scene.

"Now you tell me what it is about white people and deyr dogs!"

"What do you mean?" I asked, lost in Meriel's non sequitur.

"Daht stupid Taco Bell dog Mrs. Amy and Mr. Eric have. She treat it like it's one of de fahmily. Now she have a child and it's like she still don't know de difference between a pet and a person. Do you know she dress up daht dog like a doll? Daht dog has a raincoat—Burberry plaid—she don't even have a designer raincoat for herself—and even a little matching hat. She have a red white and blue Uncle Sam outfit coming up for de Fourt' of July. And in de winter, she tells me, it has boots so its paws don't get hurt by de salt on the streets that melt de snow. So now I get to look forward to walking a circus animal when de weather turn cold. Then she have a ballerina tutu for it that she ahsk me to put on to take de dog to a costume pahty at de dog run in Riverside Park. And de animal is a male! It almost bite me when I try to dress it like a girl. I swear to God I get embarrass when I have to walk de stupid ting."

I blushed, realizing that while our dog is never dressed like a Barbie doll, Sigmund does wear a bandanna on occasion—and when Molly was about twelve, she once tried to pierce his ears—and he does sleep on a comfy cushioned "bed" from Orvis, rather than on the floor, or outside, which is where Meriel insists dogs belong. Of course we all live in apartments, so outside is outside of the question.

"So, what I want to know before my time is up for today, so I can get a good night's sleep tonight, is—tell me what it is you white people have with your dogs?"

NAOMI AND CLAUDE

"I can't help it that I'm infertile!" Naomi snapped, at the end of her tether two seconds into the beginning of their session.

"And I can't help it that I'm Chinese!" Claude said, as rational as Naomi was peevish.

"We just found out from the agency down in Georgia that lesbian couples aren't allowed to adopt Chinese babies," Naomi said, "so we have to start the paperwork all over again. And since we can only pick one of us to be the adoptive mother, and very few single women are allowed to adopt from China, Claude thinks she has a better shot at it and she's cutting me out."

The women had tried the in vitro route, but it did in fact turn out that Naomi is infertile. Claude suffers from endomitriosis, so she isn't going to be a biological mother either. They chose to adopt a little girl from China even though the process takes two to three times longer than adoption from Latin America, Haiti, Russia, or the Balkans, because Claude feels very strongly about the ill treatment of females in her native culture and believes that adopting a Chinese girl is a political stand as well as a personal intervention. I hoped their little girl would turn out to be an absolute angel . . . and not eventually become a teenager like Molly, so sullen and angry at the world, channeling her adolescent rage into any opportunity to get attention, as if attention were something she had ever been denied.

"You are! You *are* cutting me out!" Naomi spat at Claude. "Literally! Tell her! Tell Susan what you did to me last night." She lapsed into her nervous "tic," bringing her long dark braid forward and beginning to split the ends of her hair.

"I didn't do anything *to* you," Claude replied.

"Okay, Claude. Naomi. Naomi, what do you think Claude 'did' to you last night?"

"I told you; she cut me out."

"Gee, you two, I'd love some specifics so we can work on what's really the core of the issue here. Let's revisit how you two usually handle major decisions in your partnership."

I received my answer from the more even-tempered Claude. "Fifty-fifty—most of the time. We've always been very concerned about being sensitive to that when it comes to the big stuff. But stuff like the nuts and bolts of the adoption issue is something we've never faced before, never even imagined we'd *need* to face. Since I'm now going to be the sole adoptive parent, I have to compile a bunch of photos of me that will make the bureaucrats believe I'm straight and send them to the agency for my dossier. And I have all these pictures of me and Naomi with our arms around each other and stuff like that, and . . . I had to do a Photoshop number on the ones that were on our computer and replace Naomi with the image of a guy who's a friend of ours. And with some of the old prints, I had to snip off the half of the pictures that Naomi was in, because it was so obvious she was my lover. So . . . yeah . . . I guess I did

literally cut her out, but it wasn't with malice or anything."
Claude gave her partner a much beleagured, though compassionate, look, but her attempt to connect was pointedly ignored.

"I can't even go to China with Claude unless I pretend to be
just her friend. Obviously I can't say I'm her *sister*," Naomi
fumed. "Funny, you don't *look* Chinese," she simpered. "I told
her, we should just say fuckit and adopt from another country."

"No. It has to be China," insisted Claude. "You're not changing my mind on that one."

"Look . . . I hate to shine a spotlight on the obvious, and I'm
going to warn you that I'm not speaking to you right now with
my impartial therapist hat on, but the world is what it is," I said.
"You know that's true. And the reality is that you're not going
to change it overnight. A grimmer reality is that you may never
succeed in changing it at all. So. You have a lot to think about.
But basically we're looking at two major options. In this situation you can choose to be rebels and allow your individual agen-
das to divide the two of you, or you can chose to be parents and
let the situation unite you even more. I know it may sound like
a deal with the devil, and it *is*, in some respects. I know it pisses
you off; and the stakes are really high no matter which road you
take. Frankly, I see it this way, and you're welcome to disagree
with me, but you two women—even if Claude has to be the
mom on paper—can give a, well . . . 'discarded' little girl from
across the world a loving home with myriad opportunities and
advantages. *There's* where you get to make your difference."

I flashed on my own background: being carried on my dad's
shoulders to rallies against the Vietnam War in Washington
Square Park; as a preteen marching in support of the Equal
Rights Amendment alongside my mom in matching tie-dyed
tee-shirts that we'd made ourselves in the kitchen sink, spatter-
ing Rit and Tintex all over the avocado-colored kitchen appli-

ances; carrying black balloons to my college graduation as a protest against apartheid in South Africa . . . and I wondered how all the ideals I was raised with had manifested themselves in the adult Susan Lederer. Here I am, middle-class, and technically middle-aged, since all my ancestors never lived beyond their eighties (although, as they used to say, "Life begins at forty," and I'm still waiting for something new and different to happen any day now). I've recently realized that I'm more *politically* middle of the road than I ever expected to be. Well into adulthood I've discovered that pragmatism is the thick dark border now drawn around the image that during my youth used to be boldly, colorfully, and deliberately scribbled outside the lines.

It's sort of like the kid who's a hellion hearing her frustrated mother's constant refrain "Just wait till you're a mother!" and then finding out years later, to considerable dismay, that she was right.

As I listened to Claude and Naomi argue, it occurred to me that I'd been making an incorrect assumption about identity. Naomi, who has an Italian-American background, saw herself as a lesbian first. Claude's primary cultural identity was different: she was a Chinese-American first and foremost. The adoption issue had brought the question of cultural identity into high relief, and with each of the partners having a different primary cultural identity, accomplishing a smooth resolution was going to be a tricky goal.

"You are in fact getting to make a political statement by adopting a Chinese girl," I reminded Naomi. "Even though it's currently at odds with the other one you wish to make. But one thing we really need to talk about is what kind of a home you'd be bringing this little girl into if you and Claude don't work *this* issue out."

"Baby, you know I love you," Claude said, reaching for Naomi's hand. "You're my girl."

Naomi pulled away. "I know. It's not about that. And you know it. It's a whole lot bigger than that. When the agency sends the fresh paperwork, Claude . . . ? Don't ask for my help. I don't want to even watch you fill it out."

I believed I'd said the right thing, at least I'd expressed as a compassionate friend what needed to be put on the table, but as a shrink—even though confrontation can be an effective therapeutic tool in certain circumstances—I felt like shit as I watched Naomi scowl. My unorthodox sessions occasionally drift into uncharted waters. In a totally conventional situation, couples therapists aren't supposed to appear to be taking sides.

AND THEN THERE'S MALA SONIA . . . WHO ISN'T A CLIENT

Mala Sonia is the super's wife: proud, poorly educated, a genuine Gypsy. She resents my early morning therapy sessions because she likes to come into the laundry room and use all the machines before anyone else can get to them. I have never seen a woman with so much laundry. The no-hogging rule doesn't apply to her since her husband Stevo will blacklist the tongue-wagging tenant. God help them— because Stevo won't—the next time they have a leak or require the exterminator. Mala Sonia, like her husband, calls herself a born-again Christian and does things like cross herself whenever she runs into "blasphemers" like Claude and Naomi (only she gets the second half of the gesture backward), and mutters in Romany—a language I am learning in dribs and drabs thanks to Eli, who is drawing a graphic novel called *Gia the Gypsy Girl*.

Last Sunday morning I asked him if "Gypsy" was un-PC, since he's always so hypersensitive about that kind of stuff, but he told me that his editor preferred an alliterative title to a PC one; and besides, everyone except the Gypsies still calls them Gypsies. "Now if you called them 'thieves,' that might be a bit on the un-PC side," Eli had said sarcastically, spreading Neufchatel on his whole wheat bagel.

Mala Sonia entered the laundry room and spat at the two lesbians. *"Te bisterdon tumare anava!"* She turned her back on Naomi and Claude and crossed herself—the wrong way, as usual—then sat on the couch and thumbed through an issue of *People* that was so old it featured Ben Affleck and J. Lo's engagement on the cover.

"What the hell did she say this time?" Naomi muttered crossly.

"May your names be forgotten!" I translated under my breath, and Claude laughed.

"You're too kind, Mrs. Badescu," Claude replied loudly, giving Mala Sonia a huge smile. She turned to me and whispered, "What am *I* supposed to do when she does that? Curse back at her in Mandarin and tell her that her ancestors slept with goats? What purpose is it going to serve, except to make the one doing the cursing feel . . . what? Better in some sick and twisted way?"

"Yeah," Naomi said, emptying their washer. "World peace is a goal that only Miss America contestants still think is realistic. Unfortunately."

Alice Finnegan came downstairs with another load. "These clothes are mine this week," she said to me. "Oh, are you waiting?" she asked Mala Sonia. Alice gave a resigned little shrug. "I guess I'll come back later then." Mala Sonia began to stare at Alice, who visibly shuddered under the intensity of her gaze. "What? What'd I say? Did I say something—or do something— wrong?"

"You have deep sorrows," Mala Sonia told her, wearing an Oscar-worthy expression of sheer empathy. *"A-ko isi pomo shinava tumen.* Maybe I can help you. Let me give you a reading."

"I don't need a reading. I know why I have deep sorrows." Alice then grew curious. "How much does it cost?"

"Twenty dollars. And for a full reading and a chart, three hundred. Cash. After I go to my church and meditate on your life."

Naomi drew Alice aside. "Those 'churches' are really Gypsy hangouts where they boast to each other how they took advantage of some *gaje* that day. Trust me: don't do it."

I caught Mala Sonia giving the two of them the evil eye.

"I can spring for the twenty bucks," Alice told the Gypsy. "Beyond that is out of my price range I'm afraid."

"Sar laci and'ekh vadra," Mala Sonia muttered to herself. "Like crabs in a bucket."

The worm was on the hook. Mala Sonia was a pro who knew how to turn that meager tidbit into a mighty fine dinner. She led Alice away from Naomi and sat her down at the long table. "I know your grandmother just died," she began.

"Well, you're the super's wife, so of course you do," Alice countered suspiciously. "You'd better not predict that I'll be served with an eviction notice—because my name is on the lease, so everything's legal."

The super's wife ignored the threat. "Is that a Dana Buchman blouse you're wearing?"

Alice gave Mala Sonia an incredulous look, stunned that the pulchritudinous Gypsy woman currently sporting a skintight horizontally striped tank top and orange terry-cloth shorts above tanned legs and Fredericks of Hollywood–style mules might possess an intimate familiarity with a midtown, midpriced, middle-of-the-road designer who's not exactly a household name. Actually, I suspect that Mala Sonia spends the money she makes giving "psychic readings" on terrific clothes: we just never see her in them. Or else she's gained her knowledge of Fashion Avenue from spending so much time in this depressingly downscale laundry room peopled with relatively upmarket tenants.

"I can read you like a book," Mala Sonia intoned, as though she were reciting from the Gypsy's Manual, basic readings chapter. "Your grandmother is very unhappy now."

Alice's eyes immediately began to well with tears. That's how those Gypsy "readers" do it. They tap into something pretty general and allow the mark to relate it to something deeply personal. When the mark has displayed his or her vulnerability—*pow!*

"She wants you to be happy; to find a man to love you. And there is one who you used to love who will come back into your life and you must decide what to do about it. He is very close to you now, but this time there is someone who stands between you."

Alice shivered just perceptibly enough for her reaction to register with students of human behavior—like myself and Mala Sonia. "Well, first of all, this blouse is a cheap knockoff— although it *is* a lot like Dana Buchman's designs. But if you can really read me like a book, tell me the guy's name!" Alice challenged skeptically.

Amy entered the room, carrying her son Isaac in a Snuggly. "Oh, there you are, Mrs. Badescu. I'm looking for Stevo. You remember me? I'm Amy Baum. My husband Eric and I just moved in last week? And there's still something wrong with the showerhead in the master bathroom. So can you tell Stevo to get up to our apartment right away?" She pressed a bill into Mala Sonia's palm. It found its way into the Gypsy's pocket with the speed of a sleight of hand trick. "Apartment 4K," Amy reminded her. I'm Baum, but it's under my husband's last name:

Witherspoon." She dashed out the door. "I'll expect Stevo before two. Isaac has to go down for his nap then and we need absolute quiet in the apartment except for Baby Bach."

"Witherspoon?" Alice said incredulously. "Eric Witherspoon?"

"You asked me his name," Mala Sonia said. "That's him!"

4

Alice looked totally stunned. "Eric Witherspoon lives here now? And that's his wife?" Mala Sonia nodded. "I dated him last year; we even lived together for a few months at his garden apartment in Park Slope! I moved out of my grandmother's apartment to be with him and then he ended up dumping me like raw sewage."

"*Kon del tut o nai shai dela tut wi o vast:* he who gives you a finger will also give you the whole hand."

Alice looked at Mala Sonia. "Apparently."

"Eric needed a second bedroom when they had the baby, so they moved into Manhattan," Mala Sonia said.

"My God. And she has a baby already." Alice started counting the months on her fingers. "No way that kid could have been conceived *after* they got married. That sonofabitch works pretty damn fast. I wonder what it feels like for him to move into the same building where an ex-girlfriend lives. I wonder if he ever told Amy about me."

"I know you do," replied Mala Sonia. "And he did. But she was too busy thinking about other things just now to even consider that his ex might be you. Are you sure you don't want that full reading?"

"I want a drink."

"At eight-thirty A.M. ?" I said. "You might want to reconsider such self-destructive behavior."

"Not this morning," Alice replied, and began to drag her laundry cart out the door. "I'll be back in an hour when there's a vacant washer. Totally pickled. That way I can be hung over before it's too late in the day to drink a pot of coffee in order to get over it."

"If you really want a drink, why don't you come to Sappho tonight?" Claude suggested.

"Sappho? Isn't that the nightclub in the meat packing district where straight women get to act like they're gay?" Naomi nodded. "I've never been there," Alice said, mulling over the invitation. "I've always been kind of curious about it, though. Do *you* two go there often?" I could see that she was wondering why two lesbians would frequent a club where women *pretended* to be lesbians.

"We're there every night," Naomi said. "We own it."

"Why don't you come tonight too, Susan," Claude urged. "And each of you—bring a girlfriend, if you want to. Actually, tonight would be a great night to come down. We're having a Weimar Nacht. You know, we're pretending it's Berlin in 1931 and everyone gets to act like Lili Marlene."

"As long as you don't also have people dressing up in brown shirts, I think I can handle it," Alice said. "But I've got a performance at eight. How late are you there?"

Naomi gave a little snort. "It's a *nightclub*, Alice. We don't roll up the sidewalks at midnight. By the time Claude and I usually get out of there, most people are just getting ready to *start* their day! In fact, we often come to our therapy sessions with Susan directly from the club."

"Well then, I just might check it out tonight," Alice said. "As long as you also promise me that if I tie on a few too many over this Eric Witherspoon news you'll pour me discreetly into a taxi and never mention the incident again."

"Girl Scouts' honor," said Claude, crossing her heart.

"I think that oath only applies to promising not to burn the toasted marshmallows," Naomi quipped.

Claude shot her a look. "A lot you know. That's the Campfire Girls you're thinking of."

These days Claude and Naomi could turn anything into a full-fledged blow-up. I knew that much of the tension between them was really related to the deeper issue of the adoption, but my God, could they bicker!

Naomi shrugged in disgust. "Girl Scouts, Campfire Girls, *whatever*. Funny how it's totally okay when they throw a bunch of little girls together like that and then the same people go wacko when some of those little girls begin to like each other more than they're 'supposed to,' whatever *that* means."

Claude looked uncomfortably from Alice and Mala Sonia to me and then back to Naomi. "Maybe we should save this for our next session, baby."

ME

Eli phoned at six P.M. to say that he needed to work late again—something about inking—and Ian was sleeping over at a friend's house, so I accepted Claude and Naomi's invitation to head down to Sappho. I ran into Alice, who was there with her pregnant friend Isabel Martinucci. Izzy was very anxious—once she learned that I was a therapist—that I not judge her harshly for hanging out in a bar while she was expecting a baby. "Don't worry, I don't do that," I assured her.

"Good, because we judge ourselves harshly enough!" a tipsy Alice said, raising her martini glass.

It was hard to converse above the music. Although Sappho is a very sophisticated night spot—and I did enjoy its atmosphere of elegant decadence with just a whiff of danger—I think I may be too old for this kind of thing. I was never much of a partier, actually, even in my youth.

From the sidelines I watched the women dancing with one another as awkwardly as junior high school kids, or tentatively making out on couches or plushy banquettes, unsure of what— or where—to touch, getting off on acting "wicked." Tonight, in keeping with the Weimar theme, many of the women were dressed like Dietrich, in black tie and tails, often paired with hot pants instead of trousers, and accessorized with fishnet hosiery, high black heels, and rakishly worn fedoras. Alice and Izzy, since they were both professional actresses, really got into the idea of being costumed. Alice had taken her ensemble to the theatre and changed clothes in the dressing room after her *Grandma Finnegan's Wake* performance.

"I feel like shit," Izzy announced suddenly.

"Let's find the ladies' room then," I suggested.

"No, not that kind of shit. I'm not going to puke or anything. This is only Diet Coke," she said, raising her glass. Izzy suddenly burst into tears.

Alice put her arm over her friend's shoulder and began to comfort her. "Do you want to get up? Move around a bit? Let's take a walk. How's that sound?"

Izzy shook her head. "I . . . feel so . . . unloved," she sobbed. "Sorry," she immediately added, fishing for a tissue in her evening purse. "My hormones are going insane." She assumed an expression of forced cheer. "Don't mind me! I'm okay!"

"Hey, you want to dance?" Alice asked her.

Izzy nodded. "Yeah. That's like a moving hug. And I really need a hug. Damn! I used to act this way when I was *drunk!*"

"Well, you have a different 'excuse' now," I said. "The hormones. It's okay. I seem to remember being pretty wacko both times I was pregnant too."

"How old are your kids?" Izzy asked.

"Eleven and sixteen. And as temperamentally different as two kids could possibly be. One is an angel and the other . . . isn't."

"I hope this is a girl," Izzy said, patting her belly. "They're much easier."

"It's a myth!" I snorted, wondering what the hell Molly was up to tonight. She said she was going to the movies with a girl-friend this evening, having promised on all she held sacred (so I had my doubts) that she'd do her homework first. At her age, most of her classmates go out on weekday evenings as long as they observe a curfew, so it's bootless for me to try to force her to stay at home. I did remind Molly that it was a school night, but I'm pretty confident, from experience, that my words carried all the weight of a mayfly.

Alice devoured the maraschino cherry in her cocktail, followed by several valiant though unsuccessful attempts to tie the stem into a knot with her tongue. Izzy slurped down the remainder of her diet soda, then the two of them negotiated their way to the crowded dance floor. The music was a sultry though occasionally strident German torch song that managed to simultaneously relax me and make me nervous. I leaned against the ruby-colored banquette and sipped my vodka tonic, closing my eyes—with one hand on my purse, of course—letting the tune get under my skin. A few moments later I returned my focus to the dance floor, wondering why I'd accepted Claude and Naomi's invitation. It had nothing to do with socializing in the same venue as some of my clients. In many instances, avoiding those situations is impractical.

My laundry room clients are women I've grown fond of; we frequently run into one another in the building, chatting informally when we do. To maintain appropriate boundaries, the only actual rule I enforce is that the dirty linen aired during the sessions in the basement stays in the basement.

My ambivalence tonight came from something else entirely. I just wasn't in a dancing mood and felt guilty that I wasn't enjoying my complimentary drink.

I watched Alice and Izzy doing the junior high hug-and-sway. Izzy suddenly burst into tears again on Alice's shoulder. Without missing a beat, Alice removed the white pocket square from her tuxedo jacket and dried her friend's eyes. It was a touching, unguarded moment that suddenly made me realize that I have no girlfriends whose shoulders I can cry on. In fact, I have no friends who I feel as close and connected to as I do with some of my clients. I've heard colleagues voice similar complaints: their personal life suffers while their professional one thrives, but misery having company doesn't make it any less depressing.

A tall, ponytailed blonde in the de rigueur black fedora caught my eye. She was holding her much shorter partner so tenderly; and though their dancing wasn't going to win them any Fred and Ginger (or Ginger and Mary Ann) awards, the two of them looked like they were more than just good friends. Particularly after I saw them kiss. I felt like such a voyeur, but for some reason, they mesmerized me. Perhaps it was because I was certain there was something familiar about the way the shorter woman moved, always listing ever so slightly to port, because her left leg was just a fraction shorter than her right.

When the couple turned, and her slouchy fedora slipped back on her head, I caught a good look at the blonde's partner's face. I knocked over my drink, and practically vaulted the low black granite cocktail table trying to reach them.

"Molly! What the hell are you doing here?!"

She abruptly stopped dancing and looked just as shocked to see *me*. "I could ask you the same thing, Mom."

I steered her into the corner where we'd have some semblance of privacy and plopped her onto the cushy banquette. Her friend hovered guiltily about two feet away. "Don't sass me, young lady," I heard myself say, sounding like my own mother. "Don't make me list your transgressions in front of your friend. I'm assuming this is the same Lauren you told me you were going to the movies with tonight."

Molly started to laugh. In the past few years she's perfected the teenage snort. Its very tone and delivery mocks mothers. "Yeah, right. Lauren."

"Molly, first of all—no, second of all—even though you've only got four days left until summer vacation, this is a school night. *First* of all, you're underage—in a bar—how the hell did they let you in here in the first place? And what the heck is so funny about Lauren? You haven't fazed me or freaked me out by French kissing with a girl, you know. The piercing on your . . . you know . . . was infinitely more outrageous."

"Then I'm losing my touch."

"I do, however, want an explanation. And an apology for lying to me. It's one thing to say you're going to the movies on a school night. You promised to do your homework first, and I gave you the respect of taking you at your word. But a nightclub? This isn't acceptable, Molly. And I have a feeling it wouldn't be acceptable to Lauren's mother either."

"*Lauren*," Molly scoffed again, as though I was an idiot. "We are so lucky it's so dark in here," she added, in a tone I can only describe as adolescent self-satisfaction. Are there any other mothers out there whose skin crawls at teenagers' overuse of the word "so"? There's another affectation that seems designed to annoy parents.

Molly took me by one hand and her tall blond partner by the other and dragged us all off the dance floor and into the narrow hallway that led to the bathrooms. She finally halted in an alcove housing those cumbersome chrome-plated dinosaurs otherwise known as pay phones where the light was at least bright enough to see the numbered buttons.

"Okay," I told my daughter, "talk."

Acting as though I had greatly incommoded them, Molly turned to her friend with a shrug. "I guess we better come clean," she said, removing the blonde's hat.

Now that her friend's face was no longer shaded, I wasn't sure which of Molly's lies I should be more pissed off about.

"Ma, meet Laurence."

"Laurence." I let the word sit on my tongue for a couple of moments, tasting it. It took every ounce of my willpower to refrain from reaming out my daughter in front of her friend. "Laurence. Do you have a last name, Laurence?" He mumbled something, genuinely embarrassed.

"Jacobs. Laurence Jacobs," Molly translated sullenly.

"My mother was a real Olivier freak," Laurence said sheepishly. He's lucky she didn't name him Heathcliff. "So, *Laurence-not-Lauren*, does your mother know you're out this late?" Eek, I was suddenly channeling another mother again: someone from the Eisenhower era who wore aprons and sensible heels every day instead of faded Levi's and clogs.

"Yeah, I guess. She doesn't care, though. She and my dad aren't home anyway."

"And how do you know my daughter, since she's never bothered to mention your name before?"

"Mom," Molly wailed, "stop giving him the third degree. We're not kids!"

"I'm afraid that the State of New York would quibble with you on that point."

Laurence opened his mouth to reply but received a shot in the ribs from my delicate daughter, who decided to speak for him.

"Laurence goes to Fieldston too. He's also a junior, his father is a lawyer and his mom is a realtor who's allergic to cats so they had to give theirs away last year. We met in the Environmental Club that Mr. Nivon leads after school on Thursdays, okay? So, he's, like, socially responsible."

I rolled my eyes. "And tonight would be a shining example of his social responsibility?"

"He doesn't drink."

"Yeah, but you do," Laurence quietly grunted, then immediately realized the gravity of his misstep in the loyalty department. Unfortunately for Molly, this time his mumble was articulate enough for me to decipher. While whistle-blowers are often regarded as heroes, the kid would not be someone I'd want on my side if cracking under torture was ever going to become a factor. It wouldn't surprise me if Molly broke up with him over this transgression.

"Excuse us, please, while I speak to my daughter," I said to the boy, then pulled Molly toward me so we were nose-to-nose. "What were you drinking tonight and how many have you had?"

"God, Ma!" she whined. "I'm fine."

"No. No, you're not. And I'm not just talking about underage drinking. I'm talking about lying to me. You didn't tell me where you were really going tonight—"

"Did you really expect me to? Mom, sometimes I think you are totally—"

"You didn't tell me that you actually went out with a guy."

"So now I can't date?"

"Of course you can date. Don't put words in my mouth. Dating at sixteen is fine. Speaking of which, how long have you been dating Laurence and why did you feel you couldn't tell me?"

"Since March and it's none of your business."

"As long as you live under my roof, eat my food, can't afford to pay your own tuition, and are below the age of eighteen, I'm going to have to disagree with you on that point." With Molly, no matter what she's into, if you need to ask how deeply involved in it she is, it's always safe to assume that the answer is "very." She's been pushing the envelope since she pushed her way into the world. I wasn't even about to ask the Sex Question as far as it concerned Laurence. Not in the middle of a nightclub, certainly. So I bit my tongue and chose a less inflammatory query instead. "So, why, Molly, as long as you were somehow managing to sneak into nightclubs with your boyfriend—which is another issue that I'll get to in a moment—did you choose to come to Sappho, since, it appeared to me, from your performance on the dance floor, that Laurence is a heterosexual male." I regarded Laurence's almost pretty, clean-shaven face. "And tonight he's masquerading as a straight woman who wants to pretend she's gay for a few hours." Shakespeare would have had a field day. "Either of you want to tell me what I'm missing here?"

Laurence blushed and shuffled his feet; at least his dress shoes were polished and his tuxedo pants neatly pressed. Then he reverted to teenage mumble mode.

"Sorry, I didn't hear you."

"Stop embarrassing my boyfriend, Mom!" Molly screeched. "You should consider yourself lucky that I *have* a boyfriend, instead of just hooking up, like most of my friends do!" She gripped me by the elbow just as I had done to her a minute or so earlier and steered me farther away from Laurence. Then she decided it wasn't far enough and after issuing him a curt "Wait here," dragged me into the ladies' room.

If I do find out she's been "hooking up," she's going to be grounded for life.

"I am so tempted to have it out with you right here, Molly," I fumed.

Molly lowered her voice to a whisper. "I thought you wanted to know what Laurence and I were doing in a faux gay bar."

"I do."

"Yeah, so that's why we're having this conversation in here where he can't hear us, so you can't embarrass him any further than you already have. I am *so* going to have to make it up to him after tonight."

I gave Molly a look of death. At least she had the good grace to wince.

"Okay," she said, "you asked why we came here. You want the truth, Ma? Are you sure you can handle the truth?"

"Stop paraphrasing Jack Nicholson and get to the point, Molly."

"Because he likes to see two women, you know, kissing and stuff. It turns him on, okay? And when *he's* turned on, *I'm* the recipient of that turned-on-ed-ness, okay? And that's fine with me!"

I suppose I should just act like the modern mother that I keep trying to think I am and be grateful that her boyfriend "de semester" doesn't drink, and not fret too much about his less wholesome tendencies. "Molly, you were talking a few minutes ago about social responsibility," I said, lowering my voice to a hiss. "How did you two get in here? Weren't you carded? And how do you feel knowing that you could be getting Claude and Naomi in deep shit? Everything your father and I have attempted to instill in you aside, haven't you absorbed *any* sense of ethics from attending the Ethical Culture schools for almost thirteen years?"

Molly folded her arms across her chest and narrowed her eyes, leveling a challenge at me. "The bouncer doesn't care."

"Are you telling me that you've come here before?"

"I didn't say that." It was hard to tell whether she was lying to me, particularly after her admission about Laurence's turnons. "Look," she added grumpily, "the bouncer let us in with a whole crowd of people all dressed up like we are and he didn't check IDs, okay?" *No, not okay,* I was thinking. "I didn't even see Naomi and Claude. Are they here? Why would we be getting *them* in trouble?"

"Because they own this place. And if they don't know their bouncer is admitting minors to an establishment that sells alcoholic beverages, I'm about to enlighten them."

"God, Ma! Who are you now, the FBI?"

I could have argued that the FBI had nothing to do with it and that it was the New York State Liquor Authority they'd all have to reckon with, but I didn't feel like getting into semantics with my teenage daughter.

The door to the ladies' room opened and Alice and Izzy poked their heads inside. "There you are!" Izzy exclaimed. "We wondered what the hell happened to you. Do you know there's a *guy* in here? A guest, I mean; not a bartender. Waiting right outside in the hall, in front of the pay phones."

I told them an emergency had just come up but that there was no bloodshed, everything was fine, and that they should go ahead and continue to party without me, apologizing for being unable to spend any more time with them this evening. I did not divulge that I needed to drag my disobedient and soon-to-be-grounded daughter home by her tailcoat . . . after a discreet word in the owners' collective ears.

"You don't have to act like the Gestapo," Molly moaned as I led her and Laurence toward the nightclub's exit. My patience exhausted, I chastised her for equating her Jewish mother with a Nazi, particularly on Weimar Nacht. "It's just an *expression*. You have *no* sense of humor!" she protested.

"Not tonight," I said grimly, catching sight of Naomi speaking to the bouncer. I caught her eye and she turned around.

"Leaving so soon? Hey, we're going to have a costume contest at midnight . . . Oh, shit," she muttered, recognizing my teenage daughter. "That's Molly!" She shook her head apologetically. "Don't worry, Susan, this is *not* going to happen again. Carding!!" she shrieked at the bouncer. "Carding! What have I told you about checking ID? *Every* ID. Do you want to get us shut down? I am not going to lose the business that Claude and I have been building up for seven years because some no-neck is too lazy to do his job. Next time this happens one of us is going to be facing unemployment—and it's not going to be me!"

Once on the street, I hailed a taxi and dropped Laurence in front of his apartment building. Turns out, it's around the corner from ours, right over on Central Park West. And still Molly had never introduced me to him until circumstances intervened. "You haven't heard the end of this," I warned her as we rode upstairs in the elevator. "Just wait until your father gets home."

At two A.M. Molly was sound asleep. But *I* was still waiting for Eli.

Progress Notes

Meriel Delacour: Client's focus on her employer's anthropomorphism of her pet Chihuahua is a kind of "can't see the forest for the trees" paradigm. We need to work on what's really the larger issue, the bigger picture. Client's resentment of her job situation is also rooted elsewhere. Encourage her to surmount her insecurities about her value to the workforce, not as a domestic, but as it relates to what she feels is holding her back from exploring career options, rather than accepting as the end of the line—yet all the while resenting—an unpleasant job situation. In future sessions, discuss these obstacles to risk-taking.

Naomi Sciorra and Claude Chan: The issue of adoption has created a sea change in this otherwise fairly stable relationship. Given a number of factors, including possible fear of abandonment and cultural identity, neither partner seems willing to concede any ground to the other, and each exhibits her own brand of denial in terms of the real-world scenarios or the other's sensitivity. Encourage them to function as a unified team to work through this enormous issue. Perhaps I'm not the right therapist for them at this stage because, while I'm entirely sympathetic to the hurdles facing gay couples seeking to adopt a foreign-born child, I have strong opinions on the subject, believing that all children should have the chance to be raised in a loving home, regardless of the sexual orientation of the parent(s); and therefore, even at the expense of shading a truth in order to pass muster with the bureaucracies.

Which brings me to . . .

Me: One of the cardinal tenets of being an effective therapist is to practice what you preach. How can we expect our clients to understand, and then run with, behavioral concepts that we can't master ourselves? How do I come off trying to help Claude and Naomi become good parents when I'm clearly failing, or at least falling down on the job, with my own daughter? Turning into a tyrant and grounding Molly will have an adverse effect (I know I'm backpedaling here), but if my rules remain the same as always, where's her punishment? Or, more importantly, what will she have learned from the Sappho incident, and will she apply that lesson to her behavior in the future? Who am I kidding? She's a *teenager,* not a test case!

COLD WATER

5

TALIA

"I think it'll be good for me, y'know?" Talia said. For the past several sessions she'd been foregoing the laundry room couch for the floor. She'd sit on her yoga mat with her legs in a deep second position split, which is where she was this morning as she once again underplayed her achievements.

"Good? I'd suggest popping the cork on some champagne but it has calories. Talia, it's fantastic! You've been striving to be made a principal ever since you were accepted into the company."

Talia nodded. "Yeah, I know, but champagne is too obviously . . . exultant, y'know? And I hate to jinx it," she replied, touching her forehead to her right knee.

"For the time being, let's leave superstition to Mala Sonia," I gently suggested. "You've earned this spot."

"I can't believe I'm doing the pas de deux in 'Diamonds.' I've dreamed about it for years from the wings. I've danced in the other two segments, 'Rubies' and 'Emeralds.' *Jewels* is one of Balanchine's greatest ballets and it's a big crowd favorite and all that, but the 'Diamonds' segment is the most special. I'm going to be dancing the role that Balanchine choreographed for Suzanne Farrell, and she's always been my idol, y'know?" She stretched out over her left knee.

Never in a million years, even at my most flexible, could I touch my forehead to my knee—and leave it there indefinitely. "I am so happy for you. Enjoy this moment, Talia. This entire experience. Resist all temptations to beat yourself up."

"Yeah, you're right. It's just so hard not to. Though my mother is good at beating me up—emotionally—for the both of us. I couldn't wait to tell her that I'd be dancing the 'Diamonds' pas de deux up in Saratoga this summer. And y'know what she told me when I said I hoped she'd come up to see me dance it?" I shook my head and waited for Talia to continue. "She said one of the cats is sick and she doesn't want to leave it alone." She gracefully folded her body over her right leg again. "My mother said she wouldn't trust a sitter with a sick cat and she certainly wasn't going to leave it in a strange hotel room upstate." And again over her left leg.

My thoughts drifted to Meriel's question regarding white people and their dogs. She and Amy were constantly battling over Hector the Chihuahua's proper place in the world. Most housekeepers would have gotten fired for such outspokenness, but Meriel confided to me that she was too good at her job to lose it, and Amy had admitted in *her* session that she just wasn't up to conducting interviews for someone new and that Eric liked the way Meriel ironed his shirts. "Of course I told him I'd be happy to send them out," Amy had said, "but the truth is that there isn't a decent place in the neighborhood and Eric hates the idea of some stranger touching his garments."

Any therapist who tells you that her mind never wanders during a session is lying.

Talia reached for the ceiling. "So I said to her—my mother—

'Hey, I'm your daughter, y'know. A person. Not a fucking cat. That cat's not going to take care of you when you finally get cirrhosis.' Of course the way things are going she's going to die alone of a rotten liver with her cats crawling over her, wondering why the lady who always fed them isn't moving." Talia stretched her arms toward the washers and leaned forward so that her forehead was touching the mat in front of her.

"My mother has never understood me," she added, her voice muffled by her contorted posture. "I don't know what it was she wanted me to *become*, y'know?"

"You've done remarkably well, Talia. I'd encourage you not to focus on whether or not your promotion pleases your mom, because she's one of those people who, unfortunately, lacks the capacity to share your triumph in a positive way. No matter how fast you dance—metaphorically speaking now—she won't give you the applause and the bouquet without the thorns, and without finding a way of begrudging them—or even denying them—to you. Look at what you have to be proud of: you should be very pleased *yourself* by your accomplishments. How many people get to follow their bliss in life? *And* make a living at it?" Every day I count my own blessings in that regard.

My job has its challenges, to be sure, but I meet fascinating people from all walks of life, and when they grow, I grow too. Would I have loved to become a professional dancer? At the time I switched college majors, the answer was yes, but now . . . ? I'm less sure about it. Put it this way: knowing what I know now, I've never regretted my decision.

"Well, it's not like I didn't *work* for what I've achieved," Talia said dismissively.

"I didn't say that. Or mean to imply it."

"I mean, I think I did pretty good for someone who never even went to college, y'know?" Vertebra by vertebra she rolled up to a seated position and smoothed a recalcitrant strand of hair that had the audacity to defect from her dark bun. "Most people who never go to college end up working at McDonald's or something."

"Well, that's one way to look at it," I replied.

Talia looked momentarily studious. "Y'know, I make a living doing what I love to do most and I don't even need to know how to count higher than eight. And some of the time I only have to start at five!"

It was hard to believe she was serious, but she didn't crack a smile. Talia Shaw is one of those very literal people who don't do—or tend to get—irony. Her mathematical observation reminded me of the audition sequence in *A Chorus Line* where the choreographer sets the tempo for the jazz steps with "a-five, six, seven, eight!"

"How old were you when you first started ballet lessons?" I asked her. It was just about time to wrap up our session. She'd risen and begun to dance a combination involving zillions of *pas de bourrées*.

"Four. No—wait. Four was *Ulysses* on my head." Raising her arms in an exquisite port de bras, Talia *bourréed* across the floor like the Dying Swan. "Five. I started classes at five."

"Oh, well. Too late for Molly," I muttered to myself, only half joking. I'm glad that my daughter wasn't, and isn't, one of the overprivileged overprogrammed, with a different after-school activity every day of the week since kindergarten, but my biggest fear is that Molly—who may never get to college the way she's going academically—might actually end up with a McCareer; she hasn't spent the last decade of her life in the passionate pursuit of her life's ambition. Talia was right. *Her* talent and dedication—and drive—enabled her to succeed without a college education. In Molly's case, there's *nothing* that I know of that she wants more than anything in the world. There are a number of things at which she shows promise, but she lacks all motivation. Molly will need to know how to count higher than eight.

ME

Over brunch one Sunday, Eli and I sat down with Molly to discuss her college prospects. We'd visited a few schools over the spring; and between her unenthusiastic reaction to the campuses or the students or the faculty or the food or the weather or any combination of the above, and the schools' unenthusiastic reaction to Molly and what she could—or couldn't—bring to their respective institutions, the entire experience was pretty much a bust all around. Since then she's more or less settled on her first choice. At the moment, figuring she'd have a better chance of getting accepted as a legacy, it's between Bennington (my alma mater), and NYU, which is Eli's. Although she'll take the test again this fall, her current SAT scores are lousy, her academics are worse, and she has no extracurricular activities that would set off ecstatic bells and whistles in any hallowed hall. She's never played on any athletic teams, and pooh-poohs what she calls the "dork clubs" like debating or chess, which seem to have enjoyed a renaissance since her father and I were in high school. Molly had a few poems and short stories published in the lit mag, did a couple of shows through the drama department—mostly, I think, to prove to her kid brother that she could act too—and participated in a handful of modern dance recitals. This meager résumé would even have been unremarkable back when I was applying to college; nowadays the bar has been set impossibly high for most students of modest incomes and backgrounds.

For example, some of Molly's classmates, concerned that volunteering to serve Thanksgiving dinner in a homeless shelter didn't give them enough of a competitive edge in the college admissions wars, have interned at the Supreme Court, designed and successfully marketed their own line of sportswear, had a showing of their life-size metallurgy sculptures at an edgy SoHo gallery, and one polyglot spent his school vacations as a sherpa guide. Okay, his grandfather really *is* a full-time sherpa and his father is a Nepalese diplomat with connections . . . but still. Molly could never compete with—or should I say *against*—that in a zillion years. And applying to college these days is very much a competition. I've come to regard the entire hair-raising process as a combination of filing your income taxes and running with the bulls at Pamplona.

It both worries and disturbs me that my daughter is so apathetic about something so significant. Maybe the stress that Eli and I have placed on the importance of college has somehow had the effect of pushing Molly further and further away from the subject. Last night I warned her that if she didn't focus in the coming semester and really ramp up her grades, she might be looking at Manhattan Community College as her "safety school."

"Ma," she'd whined, "they teach ESL to the freshmen! Whoever heard of a person getting accepted to a college in America who can't even speak English!"

"Well, then you'll excel academically," I said simply. She couldn't tell whether I was kidding. I'm not even sure myself.

"Maybe I'll just backpack around the world instead of college."

"What will you use for money?"

"I'll think of something. I could always sell my body."

"Don't test me, Molly." I would never force her to waste tens of thousands of dollars of our money—hundreds, by the time she graduates, hypothetically—but I'm as burned out on this subject as Molly is. If only she were hungry for something. If she were going to backpack in search of something a little less vague than "herself," it might actually sit well with me. Eli too. We realize that all high school seniors are not college material the following year, if ever. But Molly's lack of direction suggests very few options. College life should provide some structure. I hope she does apply to Bennington, and I hope to hell they'll find a good enough reason to want her. I want her to experience dormitory life, the world beyond New York City, and that middle space between total dependence on her parents and complete freedom before it's time for her to permanently leave the nest.

Eli and I reviewed the Molly college issue after we made love last night, although I have to admit that I tried to postpone the conversation as much as possible. About fifteen minutes after he'd rolled over, I snuggled up next to him and tried to get things going again. He accused me of being a sex maniac.

"Sex maniac?" I'd said. "I haven't heard that phrase since high school. And since when is wanting to have sex with your husband twice in one night being a 'sex maniac'? Whatever happened to all the inventive, creative stuff we used to do?"

"We've been married for almost twenty years," Eli said simply.

His words stung like a slap, but I ducked an argument. "So," I chuckled, trying to keep it light, "is that supposed to be an excuse? I refuse to accept that two decades of marriage and two kids *have to* take a toll on a couple's sex life. I know it's the usual, but it needn't be the norm."

"Aw, Susie, don't get all 'shrinky' on me."

"*I'm* not the one who got 'shrinky,'" I said, fondling him. Then I jumped his bones.

Finally, just before Eli was all set to roll over again, leaving that vast territory of no-man's slumberland between "his side" and "my side" of the bed, we discussed Molly.

"I told her she's really going to have to change her habits if she's got a prayer of getting into a good school, unless she wants to enroll at one of the CUNY campuses. The city doesn't seem to care much who they take these days, but it also means a degree from them will be worth shit. Even the state schools are highly competitive now. They can afford to be picky."

"Molly's Molly," Eli said sleepily. "She's always been Molly. She's never been interested in academics, has no use for sports, is generally apathetic about the performing arts—she's not Ian. She's Molly."

I stroked his back. "So you're saying you don't think she can change her attitude?"

"You tell me. You're the shrink. I 'draw comic books for a living,' remember?"

"You don't have to get snide. This is a serious discussion about our daughter, not a battlefield."

"I wasn't getting snide. You misread me. It was a joke."

It didn't sound like much of a joke to me, but I let it drop.

Eli brushed a strand of hair from my eyes. "You think too much, Susie."

"Well," I said, feeling my hackles rise, despite my better judgment, "I'm tired of being the only one doing any active thinking when it comes to a discussion about what goes on around here. I help people all day," I sighed, "I'm the problem solver, the one people expect to 'fix' them. And then I come home and I feel that I'm the problem solver here all the time too. I know you've been busy with *Gia* lately . . . you've got deadlines . . . and I don't call you at the studio every time something comes up—though Lord knows, whenever I do try to reach you I always get your voice mail anyway—but I need your support, especially on parenting issues. I feel like I'm doing everything alone most of the time."

"Well, you're so good at it," Eli replied. From the tone of his voice, it appeared to be an attempt at mollification as well as a period on the subject. Closing his eyes was another hint that should have tipped me off, but I couldn't let it go.

"I want us to work as a team: to share the responsibilities." I looked at Eli, playing possum, and waited for a response. None was forthcoming. Not only had I wrecked the afterglow, but I'd made myself crabby and tense—and even acted needy, a real turnoff—in the bargain.

"And," I added, "when it comes to Molly, specifically, more than fifteen years of experience in the field, a Ph.D., and a zillion lightbulb jokes tell me that people can only change if they want to." Actually, I believe that people can't change who they are, fundamentally, in many ways—unless of course they need medication to balance the chemicals in their brain—but they can change their behavior, which affects who they are and what they do. "Molly may always be a sullen loner, but she doesn't have to be a sullen loner with lousy study habits."

"I'm going to sleep," Eli announced, grabbing a fistful of bed-clothes. "And we may just have to let go and let Molly go her own way, even if it's not the way we want her to go. Because I still think people don't change."

I couldn't fall asleep after that. The whole postcoital conversation had made me too gloomy.

FAITH

"Look! Will you look at this blouse, Susan!"

For a split second I thought that Faith wanted me to notice a rip or stain somewhere on the fabric. Then I realized that she was crowing over another breakthrough. "It's blue!" I exclaimed, clapping my hands. "Brava!"

Faith's color heightened beneath her rouge. "Well, the sales-clerk called it 'indigo,' but it's a step. It's definitely a step!"

I'd never seen her in anything other than a shade of purple. "Yes! You took another risk and survived! You look wonderful, Faith. You should try it more often."

"Well," Faith demurred, "I almost bought an *orange* sweater for the fall. Rust, you'd really call it, I suppose. But I'm not quite ready for that yet. It's just . . . too much of a departure for me. You know, I'm the woman who dips one toe at a time into the swimming pool. Of course we have another couple of months to go until the weather starts getting cooler. Perhaps I should have purchased it nonetheless—and saved it for that rainy day! But you know my relationship to money."

"So what happened?" I asked excitedly. "I'm dying to know what precipitated the momentous decision to buy a garment that wasn't purple." Unlike some therapists who seem to thrive on their patients' anxieties so that they feel they have some-thing to "fix," I become delighted when my clients make tangi-ble progress. For Faith this forward momentum was materially evident, so to speak, in her "indigo" blouse.

"Holy cats, it looks like it lost a tooth," Faith suddenly blurted, and I worried that she had suddenly become senile. Catching my totally perplexed expression, she pointed to the line of washing machines. Until a few days ago there were six of them in a row, all white and shiny and gleaming like a perfect smile. Now there was a gap where number four—Ian's "boggart machine"—had stood. Stevo had finally removed the defunct unit after leaving the yellow "crime scene" tape across it for weeks. He's repeatedly promised the tenants that a new ma-chine is on order. I won't hold my breath. Every time someone asks Mala Sonia about it, figuring she's got the most direct line to Stevo, she makes the "crazy sign"—spiraling her index finger in front of her ear—and mutters *"dili"* under her breath. I asked Eli what *dili* was and he laughed and told me the word meant "mentally retarded."

I smiled. "Faith . . . ?"

"I know, I know. But I wasn't evading that time; I was *observing*. You asked me several sessions ago to work on living my life for myself and not for Ben's memory. Well, you'll be tickled to know that I took your advice to heart; and Susan, I've noticed that I notice more now. Truly. All since I decided it was time to take those baby steps forward. Ever since the night I decided to sleep on Ben's side of the bed. Would you believe it, now I even sleep on the diagonal sometimes! I feel so *racy*. It's terribly unlike me. And this week . . . I decided it was time to get out more; and you know how I always loved the opera and the classical concerts at Lincoln Center and the jazz series at the 92nd Street Y. So, guess what I did?" I smiled and waited for her to continue. "It was very spontaneous of me, but I called each of them on the phone, and I bought a subscription. The expense itself was *a lot* more than a baby step. It felt like a tremendous leap forward, you realize."

"You bet I realize! Faith, that's terrific! And I couldn't be prouder of you. Congratulations!"

She rose and added another two quarters to her permanent press cycle. "Goodness, it seems to cost more and more to do the laundry down here. There was a time when that same fifty cents would have bought twenty minutes of drying time. Now it buys twelve." Faith emitted a disgusted little sigh. "Uch. Inflation."

She watched her garments swirl behind the glass like purple eddies. "I had forgotten how costly the opera tickets are. My subscription to the Met is higher than my annual rent!"

"That's because your apartment is rent-controlled. But I take your point."

"I must say, I think I've taken several long strides lately with these lanky legs of mine." Pleased with herself, Faith used her right index finger to tick off her accomplishments on her left hand. "First, the bed. And an indigo blouse. And the music series subscriptions. Ouch! I think that last one hurt the most, frankly. My wallet is shrinking as my horizons expand. I'm not terribly sanguine about that, I'll have you know; however, I suppose it's all part of the head-shrinking process too." She sighed again. "But it's true, of course, that you can't take it with you. I have no children to leave it to, and I'm making sure my charities won't suffer just because I've decided it's time to spend a little money on myself." She looked dubious. "All right, I don't really believe that last remark. I just thought it was something you'd like to hear. The part about spending money on myself, I mean."

"Faith."

"Telling you what I think you'd want to hear: I suppose that's cheating."

"You're only cheating yourself." Then I told her where to find designer shoes at a discount.

ALICE

"It feels so weird, talking to someone other than Gram about what's going on in my life," Alice said. "I'm definitely not used to it yet, so bear with me." She told me about the "name game" her grandmother used to play that was Irene's folkloric way of sizing up a person. It had something to do with tea leaves. No wonder Alice had been such a vulnerable mark for Mala Sonia.

"I'm still at that place where I wake up every morning and expect her to be there." I nodded, encouraging her to continue. "I'm not even sure whether there's, like, an appropriate mourning period I should observe. I could have sat shiva for her, but she married an Irishman and never felt particularly Jewish, so I don't know who I'd be doing it for. Not for me. I'm not a religious person." Alice began to tear up. Sometimes I think I've made more women weep than Barbara Walters.

"Why are you crying now?" I asked softly.

"I know you're probably going to think this makes no sense, but every time I've ever mentioned to anyone that I don't feel any particular religious connection, I start to cry."

"What do you think that's about?" I gently continued.

"I don't know. Maybe that means I really do feel something, and I'm lying to myself. Gram didn't believe that there's some guy up there," Alice said, pointing toward the grimy ceiling, "with white hair and a flowing beard looking like something out of an Italian Renaissance painting, but she did believe in a higher power." Alice tapped her chest. "In here. Like a moral compass in a way." She took a deep breath. "I believe what Gram believed. And though I say I'm not religious, I feel a *spiritual* connection to the world and to that force inside each of us. Yet, at the same time, I do think of Gram up in 'heaven' looking down on me. Watching me. Remember what Mala Sonia said that day about her wanting me to be happy? I certainly believe that's the case."

"Well, of course it is, but you don't need a Gypsy psychic to tell you that."

Alice looked embarrassed. "I did have her read my cards after all. It was just twenty bucks, so I thought, what the hell?" She shrugged sheepishly. "I expect you want to know what the reading said."

I nodded. "Yup."

"Oh! Do you ever cry like I just did? I feel so stupid. So vulnerable. I feel like whenever I talk to you, all I ever do is cry. And I'm really an upbeat person, I swear it! Ask Izzy."

"Alice, your favorite relative—the person you were closest to—passed away very recently. It's totally understandable that you're feeling this vulnerable and your emotions are so raw. And yes, I do sometimes cry like that, and feel stupid about crying, even when I know it's stupid to feel stupid. I cry like that when people are nice to me. Spontaneous acts of kindness and generosity—and I'm a puddle. Now . . . back to you. I'm dying to hear about Mala Sonia's reading."

"She did the reading in her apartment," Alice told me. "Have you ever been down there?" I shook my head. "A total mess. Everything is filthy. And it stinks. Like sweat and cat piss and who knows what. And there's dirty clothes all over the place, like a bunch of ragamuffins did a striptease from room to room. For a woman who does so much laundry all the time, you'd think the place would smell better. I guess none of them have met a stick of deodorant. And yet, *she's* sort of sexy. Like a poor man's Sophia Loren in a way. That exotic voluptuousness, and the bright colors she wears. Yeah, she's sort of a stereotype but I think she does it deliberately. It certainly sets her apart from the rest of us drab drones."

"You're hardly drab, Alice. Or a drone."

"You never had any of my day jobs."

I laughed. "I take your point."

"Okay, so the first thing she does is yell at one of her boys in Romany and the kid cowers. Then she barks something else at her little daughter and the poor girl starts to wail. I can't begin to imagine what she said to her. So all the kids—maybe four of them—plus two mangy cats and a ferret—aren't ferrets illegal in New York apartments—anyway, they all scatter like rats at the sound of the Pied Piper's first trill, and then Mala Sonia takes a rolled up magazine and clears off her coffee table with one huge swipe, like this." Alice demonstrated the maneuver with tremendous dramatic flair. "I'm not sure Naomi's right about her, though. If Mala Sonia's ripping off *gaje* right and left, you'd think she and Stevo would live better. I'm sure they don't pay any rent, since he's the super."

The state of the super's apartment made me think about the general inattention to decor in our building. Would it kill the landlord to authorize Stevo to employ his wife's love of bright colors in the laundry room? Alice had just used the word "drab" to mischaracterize her personality. *This place* is drab. I glanced at the two-tone gray walls, darker from floor to about waist level, then a lighter hue from there to the ceiling. The uneven cement floor is painted the same slate shade as the lower walls. Fluorescent strip lights suspended over the room's center table and sofa also do little to enhance the atmosphere.

"Mala Sonia asked for my money up front, by the way," Alice said. "So I took a twenty out of my wallet, to show her in good faith that I had it, but I didn't want to pay her until she actually gave me the reading. She wasn't too happy about that, but I pretended I was getting up to leave, so she relented. Then she asked me to think of an important question—something I needed an answer to—while she shuffled the cards. 'Don't tell me out loud, just think very hard your question,' she said." Alice was a gifted mimic, imitating Mala Sonia's accent and mannerisms to perfection. " 'But I caution you this: don't use word "ever" in your question. Like "Will I ever get married?" "Ever" very bad for cards.' Then she laid out what she explained was a modified Celtic Cross: six cards instead of ten. I asked her why she wasn't giving me the full Celtic Cross, and—get this! She told me that her basic twenty-dollar reading was for six cards. For the full Celtic Cross she charges fifty!"

I rolled my eyes. Though I shouldn't have been surprised. Naomi was right. "Okay, so what was your question for Mala Sonia?" Alice hesitated. "Alice, I know we behave like this is a gabfest much of the time, but what's said in this room stays in this room. We're also in a doctor-patient confidence mode here. It's not like I'm going to tell anybody."

"Oh, all right," Alice sighed. "It was so dippy, though. All I thought to myself was, *What the hell is going to happen to my life now?* That's pretty vague. It's not like, 'Will I get involved with a great guy?' "

"Will you?" I asked, chuckling. "That would be cool."

Alice held up her hand. "Wait." She settled back into the corner of the sofa, tucking her legs underneath her. "I think what must have happened was that the hypothetical 'great guy' question pushed the vaguer one to the back of my mind. So, she's got the six cards all laid out and she says, 'Everybody looking for love. Everybody want to know will they meet love of their life. You want to know about Mr. Right, but cards may tell you about Mr. Right Now. Who may not be right for you in future. So you come back for second reading.' Yeah, right. At least I was too wise to fall for *that* trick." Alice laughed. "So I told her I wanted to change my mind. My new question was, 'Is my role in *Grandma Finnegan's Wake* going to make me a big star?'

" 'Are you sure you want to go with cards in spread?' Mala Sonia asked me. 'Cards are already laid.' I figured it was bad karma or something to change it and said yes, let's leave these cards on the table. So she tells me that the first card is one from the Major Arcana: Strength. 'This represents your experience to date,' Mala Sonia told me. 'In upright position like this is very good. You have strength and control over your situation. More than that, you have energy and determination to succeed.' So I said, 'That sounds good,' and then she tells me that the second card, representing where I am now, the Eight of Cups in the reversed position, was also very favorable because it meant that I would continue my effort until full success was attained. It would come in a holiday time where there would be joy and feasting. Now I'm thinking that there aren't any feast times coming up in the near future—Thanksgiving and Christmas are months away—and I suck at delayed gratification. And speaking of the near future, that's what the third card represents. So in my spread it was the Five of Wands in the upright position. Bad news. It spoke of unsatisfied desires in labor endeavors—which is my career, right? It gets worse. The card also represents competition, aggression, obstacles, and conflicts."

"And how did that make you feel?" I asked Alice.

"Tense. Pissed off. Cranky. Because I was believing the reading and relating it to my *Grandma Finnegan* job and the near future of my acting career. So the fourth card, which Mala Sonia explained was me within the environment of my near future, was another Major Arcana card: Justice. But, with my shitty luck, it's in the reversed position, highlighting intolerance, unfairness, accusations, a false friend and/or bad business partner . . . and my situation in the show has been really great so far, so now I was hoping that this was all a mistake. Because from Mala Sonia's reading it was looking like my *Grandma Finnegan* experience is going to turn out to be a horror show. And I went through that already with a couple of my recent office temp jobs. Believe me, job strife and false accusations are the *last* thing I need right about now! I've been thinking that things are finally looking up for me, and then I get this killjoy reading!"

"You have two more cards," I said, trying to sound positive.

Alice buried her face in her hands. "I didn't know whether to laugh or cry, because the fifth card represents the best you can hope for."

"Which was . . . ?"

"Mala Sonia tells me, 'I hate to bring bad news, but Ace of Swords in reversed position indicates *debacle*. Tyranny. Hostility. Have you ever tried to make a baby?' The question was such a non sequitur. So I just said, 'What??' She repeated her question, and I told her no, and so far I haven't had any interest in doing that. She then says, 'Just checking. Card indicates infertility, which for your question can mean impotence, powerless to act or bring to fruition your goal.' I think that was around the time I asked her to just hand me a razor blade."

"What about the last card?" I questioned, almost afraid to hear the result.

"The last card represents the outcome of the situation relating to my question," Alice said, shaking her head. "You're looking at the Queen of Failure here. Why the fuck were so many of my cards in reverse? The last card was the Eight of Wands—upside down—of course, and I might have guessed its meaning."

"Which was?"

"Discord, delay, dispute, jealousy, harassment, even domestic quarrels—and I live alone! So I started to cry a little and Mala Sonia slid the cards together and put the tarot deck away and said, 'Sorry you are unhappy, but it is not me who is cause. Cards tell story; I only interpret. Cards don't lie. Now give me your twenty dollars.' "

I can't remember when I'd seen a patient look so defeated. I reminded Alice that the cards only had as much weight and meaning as she was willing to accord them. I encouraged her to dismiss the interpretation as nothing more than twenty dollars worth of entertainment: to think of it as a couple of tickets to a movie that ended up sucking, and suggested rather forcefully that she cease referring to herself as the Queen of Failure.

"Speaking evil over yourself becomes a self-fulfilling prophecy because you train yourself to believe it. We teach others how to treat us, Alice. And if we insist on seeing ourselves as failures or lacking in confidence about whatever it is we consider 'important,' whether it's personal or financial success, talent, looks, brains—whatever—that is how the outside world will view us. Those are very treacherous waters in which to tread. Believe me, most of us go through this at some point in our lives. Parents, teachers, bosses, even jealous people who claim to be your friends, may seek to put you down. I had a modern dance teacher in college who used to make fun of my wide hips in class—in front of everyone—and I believed her when she said that I had no future as a dancer. My lousy body image kept me bulimic for years."

Alice nodded mutely, but I wasn't sure she'd absorbed the message. It's the kind of thing that takes time to actually put into practice. You can't instantly revamp your self-image just because your therapist reminds you that the world sees you as you see yourself. Oddly enough, it was the brutality of my dance instructor that catalyzed my decision to transfer out of a dance major into psychology.

"You know . . ." Alice said finally, as we began to wrap up her session. "I had a drama teacher in high school who always used to tell his students: 'If you don't believe it, I won't believe it. And if I don't believe it, the *audience* certainly won't believe it!' Why is it that I can apply that to my acting but not to the rest of my life?"

"I can relate," I assured her. "And now we have something to talk about next week," I added, unlocking the door.

*   *   *

"I suppose it's a good thing I didn't ask Mala Sonia about my love life," Alice said, once we were off the clock and speaking just woman-to-woman. "Because I did in fact meet a cute guy. Technically, I *met* him when I was going out with someone else—Amy Baum's husband in fact—God, this is becoming incestuous! Do you know a little girl in this building named Lucy? She's maybe seven years old? Has an uncle named Dan Carpenter who's an actual carpenter—and a total hottie?"

"I know Lucy," I told her. "Lucy Eyre."

"Please don't tell me her mother's name is Jane."

I laughed. "It's Diana. Diana and Jim Eyre and their daughter Lucy live in 6A. Lucy has had a crush on Ian since before she could talk."

"What does Ian think about that?"

"Well, after he went in one end and out the other of the 'ick—girls!' phase, I think he became kind of flattered. Lucy's parents took her to see Ian in *Les Miz* and she went backstage after the show, which kind of put them both over the moon. It was the first time anyone had ever asked Ian for his autograph, and when he heard the page that he had a visitor, he was twice as excited as I'd ever seen him on Christmas morning."

"You celebrate Christmas?" Alice asked, perplexed. "I thought you're Jewish."

"We're 'Christmas tree Jews,' " I replied. "Assimilated, non-practicing New Yorkers with the 'if you can't beat 'em, join 'em' mentality about celebrating Christmas. Nature made pine trees before people invented religion. Besides, history tells us that Jesus was the Jewish son of a Nazarene carpenter. I never attended Sunday School or Hebrew School; I wasn't bas-mitzvahed. Heck, I learned the names of the twelve tribes of Israel from the lyrics to *Joseph and the Amazing Technicolor Dreamcoat*."

"Speaking of *Carpenters*," Alice said, blushing a bit. "Dan Carpenter and the Eyres?"

"I don't know Diana's brother. The Eyres are never down here, though." I leaned toward Alice and brought my finger to my lips. "Diana has an illegal washer and dryer unit," I whispered conspiratorially. "Their apartment was refurbished after the rent-stabilized tenant moved out, so they've got all new plumbing in their kitchen. Of course they're also paying market value, so I don't envy them *that* much."

"Well, I've got something else to talk about in our next session," Alice said. "Dan asked me out. He's come over to the apartment a bunch of times to repair an antique settee and he finally made his move. Oh, apropos of nothing, last week I saw Ian on that commercial for the water park in New Jersey. It was on a whole bunch of times. If he keeps that up he can pay for his own college tuition! Tell him I said congratulations."

"I certainly will. Now, spill," I teased, "about Dan Carpenter." Alice shook her head. I tried cajoling. "Aw, c'mon. Just girl talk. Unofficially. We're off the clock here."

"Nope. Besides, there's nothing to share until Danny Boy and I actually have that date."

"Spoilsport." After her recounting of the disastrous tarot reading, I was delighted to see her in a better mood.

Progress Notes

Talia Shaw: A tremendous leap forward on client's career front, but she's still hung up on pleasing her mother and is devastated that her mom has elected to stay home with a sick cat rather than see her daughter dance her first principal role with NYCB up in Saratoga. I raised the subject of her mother's inability to give Talia the kind of admiration she expects from her. It remains to be seen how she fares when the dust settles. Will continue to work on the core self-esteem issue until client heads out of town.

Faith Nesbit: I'm delighted that she's continuing to actively work on everything we're discussing in her sessions. Her non-purple clothing is a bold step (yet in her own characteristically cautious way) in making a conscious effort to expand her horizons beyond living for Ben's memory. Ditto the music subscriptions. I'm also pleased that she's taking these steps in keeping with her own behavioral limits. I want to continue on the same course with her sessions, though we need to discuss how her frequent references to the financial cost of her progress may in fact impact negatively upon it, and psychologically as well as materially dampen her ability to achieve further forward momentum.

Alice Finnegan: Alice is a new client, presenting with severe symptoms of grief, having recently lost her grandmother, who was her closest relative and roommate for several years. Alice also expresses guilt at never having been able to say good-bye to her grandmother—something that was out of her control under the circumstances—and she also has job issues to work through. On that score, she has recently reached a milestone on her own, having successfully escaped the world of office temping for an Off-Broadway role. However, she's already experiencing anxiety about her stage career, as exhibited in her reaction to the negative "psychic reading" she received from the super's wife, Mala Sonia Badescu. Part of our work will be to address and focus on Alice's self-confidence issues, to allow her to securely place her trust in herself and not in others.

Me: I wish Eli were more open to discussing Molly with me—not just with reference to her college prospects, or lack thereof—but in how our parenting, both individually and collectively, isn't as effective as it could be. In believing that he's a liberal, progressive father, Eli's laissez-faire attitude vis-à-vis our daughter's behavior isn't doing her any favors. Funny, he's not that way with Ian; with Ian, Eli's always been clear about limits. On the other hand, Ian has yet to demonstrate any signs of rebellious behavior. Fathers and sons, mothers and daughters . . . fathers and daughters. It's not as though Molly's a "Daddy's girl," but Eli's way of indulging her takes the form of ignoring her bad behavior, not so much for her sake, but for his own . . . so as not to make waves, rock the boat. Eli's never been great at dealing with anything that's going to be in any way difficult or problematic. He'd prefer to play "ostrich." I can't get away with doing that. Someone's got to be the grown-up. My husband having abrogated those responsibilities as much as possible, I'm the one in the Lederer household left without a musical chair to sit on.

Maybe Molly's acting out is partly a cry for a reaction from her father. Lately, Eli has been increasing the distance between himself and the other members of his family. He attributes this to his deadlines, but he's had deadlines in the past . . . his rejection of me in bed the other night hit me very hard, and yet I let the subject drop and didn't raise it again, something I would never let one of my clients get away with.

Alice and Faith have been in mourning for those dearest to their hearts, and while I acknowledge that their pain has been (even continues to be) lacerating at times, I find myself half wishing for a familial relationship that was as tight as the bond between Alice and her grandmother Irene or half as loving as what Faith and Ben had. While our marriage is solid and essentially healthy, Eli doesn't even take out the trash, let alone kiss me good-bye on the way to the compactor. Although my mother isn't interested in knowing who Molly's become, but instead in who *she* wants Molly to be, and has never quite known what to make of Ian, and always seems bemused by Eli and me, I do admit to being grateful that I'm not constantly dancing as fast as I can in an attempt to please or appease someone like Talia's mother.

I used to think I had a relatively functional childhood. Sure, my parents argued from time to time, but it was never about the big stuff. They'd quarrel about who left the bread on top of the refrigerator, and I never grasped at the time what the big deal was. Why such a fuss about a loaf of bread? Who cares? So I'd do stuff like put the loaf in the bread box where it belonged, playing the peacemaker, the problem solver. It took years (and a couple of psych classes) before I understood that my parents' argument had nothing to do with the bread.

That's another reason I became a therapist: to try to help people get to the heart of the issue, not dance around it; to confront—which is risky and scary—but ultimately healthier than playing "ostrich" and hoping that if you hide from your problems, they'll magically go away.

If someone were to ask me whether I have a happy marriage, I suppose I'd have to answer them by saying that I am not *unhappy*. Eli and I love each other very much . . . although I'd hate to think that we've "plateau-ed." He's been working like such a demon on his *Gia the Gypsy Girl* book that he's practically fluent in Romany! I think *I'm also* using his writing schedule as an excuse to postpone talking to him about what's bothering me lately. Just because I can recognize deliberate procrastination and passive-aggressiveness in my patients, and encourage them to face and work through their issues, it doesn't mean I don't fear dealing with my own!

Who's playing "ostrich" now?

HOT WATER

NAOMI AND CLAUDE

"We checked out other agencies, but the rules seem to be the same all around," Claude sighed. "We thought it was maybe just the agency we'd selected—this place in Georgia—a state that still had a sodomy law on the books until 1988! And you have to go through an agency if you want to adopt internationally. Unfortunately, the rules are universal: no lesbian couples can adopt from China. So we're back to square one with the application process."

"We were hoping you might be able to help us fill out the application," Naomi added. "Well, I was hoping you'd help Claude, because frankly I'm still too angry to touch it."

"Is it still the idea that you can't adopt as a couple that's bothering you?" I asked her.

Naomi looked darkly at Claude. Often they sat side by side on the sofa during their sessions in the laundry room, usually holding hands. But for the past month or so, ever since they'd begun discussing the adoption, they had gradually moved farther and farther apart from one another. Today, Naomi was curled up in a corner of the couch with her bare feet tucked

under her, as though she were a feral jungle animal, coiled and
ready to pounce at a moment's notice.

"It's worse," she said. "In fact it's so much worse, I don't even
know why I'm still here. I should just pack my stuff and move
out."

"Do you really mean that?" I asked her.

Claude had tears in her eyes. She looked over at Naomi. "I
wish you wouldn't," she said softly. "I mean, I hope you don't.
It's just—bullshit: the paper. It's a form, Nay. It doesn't really
mean anything."

"Yeah? *That's* bullshit. You have to have it notarized, so it's
like swearing on a Bible in court and then committing perjury."

"Would either—or both—of you like to tell me what this is
all about?" I asked. "You just asked me to help you with the application, but I can't even help you get over today's hurdle if
you leave me in the dark here."

"I have to sign a paper," Claude began, staring at the floor.
Her expression admitted defeat; her voice was filled with resignation. She took a deep breath. "I have to swear before a notary
public that I'm 'heterosexual and actively seeking a husband.'
Which, of course, is a lie."

Wow. My jaw dropped. It's been hard enough for me to behave impartially on this issue, but caught off guard by Claude's
statement, I couldn't disguise my spontaneous expression of
amazement and disgust.

"The whole thing is dishonest!" snapped Naomi. "This is
coming from people who don't even *want* these kids—they
think they're a drain on their society—and they have the nerve
to decide who *is* allowed to want them?! Please tell me you see
the irony—not to mention the hypocrisy—in this!"

Claude continued to focus on the floor. "All the background
checks and the fingerprinting and bonding are intrusive enough,

but I can totally understand why they do them. Do you know that you have to provide the adoption agency with every address you've ever lived at since they instituted the background checks for pedophiles—all the way back to 1979 or something? And then they contact the police precincts in each one of those zip codes to make sure that your name doesn't turn up. But this paper swearing I'm straight—it's just too much for Naomi."

"It should be too much for *you!*" Naomi insisted.

"It *is*," sighed Claude. "But there's no way around it. If I don't sign this paper, we don't get our daughter from China. It's a horrible ethical dilemma. And *ridiculous*, isn't it?"

I nodded. "And it is dishonest to swear that," I agreed. "You know that old saying that everything that's good for you is either illegal, immoral, or fattening. But I suppose it could be argued that signing the affidavit fits into the little white lie category, when you think of the greater good you'll be doing by giving the little girl a loving home."

"I don't want to lie at all," Claude said. "And this lie in particular makes me sick. It's evil. Sinister, anyway. I'm totally torn. I know that if I don't pretend to be someone I'm not, something I'm not, if I don't sign the paper, I lose our daughter."

"And if you *do* sign it, you lose me." Naomi said, springing up. She turned the lock on the door and bolted out of the laundry room.

"Goddamn it." Claude put her head in her hands.

"You can't blame Naomi for how she's feeling."

"I know," Claude nodded. "I don't. And I'm not sure what I'd do if the shoe were on the other foot. I'd like to think I'd stick it out. Our whole situation, I mean. Not my foot." She tried to force a smile. "And our relationship. For a lot of reasons. We've been together for eight years, for one thing. You can't just throw that away. Well, maybe Nay can, but I want to believe she really can't and that she's just pissed off right now. And both of us really want to be mothers. So that's another reason to go through with this adoption. What would you do?"

"If I were you, or Naomi?"

Claude shrugged. "Either. Both, I guess."

"If I were you, I'd give Naomi time to come around. I wouldn't push anything. I'd muster all the patience I could. I know you're on a timetable with the adoption application, and I'm happy to help you with that. Naomi's hurting and she doesn't want any part of that right now, which is also a totally valid position. Apart from her anger about the necessity of lying in order to play the game, she's not feeling as loved by you right now as she really is. If I were Naomi, I'd want time to sort things out without feeling pressured to do so. And if I could admit to being a bit needy for your attention and affection, and your re-assurances that I'm not being pushed aside or thrown over in favor of the baby, I'd want to get that from you without having to ask for it. I know that sounds like a contradiction in terms."

Frustrated, Claude expelled a puff of air from her lips. "I feel like I'm damned if I do and damned if I don't."

"I'd say that Naomi's worried that your having to pretend you're straight in order to adopt a baby from China—having to lie, literally cutting her out of the picture—is the tip of the ice-berg. If you can do that, you can cut her out of the motherhood process and even cut her out of your relationship . . . it may sig-nal to her that even now you're choosing the baby over her and it's a sign of things to come. It's not an unusual or even an un-reasonable feeling. A lot of potential fathers feel that way when they see their pregnant partners caught up in all the prepara-tions for motherhood. It's something that they recognize there's no way they can share on a lot of levels. Yeah, it's going to be their kid too, but obviously, they're not undergoing all the physical and emotional changes that the woman is experiencing. With you and Naomi, I know you plan to co-mother the baby after you adopt her, and it's not the identical situation, of course, because neither of you is pregnant, but the feelings of jealousy and possessiveness and fear of losing the partner who's going to be the mom—and that they're going to play second fiddle after the baby comes—are still very much a factor."

Claude bit her lip. "Did you ever go through that with Eli?"

"Oh, boy!" I shuddered at the memories. "You'd think, with these 'childbearing hips,' as my former modern dance instructor used to call them, that I would have had an easy time of it. Actually, when I was pregnant with Molly, things went pretty smoothly. I rarely had morning sickness, and my one weird craving—apart from Nathan's hot dogs—was that I wanted chocolate sauce on everything." I laughed. "There are days when I still do in fact! And Eli was very into being a father; we did the Lamaze classes together and he brought the video camera into the delivery room—the whole nine yards. But after Molly was born, she was colicky and never slept more than a couple of hours at a time and was always a handful. To tell the truth, as pleasant as she'd been in utero, she was a pain in the ass as an infant; but what are you going to do? That's life sometimes. With Ian, things got weird. They're five years apart, and after what we'd been through with Molly, Eli wasn't sure we should have tried again. When Molly was a baby, I had to devote so much time to her, naturally, that he did feel very shut out. And he didn't always have the patience to handle her, so he stayed away and the whole situation became a Catch-22. I had a rough pregnancy the second time around and I needed to have a caesarian—so much for bikinis," I joked. "Of course, the irony is that the tough pregnancy turned out to be the easygoing kid, and vice versa. Eli is a fantastic man, but to say that he likes to avoid responsibility is putting it mildly. So if I'm doing the lion's share of the parenting, that's where the proportionate share of my attention is going, right? And Eli did act very resentful and hurt, and our sex life hit the skids for a while. Not only was I too tired to feel romantic, but who the hell wants to make love with someone who resents you?"

"Now I'm wondering," Claude said hesitatingly, "if we've really thought this through. Nay and I have been talking about adoption for a couple of years now. And we thought we had it all figured out. But maybe we did bite off more than we can chew."

"I think you may have factored in the bureaucratic red tape but you hadn't counted on the laws being against you, and that's what's causing the biggest problem in your relationship. I don't envy you and Naomi. You've got all the 'is it time for us to have children' issues that straights have, with the added burden of being faced with the questions of prioritizing your values and beliefs. Now you have to ask: What trumps motherhood? Traditional politics? Sexual politics?"

Claude nodded in agreement. "When we got hit with this news from the agency—the no lesbian couples policy—it threw everything into a tailspin. I think Naomi and I each have an answer to that question you just posed to me about what trumps motherhood. We even answered it in our session. The problem is," Claude added ruefully, "for now, anyway, we've each come up with different ones."

MALA SONIA MAKES ANOTHER APPEARANCE ...

 "Perhaps the question I really should ask you is when Stevo will get around to replacing all these broken washing machines! Three out of six are down now. Or should I say only three out of the *remaining* five washers are still working," Amy said with a disgruntled gesture at the empty spot where the sixth machine used to be. Washer number two had an Out of Order sign taped to its lid, and the gap remained where the fourth one in the line, Ian's "boggart" machine, had stood.

"You want to waste reading, be my guest," Mala Sonia replied dismissively. She appeared uncharacteristically elegant in one of those jersey wrap-dresses, and looked like she'd just come from the hairdresser. I found myself noticing her in a way I never had before, and realizing, to my surprise—and even to my horror— that I was a bit jealous of this uneducated, ordinarily blowsy woman who was always so comfortable in her own skin, at ease in a way I've tried for decades to convince myself *I* was.

"Stevo needs okay from landlord to replace," said Mala Sonia. "They say too many people have sneaky washer and dryer in apartment. Not enough people use machines in basement. No need to spend money when not so many people use."

"The un-sneaky of us are entitled to a full complement of building services, you know," I butted in.

"Then you write letter to landlord, Mrs. Lederer. See where it get you," said Mala Sonia with an imperious wave. Was she wearing an emerald? What happened to her ubiquitous bangle bracelets and terry-cloth Olsen-twin ensembles?

Mala Sonia graciously offered Amy a seat on a ratty old dinette chair. Amy hesitantly perched on the cracked vinyl upholstery, as though the flecking and modestly corroded foam rubber cushion might convey some bilious germs directly through her khakis. The Gypsy installed herself on a rickety café chair at the head of the table and removed her tarot deck from her large black purse.

"It's kind of bright in here," Amy complained.

"Too bright for reading? You expect lanterns and crystal balls? Tablecloths with fringe, perhaps?"

"No, too bright for Isaac," Amy said, rearranging her fussing son in her arms. "He could fall asleep," she whispered, "if we didn't have to have these ugly fluorescents on."

"Well, it is more conducive to sorting laundry than conducting séances," I said, feeling unusually peevish. I must be PMSing. I should be more careful about what I say and how I say it around one of my clients. I let my estrogen levels get the better of me. Assessing and analyzing my own remark, I think my hostility was directed more toward Mala Sonia, whom I consider a harmful charlatan, than it was toward the annoyingly whiny Amy..

"My apartment has much softer light, but you didn't want to stay there," Mala Sonia told Amy.

"It's filthy," Amy retorted. "Too dirty to expose my son to. And your rat thing—your ferret—I thought he was going to eat the baby. He kept trying to find his toes and nibble them or something."

"He's just curious, Mrs. Witherspoon."

"*Ms. Baum*," corrected Amy tersely.

"Ferrets don't eat babies. Not boy babies, anyway."

Amy visibly blanched.

"Just making joke," Mala Sonia said with evident enjoyment at Amy's discomfort. "So," she said, shuffling the deck, "you have question for cards."

"I never thought I'd be doing this," Amy said, looking over at me for some lifeline to rationality. I refused to choose sides. "Oh, you can stay, Susan. It doesn't matter if you hear the reading. You'd hear about it secondhand later in the week, anyway."

"Thanks for giving me permission to do my laundry," I teased. Sigmund had another accident that morning on the throw rug in the kids' bathroom. It wasn't exactly the kind of thing that could just be tossed in the hamper until there was more to be washed.

"By the way, if she quoted you twenty dollars, don't let her play 'bait and switch' and try to charge you fifty for a few more cards."

Mala Sonia glared at me; Amy looked grateful for something for the first time since I'd met her.

"Okay," grunted Mala Sonia. "Rich lady buys cheapest reading." Amy rose to leave, reminded the super's wife that she was still a respected litigator no matter how much her life has gone from being about briefs to breast milk in the past few months, and that put an end to Mala Sonia's derogatory quips at her "client's" expense.

"Now. You have question."

Amy pursed her lips. "Yes. I do. I might as well know sooner rather than later, so I can revise my options, if necessary." She looked down at the infant Isaac, who was fast asleep with a fistful of blankie tucked under his pink chin. "I want to know if my husband Eric is ever planning to pull his weight with Isaac, or am I doomed to single parenthood within my marriage—because this sure as hell isn't what I bargained for! Believe me, I can't wait to get back to my desk. I'd rather fight tooth and nail with a plaintiff's attorney than wipe up baby drool and shit any day of the week."

"Never use word 'ever' in your question. Bad for reading. So we just ask cards whether your husband is planning to help with baby—not 'ever' planning. You understand?"

Amy shrugged. "Yeah, fine, whatever."

Mala Sonia deftly shuffled and cut the deck, fanned the cards out in a giant crescent, then asked Amy to select six without touching any of them. Amy pointed to a half-dozen cards in evenly spaced intervals within the spread, and Sonia laid them on the table in the same simplified version of the Celtic Cross that she had used for Alice.

I sat on the couch and eavesdropped on Amy's reading, while washer number one rid my bathroom rug of Sigmund's fetid gift to the Lederer family. We learned that the Page of Pentacles represented where Amy's life had been until now, apparently filled with the desire for study and the application of learning.

"Well, that doesn't surprise me," Amy snorted indelicately. "Four years of college and three of law school, a year of clerkship for a Supreme Court judge, then an associate at Newter & Spade. And even now, I'm learning something new every day. Mostly about different textures of poop." Funny how she could act like such a sentimental mush-brain with Isaac when he was awake; and when he was asleep, or out of her line of vision or earshot, the other Amy emerged: the sarcastic one, dark and angry and full of contempt for motherhood.

The new mom didn't like hearing one bit about where she was in her life now. The upside-down Six of Wands referred to indefinite delay, apprehension, disloyalty, and only superficial benefit with inconclusive gain. Amy shook her head. "I had a feeling," she said dolefully. "That's why I asked you for the reading."

"Cards don't lie," replied the Gyspy smoothly, echoing the rote phrase she'd given Alice. "But look, this is good news," she added, pointing to the card representing Amy's near future. "Knight of Swords is bravery. Imagine a strong, dashing hero fearlessly coming to the rescue."

Suddenly Amy's eyes shone. "Okay, so maybe I was a bit hasty. I'm still hormonal, I suppose. It must be all that breastfeeding. What's *that* card?" she asked, pointing to the fourth one Mala Sonia had laid.

"You in environment of near future—reversed Three of Pentacles. I hate to tell you, but will be sloppiness, money problems, lack of skill, lower quality, and preoccupation."

"So I get my knight, but maybe he's not such a pro after all? Is that what you're saying? Leave it to me to get saddled with a second-rate hero," Amy groaned.

"You're not *believing* any of this?" I muttered under my breath. PMS had most certainly taken over today. Although, I kind of like being uncensored. It's honest, it's real, and it's fine— as long as I'm not with a patient—when, while I'd like to think I'm still being "real," every word must be chosen carefully or it could upset the emotional and psychological apple cart.

Amy's fifth card, standing for the best she could hope for in her question scenario, was the Emperor in the reversed position, indicating immaturity and lack of strength, and a weak character or wishy-washiness, bolstering the information she received from card number four. So, if Eric Witherspoon was expected to come to the rescue of his overworked, overwhelmed wife and devote some serious quality time to his family, Amy wasn't about to get the man she'd bargained for. In one of her sessions, Alice Finnegan had explained her late grandmother's "name game" analysis of people's personalities based upon their names, using her ex-boyfriend—Eric Witherspoon—as an example. I seem to recall that Irene Finnegan had warned her granddaughter of the man's lack of resiliency.

"Oy, just my luck," Amy muttered to Mala Sonia. "Hey, do you ever give *good* readings? Positive ones, I mean, where things turn out wonderful in the end?"

"Last card," smiled Mala Sonia, pointing to the upside-down King of Swords. "The outcome to your question."

"So, *nu?*"

Mala Sonia tut-tutted. "I think you are already unhappy. I

think maybe you just pay me and we call it a little cheap entertainment."

Amy frowned. "But *you* take these readings seriously, right?"

"Cards don't lie," repeated Mala Sonia. "I just have gift to interpret."

"All right," sighed Amy. "Just tell me the damn outcome so I
can go upstairs and put Isaac down properly."

"*Bi-lacio.* No good. Twenty dollars before baby naps," the
Gypsy reminded her.

"Here!" Amy thrust her hand into her pocket and withdrew
a crisply folded bill. "Now, the last card, please."

"Outcome: reversed King of Swords," Mala Sonia repeated.
"Oh, sorry, you not like, but you said you want to know to make
decision in advance. Outcome is cruelty. Conflict. Selfishness.
One who causes pain and sadness."

To me this all seemed a bit too familiar. Hadn't Mala Sonia
given Alice a similarly dire prognostication?

"Right, then. Thanks for your time," Amy said dispassionately.
She looked like she was trying very hard not to cry. Perhaps
someone had told her back in law school that there's no crying
in moot court or something. Isaac still slept like the innocent he
was. "Well, Mommy's got some thinking to do," she cooed to the
slumbering infant. "It seems like Mommy just confirmed that
she actually has *two* boys at home."

I can relate, I wanted to tell her, but she left the room too quickly.

The heavy scent of Mala Sonia's perfume, something laden
with musk and citrus, lingered in the air like a pall over the
reading. "Did you have to be cruel?" I asked the Gypsy. "She's
already going through so much now as it is."

"Then you profit too, from negative reading, Mrs. Lederer.
Ms. Baum will talk about it with you privately, yes?"

"But I don't charge her for my advice. There's a difference.

One of many between us, for starters. Look," I sighed, running my hands through my hair, something I always seem to do when I'm a bit at sixes and sevens. "For a pragmatic woman, schooled in the law, she seems to really believe in your superstitious hocus-pocus. The reading clearly upset her. Couldn't you have softened the blow at least? Maybe lied to her just a little about what the cards represented?"

Mala Sonia invoked her litany. "I interpret cards. *Cards* don't lie. You think it's just *darana swatura*—magical and superstitious stories? Hah!" Her dark eyes were filled with disgust. "Like you, I am a professional," she added, waving her manicured hand so that the emerald refracted the light from the fluorescent tube overhead. "You tell me, would *you* ever lie to one of your clients—to 'soften the blow'?"

TALIA

Navigating on crutches, Talia propelled herself into the laundry room. "This is why they never tell dancers to 'break a leg!' "

I blanched and my hand flew to my throat. Her right leg from toe to thigh was encased in a huge brace. "Jesus, what happened?!" I gasped.

"I tore my ACL."

"My God, I am so sorry." I shook my head. "I'm not even sure what that is."

"ACL? Anterior cruciate ligament. There are four key ligaments that connect the bones to the knee joint, y'know? Well, the ACL is one of the most important of them. It provides stability to the knee and helps minimize stress in the knee joint. A tear can happen a lot of ways, like from overstretching it."

"You poor baby." I felt awful for her. "Is that how it happened?"

"I did it coming down from a jump. I twisted my knee as I landed, and *pop!* You could practically hear it, I swear. Just my fucking luck, y'know! A complete tear; not even a partial one. They did an MRI and said no way it could heal on its own, so I had to have surgery. The doctor said I probably had it coming since I'd been stressing out my knee for a while. Before the tear, I never told anyone in the company about my knee pain because I've had a hard enough time getting cast. I don't want them to see me as injury prone. Then I had a choice: to stay up in Saratoga to get it repaired or to come back to the city for the operation, and my mother—who never did see my performance in *Jewels*—decided that she knew best and insisted that I stay upstate. And get this: did you know that female athletes—and don't ever let someone try to convince you that a ballerina isn't an athlete—are more likely than men to suffer an ACL injury?" Talia rolled her eyes heavenward. "Oh, goody," she added sarcastically. "And, y'know, athletes who are loose-jointed run a higher risk than those who aren't. Dancers again. Double goody." She pointed to her leg. "You're looking at a complete surgical reconstruction."

I gave her a sympathetic look. "My God, I'm sorry." I hesitated to ask the burning question. "Are . . . will . . . when are you going to be able to dance again? You are going to be able to, right?"

Talia frowned. "I'm looking at several weeks of P.T.—physical therapy. After that, who knows? The doctor told me it'll take six to eight weeks before I can resume 'normal physical activity.' But 'normal' for me isn't exactly 'normal' for other people, y'know? So," she added, "since I hate to talk and since I can't sit here and do it without moving around, I'm out of here. Sorry about the therapy sessions, but I'll see you back down here

again *whenever.*" She turned on her crutches and hobbled out of
the room before I had the chance to suggest that she reconsider
her decision.

ME

"I so don't want to do this," Molly moaned. "None of my
friends have family picnics."

"Can I bring my sketch pad?" Ian wanted to know.

"Of course."

"I want to draw the fat Russian people!"

"Ian!"

"What?"

"That's not nice. And we're headed to Coney Island, not
Brighton Beach."

Ian shrugged. "Same difference."

"Not!" Molly sneered.

It never ceases to amaze me how my intelligent, extremely
literate kids regress by the decade whenever it comes to family
outings. I've had enough to deal with from Eli, who's been
hemming and hawing about whether he'll be able to join us this
year, because of his looming *Gia* deadline.

It's a tradition in the Lederer family—an annual homage to
my Nathan's hot-dog cravings during my pregnancies—that on
a sultry August Sunday we all schlep out to Coney Island on the
subway with a picnic hamper (containing a full complement of
Zabar's delicacies—for those of us, like Molly, who disdain the
"dogs"). We dine on the beach, take a dip in the surf (at least an
hour after eating, of course), stroll the boardwalk, and ride the
Cyclone (a *couple* of hours after eating).

Eli had really disappointed me—and he knew it—when he

said that he wasn't going to be able to make it. "Maybe you and I can go out to dinner sometime or something, to make up for it," he offered, somewhat noncommittally.

"At the risk of sounding like our adolescent daughter, it's not the same thing," I replied, trying to avoid slipping into an angsty whine. I steered him into the kitchen and lowered my voice. "We do this every year; you've had deadlines in the past and never missed a celebration. Is . . ." I felt my stomach clench. "Is . . . there something . . . I should know about?"

Eli briefly glanced at the microwave before looking me in the eye. "No. No, there's . . . nothing. It's . . . I'm on unfamiliar turf with this *Gia* novel and it's taking me longer than usual to finish the book. Susie, the muse doesn't always sit on your shoulder whispering creative things in your ear. I can spend all day and half the night at the studio and still get nothing accomplished. Writers block can strike graphic artists too, you know. And when I'm not working on the book, when I know a deadline is looming like the shadow of Godzilla, I have to be honest with you—since you're always trying to analyze everything anyone does or says—I have to say that it makes me feel guilty to take time off and . . . and *party*, when I should at least be *trying* to get some writing done."

I slipped my arms around his waist. "Coney Island is one day a year," I said earnestly. "Hey, you missed our anniversary this year. Can you at least give me—or if not me, the kids—their beach day?"

"Molly doesn't even care."

"She's at the age when she doesn't care about anything related to family or tradition or something that might smack of 'dorkiness,' which she'll never live down at school, should someone find out she actually spent a day hanging out with her parents and her kid brother."

"So, basically, you're agreeing with me?"

"Eli. Oy." I sighed. "It's rare enough to get the whole family together for anything these days."

The conversation ended with his reluctant acquiescence to accompany us. Ian, a budding caricaturist, sketched everything in sight, Molly grabbed the binoculars and scoped out boys, I scarfed down three hot dogs and a large order of crinkle-cut fries (I love those little forks they give you), and the only place Eli didn't anxiously check his watch every few minutes was in the Atlantic Ocean.

"I really feel like I should be getting back to work," he said, before it was Cyclone time.

As he headed toward the subway bound for Manhattan, it felt like I had my very own roller coaster dropping and dipping and swerving in my gut. Or maybe it was just the hot dogs.

MERIEL

Meriel laughed, exposing the gap between her top front teeth. "I tell you, it just get worse and worse," she said. "Another one bites de dust." She pointed at the line of washers. "We now down to four machines and Mrs. Amy worry daht I won't get de laundry done for her before it's time to walk Taco Bell. Now almost every day is another row wit' her. Fighting. Fighting. And every day I go home to Brooklyn wit' a pounding headache. I know de fighting is mostly because Mr. Eric never home and she feel overwhelmed. I offered to help wit' Isaac but she look at me layk I never have children. My son William is tirty years old, and he have a baby girl too." Meriel took her wallet from her apron pocket and withdrew a photo of an adorable child, posed formally against a mottled drape: a department store portrait.

"Daht's Julia," she beamed. "She four years old now. She going to be in de kids' carnival tomorrow. Always de Sahturday before Labor Day. And den we have de West Indian Day Parade on Monday. Every Labor Day, you know, we pahty till de cows come home. Almost forty years now we do it. Daht's another ting Mrs. Amy fight wit' me over. We have all de preparations daht start weeks before de parade. We have de rehearsals for de dances and the bands and make de costumes. Every night for de past two weeks, we pahty. And Mrs. Amy tell me I come to work too tired. She don't layk it one bit."

Her face relaxed into a grin. "My late husband Leon used to enjoy de pahties so much. He had de diabetes, you know," Meriel added, changing the subject on a dime. She shook her head. "Left me for God when our boy William was only tirteen." A memory made her laugh. "And Leon fight wit' his bosses, too, before Carnival. But he never care. Dey never ahngry for too long."

"You, know, I don't think you've ever told me what Leon did for a living."

"He worked for de MTA on the trains. Not a conductor—he drove de train. You know . . . what do you call daht?"

"A driver?"

Meriel laughed again. "I guess so. Leon always fighting with his bosses. Didn't have to be Carnival time. Because he was very ahktive wit' de union. I used to tell him we have de same temper, he and I. But he was not from Jamaica like me. He was Haitian."

"So how did you meet him?"

"We met here in de States, at a disco out in Coney Island. I tell you, Mrs. Susan, Leon was such a good dancer. He had all de moves to sweep a convent-educated girl like me off her feet." Meriel blushed like a schoolgirl. "So when I get married and take his name and become Meriel Delacour from Meriel Robertson, my family tink I put on airs because Leon's name sound so French. Our son William use de name Robertson, though. He love his Jamaican heritage."

"Is William going to be playing with one of the bands in the parade?" I asked her.

Meriel shook her head. "No, William don't do de mas bands. He do his own ting. He want to be a chef and open a Jamaican restaurant, but all de time, he ahsk me for de old fahmily recipes I always make for him when he was growing up. I tell him *I* should be de chef and he should just sit bahk and collect all the money from de customers!"

I sighed. "I wish Eli could cook. After almost twenty years, he's mastered cold cereal and the occasional omelet. Is William a good cook?"

Meriel winked. "Not as good as me! No one as good as Mama!" She leaned forward. "I tell you, Mrs. Susan, you come to de parade and see for yourself. Bring your fahmily. William gonna have a tent wit' his Jamaican home cooking, right across de street from de Brooklyn Museum. I'm going to be one of de Sesame Flyers mas dancers. You'll see me in my spangles and spandex." She hefted her large breasts with her hands and looked down at her round belly. "All daht lycra gonna be workin' overtime on Labor Day, I tell you daht!"

7

ME

Molly evinced no interest in trekking out to Brooklyn for the West Indian Day parade. She claimed to hate crowds, a new development, considering her penchant for sneaking into nightclubs. I asked her to use the time to review her downloaded college applications so we could talk about what needed to be done when I got home. I have little faith that she'll accomplish the assignment. I'd dropped off Ian earlier at a rehearsal in midtown for a backers' audition of a new musical, an adaptation of the first Harry Potter book. In a clandestine attempt at method acting, he'd made an unholy mess of the bathroom by dying his blond hair black for the occasion and had been working on the role at home by sporting a pair of wire-rimmed spectacles with the lenses removed so that he could better see his script. Eli, opting to work at home rather than down at his studio space, said that the quiet house would give him an opportunity to work on *Gia*, uninterrupted, an odd comment, since I never interrupt him when he's drawing. At least he agreed to pick up Ian after the backers' audition. So maybe he *did* hear me when I expressed my need for his parenting presence.

In the lobby, I ran into Faith, looking very jaunty in a tee-shirt the color of an early September sky with a lilac colored scarf at her throat. "Hey, Faith, that blue looks fabulous on you!" I told her.

"Moving on from indigo," she said proudly. "This is about seven shades lighter. I still have my security blanket, though," she chuckled, touching the purple scarf.

"Where are you off to on such a glorious day?" For some reason, I felt like one of those barnyard characters who asks Henny Penny where she's headed.

"I'm going to the park. There's a concert over at the Summerstage this afternoon, but I thought I'd sit on a bench and read a little before it starts." She patted her Channel 13 canvas tote. "And you? Where is this magical weather taking you today?"

I told her about Meriel's invitation to the West Indian Day parade. Faith gave me a thoughtful look. After a few moments she tentatively asked, "Susan, would you mind terribly if I joined you?"

"No, not at all. That would be terrific. My entire family bailed on me, so it would be wonderful to have a friend to share the experience. I've never been to this parade; have you?"

Faith looked shocked. "Me?" She laughed. "But you're always telling me I should broaden my horizons. I'll be right back—unless you want to come with me. I must get a hat. You should have one too, Susan. We'll be standing in the hot sun for hours."

Her maternal solicitousness was sweet. "No, thanks, I'll be fine," I demurred. "You go ahead. I'll wait right here."

A few minutes later Faith reentered the lobby wearing a wide-brimmed straw hat. Between the chapeau and the scarf knotted at her throat, she looked like she was going to spend the afternoon painting wildflowers in a field in Arles rather than hanging out on Eastern Parkway immersing herself in the colorful culture of the Caribbean.

It was a glorious September day. Even the subway, which was running on a holiday schedule, seemed obliging. We shared the ride out to Brooklyn with a number of people clearly headed for the same destination, outfitted with pride in their island's official colors, or sporting its flag somewhere on their anatomy in every possible manner, from do-rags and headbands to shawls and shortened versions of pareos, tied at the waist and emphasizing the butt. A number of young women were all kitted out to shake their booty for Barbados—or wherever.

"And yet . . . if those were American flags, there are those among us who might consider that desecration," Faith whispered to me. "My ancestors in the DAR among them."

"But it's the opposite," I argued, sensing Faith's internal struggle with the issue. "This is *celebration* of the colors, not desecration. I, for one, love it."

As the train pulled into the Eastern Parkway station, many of our fellow passengers began to make their way toward the subway car doors, bursting forth with a rush of high-voltage energy as soon as they were opened. Faith and I were caught in the crush, shuffling along with perhaps a hundred others toward daylight, the heady aroma of frying fish hitting our nostrils even before we ascended to the street. The sweet sound of steel drums wafted down the subway stairs and filtered into the subterranean passageways, heightening the party mood of the spectators who were all too eager to see the sun once again.

Faith's hand clamped down on my forearm with remarkable strength. With her free hand, she clutched her sun hat to her head. I had a feeling she wished for a third appendage to more properly secure her purse. "Don't lose me," she whispered desperately.

"Don't worry, I won't. Another dozen steps or so till we get to the sidewalk." I regarded her tensely set jaw. "Are you all right?"

"Yes," she assured me nervously.

"This was your idea, remember."

"I do. I just feel a bit . . . overwhelmed . . . is all. I'll be right as rain once we get outside."

Once on the sidewalk, gulping some fresh air, Faith did indeed relax. I was surprised at how sparse the crowd seemed to be, since we'd arrived more than a half hour after the parade's scheduled start time. We'd emerged just across the street from the Brooklyn Museum and had little trouble securing a curbside spot just a few yards from the reviewing stand, with a terrific view of the festivities. An elderly gentleman in embroidered guyabera shirt and dapper Panama hat ceded his place to Faith with an elegant flourish. "Dis is my day," he explained courteously, his voice as tuneful as any melody played on a steel drum, "so you should stahnd here where you can see de best."

Faith, charmed, flashed the man a dazzling smile. "Where is everyone?" she asked him, looking up an empty Eastern Parkway. "Where's the parade?"

The gentleman's laugh was echoed by a half-dozen spectators around him. "Oh, dey're all on Caribbean time! No one wants to start de pahrade too early because it end just down de street at de Grand Ahrmy Plaza." He pointed to our right. "Once dey get to the Grand Ahrmy Plaza, it's time to stop de pahrty and go home!"

"So when will everyone walk by?" Faith was accustomed to Yankee punctuality.

"Well, you get all de politicians first and all de local groups, like de hospitals and insurance companies daht have deyr own little float. Once dey all get by," the man grinned, "dehn de real fun begin!"

"I hope I can hold out that long," Faith sighed to me.

"You'll be fine," I assured her. "And anytime you get tired, we'll just start to make our way back home."

Faith scowled. "Not without seeing Meriel first! I haven't come all this way for nothing."

So, just as Panama had foretold, the procession of politicians passed: the mayor and the police commissioner, each looking as incongruous as a lobster dinner at a bar mitzvah, marched by, and bailed just past the museum, sneaking inside its grand glass facade when they thought no one was looking. Finally, after we'd been standing in the hot sun for about four hours, the first of the mas bands approached. And what a spectacle it was!

"It was worth the wait, huh!?" I shouted to Faith, trying to be heard above the din. A huge soundtruck was blaring reggae from speakers the size of refrigerators. Hundreds of dancers, clad in fatigues and paint-spattered tee-shirts dirty-danced to a song that had the men and women around us in fits of giggles.

"I'm sorry, I'm not getting it," Faith said apologetically to the man in the Panama hat. "What is the lyric saying?"

Panama laughed again. "It's in de patois," he said. "Dey're making it about de sugar plant, you know . . . 'you cannot go for cane,' but it sound like someting else, yes?"

I thought about it for a couple of moments and figured it out. Faith clapped her hand to her mouth. "Oh, my goodness!" she exclaimed. "You cannot go fuck-ing!" she said in a shocked whisper intended for my left ear only. "That's what they're saying! No wonder they're all dancing so . . . naughtily."

"Welcome to de West Indies!" said Panama with a grin. "You like?" he asked Faith.

She blushed under her wide-brimmed sun hat. By that time I was wishing I'd taken her advice and worn a hat as well, because the skin exposed by my V-necked tee-shirt had resulted in a sunburned triangle that was beginning to sting. My reddening arms didn't feel so great either.

The sugarcane rebels made their way toward Grand Army Plaza, and for a few minutes the street was quiet. Then a cheer went up as the Sesame Flyers International approached. They were led by dancers costumed in enormous feathered head-dresses. Their voluminous skirts were stabilized by elaborate harnesses on wheels that enabled the wearers to glide along the avenue. The effect was magical. Then a pair of turtle doves twelve feet high, with wings of pink and gold, sailed past us as a human float; how the dancer within it managed all that weight for so many miles in the blazing sun was beyond my comprehension. Some of the headdresses and harnesses resembled Native American tribal costumes, but in blindingly vivid colors: pinks, blues, yellows, and greens in neon shades, and reds and oranges so vibrant you practically needed to squint. It was as close as I was ever going to come to Rio.

And then came hundreds if not thousands of revelers, garbed in scanty costumes that would have made a belly dancer feel overdressed. First, we were entertained by a spectacular sea of dancers in red lycra and golden beads, set dramatically against chocolate-colored skin. Every color of the rainbow was represented by huge blocks of people, the design of the costumes differing for each color. The carmine-clad dancers swept by us, about ninety-five percent of them women. All ages and figure types were represented—with a much healthier attitude toward body image than we white chicks have ever had! Most women I know wouldn't have been caught dead in public in ten times the amount of spandex sported by the Sesame Flyers. And the workmanship that went into the building of all these costumes was extraordinary. It had to have been immensely time-consuming. How long, I wondered, did it take them to add each ruffle, string of ricrac, or rope of beads to thousands of one-of-a-kind outfits? The bright, feathered headdresses made every woman resemble an exotic bird of paradise, and I found myself envying their fun as much as I delighted in it. The view from the helicopter circling above us must have been remarkable as it filmed the ribbon of revelers, a moving rainbow undulating along the roadway.

The women in yellow and black performed a dance that had found its way to the Caribbean by way of Spain, their butts barely concealed by a cascade of golden ruffles, their fans and lace mantillas their only semblance of modesty. Dancers in purple, green, and gold trailed their lilac-colored scarves about their bodies and performed a number that could have come to Flatbush straight out of the Arabian Nights. Many of the costumes were given personal touches by the wearers, who displayed their native island's flag or colors as wristbands, head scarves, or draped over their fannies, just as we'd seen the spectators do on the subway. "Meriel must be out there someplace," I shouted to Faith. Neither of us could hear anything above the music. "I think this is her group."

"How will we ever spot her?" Faith shouted back. "This makes the marching bands at the Macy's Thanksgiving parade look like small potatoes."

"And more feathers, sequins, and sparkles than the Gay Pride parade," I added. "Too bad Naomi and Claude didn't join us."

"You know something? I'm feeling a bit peckish," Faith said suddenly. "The last thing I ate was a bowl of bran flakes at breakfast. And I think I need to move my legs a bit. Would you like anything?" I shook my head as she scanned the row of food stands behind us and frowned. "It's so dreadfully crowded, I'm not so sure I'll make it through the crush. If I'm not back in fifteen minutes, call the National Guard," she joked.

Faith had been gone for about a third of that time when Meriel came huffing over to the curb, resplendent in indigo spandex and enough gold beads (had they been genuine) to remortgage Manhattan. Although her costume was untainted, her exposed limbs were coated with dried paint in white and bright, primary hues.

"Oh, dese dogs are tired," she said, enveloping me in a sweaty embrace without losing her grasp of an adorable little girl. "Julia, say hello to Mrs. Susan."

Meriel's granddaughter, also dressed in blue and gold, with a feathered headdress that must have weighed half as much as she did, shyly hid her head in the shadow of her grandmother's ample hips.

"We been walkin' for miles," Meriel told me, standing first on one white-booted foot and then the other, shaking the free appendage to release some of the pavement pounding tension. "Julia here has been a very big sport. Am I right?" she asked the child, who seemed to have finally wilted from the heat, the long march, and the perspiration-stained polyester bathing suit.

"Hi, Julia," I said, extending my hand to her. "I'm Susan. I'm a friend of your grandma's."

"Nana, I'm thirsty," said Julia, ignoring me in the way only an exhausted four-year-old can.

"Okay . . . we get you someting to drink, sweetheart. Your daddy's stahnd is right over dere." She pointed to the sidewalk in the direction Faith had headed a few minutes earlier. "Susan, you come wit' us. I like you to meet my son William."

I hesitated, only because I was afraid that if I couldn't locate Faith, she might return to our spot and find me gone, and I didn't want to lose her in the crowd. But I figured she couldn't have gotten too far, given the mob scene behind us. Her giant sun hat and trailing purple scarf would at least give me a landmark to look out for.

"Oh, I can scarcely keep my eyes open," Meriel complained, though a grin was plastered on her face. "Two in de A.M. I was up for de j'ouvay. Of course, being on Caribbean time," she laughed, "dey didn' start until four!"

"What's the 'j'ouvay'?" I asked, mimicking Meriel's pronunciation, and she explained the predawn celebration of J'Ouvert, or jour ouvert, meaning "daybreak," which traced its origins to Trinidad. Throwing colorful powdered paint at one another was part of the tradition, as was blowing a whistle to complement the rhythm section of the bands. "Oh, you know, we have to keep de pahrty going, no matter what," Meriel said, laughing again. "Don't quote me on dis, because I'm not sure, but de paint come from de old days when de slaves would paint dere skin white on j'ouvay to imitate dere mahsters. Now we got all sorts of colors. Blue for de blue devils. And in de old days, on the islands, de slaves would wear dere worst clothes and cover dem-selves in mud to dress up for Carnival and de j'ouvay. It's when de creatures of de night come out, and de boogeymen too. Like Halloween and Carnival all rolled into one."

"It was scary!" Julia avowed enthusiastically.

"You let her stay up that late? Or get up that early?" I was surprised.

Meriel nodded. "She was too excited today to sleep anyway. Dis is so much bigger dahn de kids carnival she did on Sahtur-day. It's her first time marching in de pahrade and she love to see all de excitement."

"Ah, here you are!" Faith exclaimed when we practically bumped into her in front of the "No Problem" Jamaican food booth. She shoved a plastic plate under my nose; it was loaded with cubed meat spooned over a generous helping of white rice. "Smell this, isn't it divine?" I inhaled a snootful of aromatic spices. Faith took a bite of meat, then speared another cube and in an excited, aggressive manner that was entirely new to me, she practically pushed the fork into my mouth. "You must taste this!" she gushed. Compliantly, I chewed the meat. It tasted a bit like beef goulash smothered in a delicate curry sauce.

"Isn't it delicious?" Faith crowed. I'd never seen her so giddy over anything.

"What did you just feed me, Faith?"

She beamed triumphantly. "Curried goat!"

My brain considered spitting it out into a napkin, but my taste buds rather enjoyed it, surprisingly. I didn't have the chance to do more than swallow the bit of goat meat anyway, because Meriel turned around and said, "Oh, you're eating William's specialty! How you like it?"

Faith answered for both of us. "Delicious! Susan, I think this is my biggest breakthrough yet!"

"Of course I make it even bettah," Meriel said, winking at us. "But my son, he's not so bahd in de kitchen!"

"Did you know it was goat when you bought it?" I asked Faith.

She pointed to the hand-lettered menu and nodded emphatically. "I wanted to try something new that never in a million years would have been assayed by the old Faith. Although," she added hesitantly, "I didn't have the guts to try the oxtail stew. Please tell William I want to taste the sorrel too," she said to Meriel.

"Sorrel?" Suddenly Faith the inflexible Yankee stalwart was an international gourmand.

"Oh, you'll love it," William told us. He was a very nice looking, muscular man who still managed to look cool and collected in a bright white tee-shirt emblazoned with the Jamaican flag. He had his mother's smile. "And you met my little Princess, right?" He gestured to Julia, who was sucking down a lemonade next to the cash box. William poured two glasses of a bright red liquid from an enormous plastic jug. "Sorrel is made from the brewed leaves of the sorrel plant, which give the beverage this color," he explained. "It's usually mixed with ginger, and sometimes with spirits like rum, but we can't sell alcohol at the parade: New York City law."

I toasted Faith's courage and tasted the cool drink, which resembled a stronger version of ginger beer. "Yum." It packed a bit of a kick, even boozeless. The ginger in it burned the back of my throat like a good swallow of brandy.

"Give dehm a slice of my black fruit cake," insisted Meriel, and William handed over a Saran-wrapped slab of what looked and felt like a very dark, dense pound cake.

"Wait, let *me* taste it first," demanded the gustatory adventuress once known to me as Faith Nesbit. After this display of bravado, she unwrapped the slice of cake and took a small, tentative bite. I guess I was a teensy bit relieved to learn that her baby-steps method of change, while having quickened its pace somewhat during the afternoon, was still behaviorally consistent.

"*Umhnh,*" she murmured, gracefully dabbing at a corner of her mouth with a paper napkin. "Lots of prune. You know," she said, addressing Meriel, "you could really market this cake to seniors with a sweet tooth!" She broke off a piece and offered it to me. It did taste very prune-raisiny. With maybe a hint of rum. Or perhaps that was merely wishful thinking on my part.

"So, you tink my William can run his own restaurant?" Meriel asked us, leaving no room for any response that was less than wholeheartedly positive.

"With Mama in the kitchen?" I asked her.

"Oh, no," Meriel laughed. "I tink I'm the bettah cook, but we kill each other in de kitchen. Only one chef at a time in dis family!"

"And this one is my dream," added her grown son. "Right, peanut?" He turned to his four-year-old daughter for confirmation.

"I'm tired, Daddy," came the nonsequiturial reply.

"I think the sun has bested me," I said, realizing how red my chest and arms had become. "Maybe we'd better head back," I suggested.

"Wait. Not until I find out what jerk chicken is," insisted Faith, reading the No Problem menu. "It sounds like what the nasty boys used to call each other when I was growing up."

William laughed and gave Faith a taste of the drum-grilled chicken. Meriel helped herself to a taste and told William that it was good enough but that his sauce needed a little work. "Mama knows best," he said, miffed that his mother kept openly critiquing his recipes, particularly in front of a couple of white women who were clueless when it came to Jamaican cuisine.

"Oh lookit!" Julia exclaimed, perking up at the sight of a cluster of colorfully attired stilt walkers making their way along Eastern Parkway. "The moco jumbies, Nana!" They were dressed like ninjas. Either that or Iraqi war survivors in endless swaths of bandages. I wasn't quite sure. They were dancing and swaying in unison, and their choreography—let alone the sheer ability to get up on the stilts and stay there—blew me away.

"It's a good way to top off de ahfternoon," Meriel told us. "De moco jumbies are a big tradition at Carnival in de islands. A lot more mas bands be passing by for a while, but you've seen de best one," she laughed, pointing to her chest and mopping her brow with one of William's paper napkins. "Mrs. Amy gonna be very annoyed wit' me next week because I'm dragging like a rusty beer can on a cat's tail."

So Faith and I said good-bye to Meriel, William, and Julia; and with an eye toward the subway station, we threaded our way through the thousands of others still enjoying the Labor Day festivities.

"I'm so glad I tagged along today," said Faith as we boarded the train. "Didn't you just love all the dancing? So spirited, so free. I wish I could have joined them."

"A 'tough old Yankee bird' as you call yourself, who resembles Marian Seldes? Yeah, you'll blend," I joked.

"A lot you know," Faith shot back jovially. "I can dance the 'jerk chicken'!"

I'm convinced that all school guidance counselors are churned out of a mold: balding—including the females— a bit stooped in the shoulders, Coke-bottle lenses, generally out of touch with both the student body and their parents. That said, Molly and I shared pretty much the same reaction when we each received a summons to meet with Mr. Bernstein, Fieldston's guidance counselor, to discuss Molly's college prospects. It was the summit meeting we'd both been dreading.

I met Molly up at the school's bucolic seventeen-acre campus in Riverdale. We mounted the stairs of the Administration Building with our game faces on and were greeted at the second floor landing by the school receptionist, who led us into Mr. Bernstein's sanctum with its healthy ferns, Kilim carpet in tastefully muted earth tones, mahogany office furniture, obligatory Vermeeresque sunlight streaming in from a window situated to the left of the desk, and Rothko lithographs on the wall. In short, it resembled the traditional Upper West Side psychotherapist's office.

After the initial pleasantries were exchanged, Mr. Bernstein opened with, "Well, you know that SAT scores aren't everything." From watching the sweat stains on the counselor's pale blue shirt grow the way Pinocchio's nose did when he was caught lying, it was clear that even Mr. Bernstein didn't believe a word he was saying. "What schools are you considering?" he asked Molly.

She mentioned NYU and Bennington, then made a crack about applying to Manhattan Community College as her "safety."

Bernstein burst out laughing. "God, that's funny. You have a terrific sense of humor, Miss Lederer. It's a shame we won't be seeing you in the senior class comedy this semester."

"The senior class *is* a comedy," muttered Molly dryly.

"She wasn't really kidding about MCC," I said.

"Oh, you don't have to worry about ending up there," Bernstein said cheerfully.

"Good," sighed Molly, feigning relief. "Because they never ended up mailing me the application after I asked them three times. I really don't want to go to a school that doesn't want me *so* much that they don't even send me the application."

"You can always apply online," I said grimly.

"Well, I think you can shelve the community college fail-safe," said the college counselor. "I can always make a phone call and they'll take you *somewhere*. Fieldston graduates *always* go on to a respectable college."

"Nice to know," Molly said. "That *some* college *somewhere* will accept me—not to save my lousy SAT-scoring ass, but to save yours."

I leaned over and whispered to her that it might be a good idea to can the attitude; that Mr. Bernstein was trying—in his dorky way—to be helpful. The poor schmuck was just doing his job.

"Well, let's talk about Bennington," said Mr. Bernstein.

"Assuming—'in the best of all possible worlds,' to quote Voltaire"—this is when Molly dramatically rolled her eyes— "that Bennington decided to accept your application. Why do you think you would fit in there? And how would you complete a foolproof application?"

Molly visibly squirmed. "I'd fit in because they encourage freedom of self-expression. In our society, convention is winning out over individualism. And convention is so not me. The application thing? I haven't a clue. Am I supposed to second-guess what they want from me?"

Mr. Bernstein leaned forward and rested his hands on his immaculate green desk blotter. "Well, I hate to break the bad news to you, but Bennington isn't quite the flakes and nuts school it used to be in your mother's day. They don't even offer a Creative Writing major anymore." Molly's face fell. "Although if you got accepted, you could always major in English."

"That's like majoring in unemployment," replied my daughter sulkily.

"Well, what's your favorite subject here?" Bernstein asked.

"English," admitted Molly, blushing for the first time in years. "I like to write."

"Fiction? Essays? Plays? Poetry?" I could see that the counselor was struggling to hook into something that made my daughter's bells and whistles go berserk. I wished him luck, because her father and I had yet to discover this silver bullet.

Molly shrugged. "Whatever I feel like. I dunno. I just write. Whatever's on my mind?" she added, with the annoying upward inflection that makes statements sound like questions. If it were in my power to ban "uptalking," I would.

"Do you blog, then?" the guidance counselor asked helpfully.

Molly rolled her eyes again at Mr. Bernstein's pathetic attempt to appear hip. "That's *so* everyone-else-and-his-ferret-is-doing-it. But at least I don't write sucky poetry like my mom used to."

My jaw dropped. "How do you know . . . ?"

"Get a grip, Ma. I found it when I was sneaking through your desk drawers like a hundred years ago."

"Ugh. Busted," I said, trying to make light of it, but wishing I could crawl under my chair. I knew I should have tossed my angsty college efforts at free verse. Either that or locked them in our safety deposit box over at Citibank.

"Please don't try to sound like a teenager, Mom," Molly said, in the loudest stage whisper I've ever heard. "It doesn't work."

"I'll have you know that angst is a manifestation of one's acknowledgment that all's not right with the world—or at least your world—and *that* acknowledgment is the first step on the road to enlightenment."

"Yes, grasshopper," Molly muttered mockingly.

Bernstein sought to regain control of the meeting. "Well, Mrs. Noguchi says you're doing very well so far in her Faulkner, Fitzgerald, and Hemingway class."

"We've only been in school three weeks," Molly replied tartly.

Undaunted, Mr. Bernstein continued. "I understand you got an A on your first paper, though. The one where you were supposed to write the next chapter of *The Sun Also Rises.*"

"I'm glad Mrs. Noguchi didn't think it was too much of a stretch that you had Lady Brett Ashley decide to stay in Spain and learn bullfighting," I said to my daughter. "So, Mr. Bernstein, how can we parlay Molly's talent into a successful college application?"

"Well, I have to say, Molly's going to have to have a lot more going for her than good grades on a couple of English papers and a moderately respectable showing on the essay section of her SATs. All of her competition does. Have a lot more going for them, I mean. With her otherwise lackluster test scores and equally uninspired grades in every subject except English, she'll have to find a way to stand out from the pack, and I'll admit that it won't be easy. Her math and science grades are very weak, even for a typical liberal arts major."

"We have to film our new Hemingway chapter, next," Molly said. "I'm going to do it with my cell phone."

Mr. Bernstein winced. "Weeellll, I'm not sure that'll cinch it. Even if you somehow managed to get real bulls."

"You're the expert," I said to him. "What suggestions do you have that will get Molly into a college of her choice—not *your* choice?"

"Well, I'm afraid there are no quick fixes," the counselor sighed, and I briefly flashed on a few of my lowest-functioning clients who expect a quick fix from me as well. "You can't just whitewash years of underachievement by suddenly doing something grand at the eleventh hour, like winning public office or writing a Pulitzer prize winner."

"Although classic underachievers have gone on to become president," I muttered.

Bernstein ignored my editorializing. "I don't need to tell you that it's a very competitive market out there. Molly's classmates have been building their résumés since pre-K."

"While Molly's just enjoyed her childhood. You poor kid," I said sympathetically, patting my daughter's knee. "You poor, somewhat normal kid."

Molly abruptly rose. "Let's go, Ma. I feel like we're being interviewed by a parrot."

"On, the other hand," said Mr. Bernstein, rising, "the colleges and universities don't want you to lie or pretend to be someone you're not. They'll see right through it. They want to be interested in you, not in the person you think you need to be."

Funny . . . therapists operate the same way.

"So, we're hoping Bennington is really into accepting under-achieving slackers," Molly said sarcastically. "And maybe the fact that I'm an underachieving slacker at the insanely overachieving Fieldston gives me a niche of my own, don't you think?"

"I really didn't mean to come off as an ogre," Mr. Bernstein apologized. "But I feel it's incumbent upon me not to paint a rosy picture when, in Molly's case, there's just not enough pink on our palette."

We decided to walk down the long hill to the subway station rather than take the express bus back to Manhattan; both Molly and I get dizzy from the diesel fumes. At least she inherited *something* from me besides the ability to stick out a curled tongue.

"Did you download the Bennington application?" I asked her as we rumbled past Dyckman Street. She nodded. "Did you look at it yet?" She shook her head. I figured as much. "Meet me at the dinette table after you've finished your homework," I told her. "We're going to prove the smug Mr. Bernstein wrong!" I held up my hand for a high-five, and Molly, embarrassed, slapped it halfheartedly as the subway descended from the ele-vated track into the subterranean gloom.

Our mailbox yielded up the community college application that evening. I'm fairly sure that its ultimate materialization—more than the meeting with her college counselor, or anything else that was banging around in her rebellious adolescent head—spurred Molly to honor my demand to sit down after dinner so we could review the Bennington application together.

"Oh, my God, it's like thirty pages!" my daughter exclaimed. How she could have downloaded this massive application without even looking at it escaped my logic. "Were college applications this big when you were my age?"

"If memory serves, I'd say they were probably about half the length," I replied. "Then again, college was also half the price." Molly flipped through the pages, sighing heavily. "Well, since you found something wrong with every school we visited except for Bennington, I'd say this is your last best hope for not living at home for the next four years."

"Let's get cracking!"

Molly can be a particularly maddening young woman when it comes to the typical teen surliness, and in not making any effort or attempt to attain her potential—as anything—but I must admit that I am so glad I'm not a high school student, especially a graduating senior. Those are years I would never want to revisit. The Bennington application, which is pretty much on a par with other colleges of its ilk, was truly daunting. And in order to keep Molly's spirits up, I tried to pretend it wasn't, which wasn't working as well as I had hoped.

"I am so totally fucked," she said, on reading a preamble to the application that set forth its goal of encouraging individual expression within the application format, urging the student to provide the school with a sense not only of what they've accomplished thus far, but who they hope to become. "Which is worse," she moaned, "not having accomplished anything these ivory tower people want to read about, or not knowing who I want to become? Please don't tell me I'm the only high school senior in America who feels this way."

"I'd venture a guess that you're in the majority," I told her, "but don't defeat yourself before you even start the process. That kind of attitude has a way of becoming a self-fulfilling prophecy." I tell the same thing to my clients.

"Don't get all shrinky on me, Ma." Molly turned the page. The three essay options sent her into a tizzy. The only saving grace was the ability to supplement them with other media, such as photos, poetry, artwork, or anything else a clever student might devise. One essay quoted Aristotle on the use of metaphor and requested the applicant to prove *themselves* a "master of metaphor."

"That is, like, so stupid," Molly commented.

"And *that* is, like, *so* like a *simile*. They want metaphor, kiddo."

"You're not funny, Mom. You're just not a funny person, okay?"

Essay option two asked the prospective Bennington freshman to design an experiment that would prove that toads could hear.

"You could play Bach for them and see how they react, and then make them deaf with hip-hop," I suggested. "Hip-*hop*? Toads? Get it?"

"I hate to say it, Mom, but that's probably not such a stupid idea. It's better than essay option three. 'Select an issue about which you have strong convictions that extends beyond your family, yourself, and your friends.' This is like dork debate class. Pick something important and get the rest of the world to see your point."

I tried to convince my daughter that not everything is "dorky." "Molly, each one of these essay choices gives you the opportunity to think in a different way, to use the best part of your brain to its strengths, whether it's scientific, rational, or creative. Left and right brainiacs get an equal shot here. And look at it this way," I said, giving the community college brochure a quick scan. "If all else fails, you can study creative writing *here* and take advantage of the free theatre tickets they set aside for their students. Not only that, their women's volleyball team took the City University championship. And, from

looking at their application, the clincher is that they don't seem
to require any essays."

"That's probably 'cause their students don't know enough
English to write them." Molly sighed. "Okay, this may boil down
to the toads after all. Where do they come off with such dumb
topics? What kind of essays did you have when you were
applying?"

"We only had one choice. 'In John Donne's Meditation XVII,
he claimed that "No man is an island." Discuss.' "

"I don't even know what the fuck that means."

I laughed. "I've got a confession. Neither did I."

"So what did you do?"

"Supplemental materials. Lots of 'em! Actually, I wrote an
essay on Hemingway." Molly gave me a blank look. "I'm surprised you don't recognize the connection, Ms.-Hemingway-
star-writer-for-Mrs.-Noguchi. 'Never send to know for whom
the bell tolls; it tolls for thee.' "

"Huh?"

"It's the end of the 'no man is an island' meditation. Basically
I wormed my way around the essay. I think it was the interpretive dance I performed at my interview that nailed it though. I
called it 'Loneliness.' "

"Are you kidding?"

"Alas, no."

"Was it as angsty as your crappy poetry?"

I nodded. "Although I think you should be kinder toward my
creative efforts. They did get me into college."

"I am so not doing an interpretive dance."

"Then we're back to the toads." I turned the page. "Let's
read on."

As we perused the application, I shuddered to think of the

crates of materials that must get scrutinized annually by admissions committees all over the country. In addition to the usual test scores and transcripts, the required essays and teacher recommendations, the pages of short-answer questions, and the supplemental materials that we hoped would be that make-or-break silver bullet, Molly would have to provide Bennington with a graded analytic essay and a performance report from her college guidance counselor—and I didn't get the vibe from Mr. Bernstein that he was too crazy about us. From our brief meeting in his office that afternoon, I sensed that he wished it wouldn't require so much effort to report enthusiastically about my daughter to the college of her choice—or even to the college of *his* choice.

After spending an hour and a half reviewing the application, Molly leaned over the dinette table, folded her arms in front of her and buried her face. "My favorite question is the one where they ask if you have any relatives or close friends who attended Bennington. Are you *sure* I can't just backpack around Europe for a year? You're always telling your clients to take risks—like that's the most important thing in the world. So why can't you do in your personal life what you do in your professional life and let your own daughter take one?"

"For one thing, my clients aren't minors who happen to be related to me. And for the time being, given everything Mr. Bernstein said this afternoon, don't you think it's risky enough to try to get accepted to Bennington?" I flipped through the application's numerous pages. "At least you don't have to sign an affidavit swearing that you're heterosexual," I muttered grimly.

"What?"

I'd been thinking about Claude and Naomi's international adoption procedure, and their request for my assistance in completing the sheafs of complex paperwork. For all their left brain/right brain teasers and myriad questions designed to probe a person's psyche as much as ascertain their bank balance, do these voluminous applications really measure the sum of a person? Their values, their strengths, their potential to improve mankind? "Nothing," I mumbled to Molly. "Never mind."

ALICE

"If Mala Sonia ever gives you a prediction, you should take it seriously. And it doesn't give me any satisfaction to say so." Alice threw up her hands. "I was this close," she said, "*finally* with a steady acting job. Okay, Off-Broadway wasn't making me rich, but I suppose that falls into the 'be careful what you wish for' category. I wanted to be a full-time, working actress, instead of an abused office temp. I got my wish. I just didn't know how short-lived it would be."

"Is *Grandma Finnegan's Wake* closing?" I asked her.

"Not exactly. Listen to me; I sound like one of those old Hertz commercials. I play Fionulla Finnegan, a former *Star Search* winner. She's totally outrageous. I get to sing too. It's a wonderful part. A lot of the show is improv, which leaves lots of room for spontaneous reactions and interactions between the characters and with the audience. I went into the show as a replacement for the original actress, a bitch named Bitsy Burton who left to join the Chicago company, which apparently died a premature death, so she's back in the Off-Broadway production again. They couldn't give her her old role because *I* was in it, but

one of the other actresses in the New York company got a better job somewhere. So they ended up putting Bitsy—who had
originated my part—into the vacated role of Megan, Fionulla's
very unsexy cousin—who's a therapist—sorry—and who has to
dress like the stereotype of an Upper West Side shrink in thick
glasses, Birkenstocks, and unflattering dirndl skirts."

I glanced down at my own attire. "Dirndls camouflage wide
hips. Don't knock them."

Alice blushed. "I am *so so* sorry. Open mouth, insert foot,
swallow whole."

"It's okay," I ribbed her. "I wear soft lenses and my Birkenstocks are at the cobblers. Anyway, I'd rather hear about what's
going on with the show than a dissertation on the inherent lack
of fashion sense of Upper West Side psychotherapists."

"It's a nightmare. Remember how Mala Sonia had told me
about all this job strife and internal jealousies of coworkers and
all that crap I had coming to me in the near future? Well, Bitsy
had it in for me from our very first performance together. About
a third of the show is actually scripted, but like I said, the rest
of *Grandma Finnegan's Wake* is improvisational. So from the
get-go, Bitsy started accusing me of improv-ing during her
scripted speeches and dialogue—which I wasn't doing, beyond
what was required of Fionulla's character in the show. I was just
doing my job. As the days went on, I discovered that *nobody*
likes this actress. Back when she was playing Fionulla, she used
to make life hell for any new person who came into the show. I
get along great with everyone—the actors, running crew, et
cetera—and that pisses off Bitsy as well."

"Well, can't you just do your role and go home? I know that
actors like to socialize with each other after the show, unwind,
and all that, but can you just try to keep this to the most professional level? Think of it as one of your former day jobs? Just

do your work and go home and get on with the rest of your life until it's time to go to work again?"

Alice sighed. "I wish it were that easy. I hate feeling like Bitsy's rude and unprofessional behavior is rebounding on me, punishing me for getting along well with my colleagues. But it's bigger than that. Mala Sonia spoke to me of false accusations leveled against me, remember? Well, Bitsy took it upon herself to maintain a journal of my 'improvisational transgressions' during performances and took it to Actors' Equity, where she's preferring charges against me. So now I'm in deep shit with my union just for doing my job. And because the *Grandma Finnegan* writers don't have every single moment of the show parceled into 'improvised' and 'scripted' sections—I mean, there's a lot of gray area that can be open to interpretation—I don't have much to hang my hat on when it comes to mounting my defense. What this is really all about is that Bitsy is angling to get her original role back, and, face it, I'm prettier, more talented, and everybody likes me—which gets her goat even more."

"So, where do you currently stand?"

A huge tear traveled down Alice's right cheek. "The union hearing is next week. And I haven't been able to get anything resembling a good night's sleep since this *literal* character assassination thing began. A couple of years ago I went through something like this after I got canned from a lawyer's office and filed for unemployment benefits. I'd rather slit my wrists than go through that again. But this is much worse than the day job hearing because this is my real career. If I get a blemish on my record as an actress and Equity agrees with Bitsy that I behaved unprofessionally in a show . . . that's it. My acting career is dead. No one wants to hire a problem—at least not if they're an unknown. If you're a *famous* pain in the ass, that's another story.

But in my position . . . ? If the ruling doesn't go in my favor, there are too many other good actresses out there for a producer or director to bother to go out on a limb for me." I took a packet of tissues from my pocket and handed them to her. "You do that a lot," Alice said, trying to chuckle between sniffles.

I went over to sit beside her, something I never do, even with my laundry room clients. But poor Alice had suffered a Job-like existence these past few months: losing her closest relative, and, finally transcending years of temp hell to reach her goal of being a working actress—only to find the triumph short-lived and slipping through her fingers like grains of sand.

"Remember when Mala Sonia told me that everything would finally turn out all right during a time of feasting? Well, I thought my first date with Dan Carpenter—remember him—would do the trick."

"That's right!" I exclaimed. "You had that date with Dan. Your love life kind of got buried under all the job stuff. So?"

"He's wonderful," Alice sighed. "I could really like this guy. You know, when we first became acquainted there was this current between us, but he never made a move. It was like he sensed I wasn't ready. He gets lots of points for that. Anyway, we had a wonderful dinner at Il Pomodoro—except that most of the time all I talked about was the shit that's going on with me and *Grandma Finnegan's Wake*. The poor man was bleary-eyed by the time we got to the tiramisu."

"In my experience, if Dan's a sensitive guy, he'll cut you some slack. You're going through a rough spot and needed to talk about it. Don't beat yourself up over it. Of course," I chuckled, "that said, there is a line in the sand between *sharing* your tribulations and dumping-and-venting mode."

"Oops," said Alice. "I have a strong feeling I crossed it. Big-time."

"Share with Dan; dump-and-vent with me. That's what I'm

here for. Has Dan called you since this ill-fated Il Pomodoro dinner?"

Alice shook her head. "He gave me a very nice good-night kiss out on the sidewalk in front of our building, so I certainly had my hopes up."

"I'd agree that all signs would be encouraging." *God, I sound like the Magic 8-Ball.*

"But of course, Il Pomodoro happens to be the famous *Seinfeld* 'break up' restaurant, so we may have started out on the wrong foot; begun at the end. And now there's a new little wrinkle that may put a major crimp in my love life, or sex life, assuming I ever get to have one again."

"Which is?"

We both nearly jumped out of our skins when we heard the frantic knock on the laundry room door.

"Probably that," Alice said, gesturing toward the sound.

"I guess I should unlock it."

"You know, all my life I've felt like I was one of those circus performers, trying to keep a dozen plates spinning in the air at once without letting any of them drop or lose momentum. And I thought I'd gotten pretty good at handling it. I was kind of proud of my multitasking abilities, in fact. Well, now I feel like someone tossed in a thirteenth plate, and my whole act is going to shit."

"One thing that I've found very useful is to try to tackle one hurdle at a time, rather than trying to take on everything at once," I said, heading for the door. "You're dealing with a budding romance—"

"Well, what I *hope* is a budding romance. I really like Dan. Spending time with him is like wearing a favorite old sweater. Well, a six-foot-tall, hazel-eyed, muscular-yet-sensitive favorite old sweater."

I laughed. "Remember when we first officially met, I congratulated you on retaining your sense of humor. This is good. You've done that. Keep it up. So you've got Dan, and then you've got the *mishegas* with *Grandma Finnegan's Wake*, Bitsy, and the ogres at Actors' Equity on your front burner—" I opened the door to find Alice's now rather pregnant friend Isabel sobbing into a shredded Kleenex.

"And Izzy," Alice added. "Susan, meet my new roommate."

"Yeah, meet the bull in the china shop," Izzy said, kicking the doorsill angrily and stubbing her toe in the process. "Fuck a duck! Ouch! Can I come in?" she asked tentatively. I looked to Alice for the answer, since we were in the middle of her session.

"Might as well, since you've become one of my 'issues,' " Alice said.

"Oh, lovely," Izzy groaned. "I'm cutting to the chase. I figured I'd tell you sooner rather than later, because I'll be halfway out the door on the way to medical mal hell at Steinbeck and Strindberg by the time you get upstairs and see the pieces all over the floor."

"Pieces?" Alice looked both puzzled and horrified.

"Your grandmother's Balloon Seller. The Royal Doulton figurine she loved so much." Izzy shook her head woefully. "Dust. I knocked into it by mistake when I was reaching for the teapot. Which isn't in great shape either."

"Oh, no!" Alice's horror morphed into new tears.

For the next fifteen minutes she vacillated between saying she didn't know whether to hate Izzy forever for breaking a cherished heirloom (or two) or forgiving her for being in such a bad state herself. Izzy and her husband Dominick had quarreled frequently since "they" had become pregnant. Dominick couldn't handle the emotional roller coaster of Izzy's newly rampaging hormones; he felt she'd become another person entirely.

"He says it's like my body is possessed by some demon from a sci-fi movie," she raged. "Can I help it? This is what happens to pregnant women. You've got kids. Were you like this?" she asked me.

I admitted that Eli had threatened to move back in with his mother during each of my pregnancies. And had really resented trekking all the way out to Coney Island to satisfy my occasional cravings for those Nathan's hot dogs—which had to come *only* from the original Nathan's location—*only* an hour or more away by subway—in each direction. And naturally, they'd no longer be steaming hot when they arrived on the Upper West Side, and I couldn't stand to have them reheated—particularly once I'd drizzled chocolate sauce on them. The memories made me wonder if Eli's increasingly frequent absences from the dinner table were an extremely belated form of payback, an "acting out" for all the estrogen and progesterone-related acting out I'd done so many years ago.

So Alice, who now had a spare bedroom, had graciously taken Izzy in until she and Dominick could cool down. Unfortunately for both women, Izzy confessed that she couldn't foresee any specific time frame for this temporary sojourn. "Right now we never want to see each other's ugly mugs again."

Alice, who hadn't yet adjusted to living without her grandmother, or to living alone, which she had never done before in her entire life, admitted that she loved Izzy like the sister she wished she'd had, but that she hadn't yet figured out how these new living arrangements would work out to her satisfaction. She couldn't give Izzy her recently departed Gram's bedroom because it still held shrinelike connotations for her and it felt too much like moving on too fast. On the other hand, she couldn't give Izzy her own bedroom because she'd been comfortably ensconced there for years and everything had been dec-

orated and set up to her liking and she wasn't inclined to dis-
mantle the room, because it was (a) inconvenient, and (b) where
would she put everything? Gram's room, which still had Gram's
furnishings in it? And if she did move all her stuff out of the
room, what would Izzy do? Buying new furniture made no
sense.

"I have to say that on one hand I couldn't refuse Izzy. Your
sobbing, pregnant best friend shows up on your doorstep like an
orphan in the storm? It was a no-brainer. Of course I took her
in. On the other hand, yeah, it is an inconvenience. I guess a part
of me secretly wished that she'd spend the night on the couch
and in the morning her fight with Dominick would have all
blown over and they'd kiss and make up over the phone and
she'd go home."

"When did you move in?" I asked Izzy.

"Last week."

"The night after my last session with you," Alice told me. "So
this is the first chance I've had to talk about it in therapy."

"Excuse me," Izzy said, and bolted toward the bathroom.

"Her morning sickness is pretty horrible," Alice whispered.
"She's one of those women who still have it after the first
trimester."

A minute later Izzy staggered out of the bathroom, her com-
plexion pale. "Maybe I should call Schmuck and Schmuck and
tell them I'm too sick to come in. I can't read hospital charts
and doctors' reports about their clients' gastrointestinal problems today." She turned to Alice. "You know, *I* really wish I were
back home too. I hate barfing in other people's bathrooms. But
I think it's gotta be bad for the baby if every minute of my life
is all about Dom and me yelling and screaming at each other.
Pick a topic: we fight about it. The other day he dragged me into
an argument about the fact that we both wanted steak for din-

ner. I ask you, how does a man get away with picking a fight when you're both on the same side?! Oops. Sorry." She dashed back into the bathroom.

"I really feel sorry for her," Alice whispered to me. "And I'd like to think that there's nothing I wouldn't do for her. But I'm in such a transitional place myself right now that it's all too much to handle."

"There's a philosophy that says that the universe never gives us more than we can handle, even when we really feel we're being completely dumped on."

"Well, Susan, I've got a philosophy that says that *that* philosophy is total b.s."

We shared a laugh. "Not that it's the same thing, but there was a time when Eli's mother came to visit for a week and ended up staying three months. She never liked me, and in the beginning I was tearing my hair out trying to be particularly nice to her, and then giving up trying altogether because it wasn't going to change her lousy opinion of me. So I started taking things one day at a time, grateful for every day I got through with no bloodshed on either side. At least you don't have someone telling you every five minutes that you're not raising your kids properly and have no clue how to be a mother.

"Anyway, where I'm going with this is the opinion thing: something it takes an awful lot to change. Izzy loves you and I highly doubt she's going to change her mind about that and suddenly end your friendship just because you're going through a lot of stuff yourself right now. Even from the few minutes she was sitting here, I didn't get the sense that she expected you to *take care* of her to the exclusion of your own needs. Just being there for her is important to Izzy. She sought a safe haven with you; a place where she feels appreciated and supported during this enormous turning point in her life. You're both going through highly charged emotional periods. You're just beginning to heal from a death and you've got significant romance and career changes going on as well. She's carrying a life, and her own will never be the same in a few months' time.

"Now what you want to do about who-gets-which-bedroom and how it would impact things to have Dan Carpenter shuffling around the house in his boxers on a Sunday morning is up to you and Izzy to work out, but at the risk of sounding 'shrinky,' I think both of you women can learn and grow from this giant hiccup that's been tossed in your path. You sort of have no choice, in fact, because the apartment isn't big enough for either of you to play 'ostrich' and hope that your issues evanesce while you've got your heads in the sand."

I glanced at Alice and spontaneously decided to employ a methodology that I thought might help her work through one of her biggest issues. "I want to try something a little different this morning, so bear with me. Since you're an actress, I think you'll respond well to some role-playing. You've expressed feelings of sorrow and regret, even of guilt, that you never had the chance to say good-bye to your grandmother, since her death was so sudden."

I went over and switched off the fluorescents. "I want you to take a moment or two to think about what you would have liked to have said to her, if we turned back time and you could speak to her face-to-face. You can look at me, if you want to, or you can focus on something else in the room. Okay?"

"Okay," Alice replied. She took a deep breath. "This isn't going to be easy. I think I'll use you. I can relate better to a warm and nurturing woman than to an ungainly, malfunctioning household appliance." She closed her eyes and sat up straight, resting her hands on her knees.

"Gram . . . ?" she began, opening her eyes and focusing them on mine. "I'm going to really miss you. You've taught me so much . . . about human nature, about myself, about the importance of contributing to my community . . . and about following my heart's desire, instead of playing it safe. They don't make 'em like you, Gram; they broke the mold. Ever since I was a little girl, you've always led by example, demonstrating the true meanings of humanity, compassion, generosity, and tolerance. When you were ill, you maintained a positive attitude that put healthy people to shame. I . . . I wish you didn't have to go, Gram. We could use someone like you running the country. But I know you'd really miss your favorite sound—the carriage horses clip-clopping past our windows—if you lived at 1600 Pennsylvania Avenue."

Alice blew her nose loudly. "You were always so political, Gram, that I thought I'd throw that in. I want you to know that I will always carry your lessons in here," she said, placing her hand over her heart. "No one could have left me a greater legacy. You know how much I love you—and I'll never stop—even when you're gone. But maybe even more than that, I know how much *you* love *me*, and I know you aren't finding this any easier than I am. But maybe we can both move on, knowing that your granddaughter will continue to cherish, and embody, your values and beliefs for as long as she lives . . . no matter what she may end up doing with your tchotchkes."

Alice wiped her eyes. Her lids were puffy and red. "Thanks for putting me through hell just now," she said to me.

I gave her a hug. "Do you feel any better about things?" I asked softly.

Alice sighed deeply and remained silent for a few moments. "You know something? Actually . . . I *do*."

When I heard the whimper of an infant, I freaked out for a moment, until I realized that the sound was coming from the doorway. In the commotion of Izzy's hysteria over breaking the cherished figurine and then instigating the role-playing exercise with Alice, I'd forgotten to lock the door again. Amy stood there with her son in one arm and a diaper bag in the other. "Oh, I thought you were officially open," she said to me, then checked the sign posted outside the door. "Well, so I'm two minutes early. You can't expect me to stand here holding Isaac for a hundred and twenty seconds. And by the time we got all the way back upstairs it would only be time to come back down again. And believe me, I'm not anxious for the extra exercise." She cooed some nonsense syllables to Isaac then glared at Alice.

"I'm not a selfish person," Alice said pointedly, glancing at her watch. "So, come on in and wash Eric's son's stinky diapers." She looked at me and it was very hard not to laugh. Next session—for each of them—it might be a good idea to deal with what was going on with Alice and Amy. "We were pretty much done anyway," Alice added.

Izzy emerged from the bathroom. "I figured it was probably a good idea to camp out in there for a little while longer, to give you some privacy. I think I just lost the last ten meals I ate."

"Oh, hi. Welcome to the club," grinned Amy. Izzy grunted wearily. "How far along are you?"

"I'm due in mid-February."

"And you're still throwing up in your second trimester?" Amy tsk-tsked and Izzy winced. "Don't feel bad. I did too. Barf, I mean. You get used to it. You're carrying pretty well; you don't look like the Goodyear blimp yet and your feet haven't swollen to the size of sausages that you couldn't squeeze into Michael Jordan's Nikes. No, you haven't put *too* much weight on—but just wait. Wait for the weight, get it?" Amy emitted a forced laugh. "Sorry, I don't get to talk to adults too often these days. Except my mother, who really doesn't want to hear about the baby. She says she's sick of my discussing Isaac like he's some sort of miracle. 'Everybody has babies. I had three of you. Big deal.' That's what she says. But you *are* a little miracle," she gurgled to her son, "aren't you? You *are* a little miracle, *yes* you *are*." I almost gagged. I hope I wasn't this way when Molly and Ian were babies. "Yes, you're such a little miracle," Amy murmured, "because it's a miracle that Daddums was home long enough to even *get* Mom-ums *pregnant*. But we'll talk about that in our next session with Smart Susan, won't we?" she added. I noticed Alice suppressing a smile.

"Wow," Izzy said. "Having a baby is one of the ultimate mutual decisions a couple can make, but then when we get pregnant, our husbands act like it was entirely *our* idea and they take a powder. What's that about? You think you've gotten past that fear of commitment thing when they finally marry you. Then you get pregnant, and bang! They freak out all over again."

"Are you bonding with *Amy?*" Alice hissed, drawing her friend aside. "She's the one that slime-bucket-pond-scum-asshole lawyer Eric Witherspoon married after he dumped me! And doing the math, there's no way she got pregnant *after* he stomped on the glass and their families danced to 'Hava Nagila' and stuffed their faces at a Viennese table."

"Oh don't give me that 'I can't be friends with both of you,' thing," Izzy responded. "That is *so* kindergarten!"

"She already stole my, well, ex-boyfriend. Now she wants to steal my best friend too. She's diabolical. Don't let her insidious grin and solicitous Mommy questions fool you!"

I think this was the point where I realized that it might not be a bad idea somewhere down the line to offer group sessions in the laundry room. Sometimes it's the most effective—and healthiest—way for people to air their dirty linen.

Progress Notes

Naomi Sciorra and Claude Chan: Naomi is still resentful over the new wrinkle in the adoption issue, but she and Claude are faced with an even greater dilemma, ethically and personally, because if they want to adopt from China, Claude will be compelled to tell a lie on a formal document, essentially denying or repudiating her sexual orientation. Despising the hypocrisy of the whole situation, I found myself in a difficult position, encouraging the lie for the greater good of gaining the little girl. That may work for the woman, but not for the therapist, where I took sides, with regrettable results. I'm not sanguine about this; not at all. The three of us need to actively develop ways to reconcile the two partners, as well as reconcile all the implications inherent in Claude's acquiescence (by signing the "heterosexual" affidavit) to a system that insists she conceal her identity. The more immediate goal, however, will be to help Naomi realize that she's a valuable and vital part of the process.

Talia Shaw: I've never lost a laundry room "client," so this is a first. Talia's convinced that her leg injury precludes her from continuing with her therapy, as it severely hampers her ambulation; and she believes that if she can't dance during her sessions, then she can't articulate her issues either. So far, I haven't been successful in making much progress, if any, on her self-esteem issues. I need to help her see, and believe in, her worth beyond the dance world; but she walked out on her last session and has not resumed therapy. Beyond my assurance to her that the door is always open, I fear that pushing Talia to remain in therapy will be counterproductive at this point.

Meriel Delacour: Job issues persist: she hasn't discussed these issues with her employer directly when employer has presented them to her. Instead, Meriel has been passive-aggressively dealing with the situation, acknowledging in her sessions that these issues have been troubling her employer while nonetheless continuing her "unacceptable" behavior (in employer's eyes). In the present situation, the locus of the disagreements between client and her employer have a cultural root. I need to encourage client to explore a cool-headed open discussion of her job issues with her employer directly. There's something deeper that's operating here, though. Meriel is unfulfilled in her employment, and her discontent is breeding resentment and acting out, as evidenced by her tardiness and sluggishness on the job due to her West Indian Day carnival preparations.

Alice Finnegan: Alice is experiencing so many changes that have hit her simultaneously that it's difficult to focus on a single issue during her sessions. She's still grieving for her late grandmother, a major issue in itself, but I believe the role-playing we did in her recent session will have a beneficial effect insofar as helping her move on. With career strife, a new man in her life, and the sudden appearance on her doorstep of her pregnant friend Isabel seeking sanctuary from her own domestic woes, Alice is totally overwhelmed and our key task will be to work on maintaining her equilibrium in the face of such upheaval, and not self-destructing under its weight. Need to work on Alice's confidence that her own inner strength will carry her through her present morass one step at a time—rather than allowing the contemplation of all these life crises striking her simultaneously to generate anxiety attacks, impulsive behavior, or depression. With so much on her plate right now, she'll have to make a deliberate and conscious effort to retain her emotional balance.

Me: The irony has not escaped me that I've been able to help other people navigate their way through life-changing issues like death and divorce, but when it comes to taking care of myself, I neglect to do something as simple and basic as putting on a sun hat. And at the parade the other day, Faith was gustatorially bold, where I was not.

I am proud of myself for attempting to be more direct with Eli, even though I could barely get myself to articulate what's been an annoying little bug buzzing around the back of my mind. And when he insisted right to my face that there was nothing I "should know about," I accepted his words at face value. Am I in denial about something being "off"? Immediately devaluing or invalidating my anxiety and intuition because I want to believe that Eli is just having a lot of difficulty completing this particular graphic novel? I'm angry with him—but angry about what's in my *imagination*, rather than what may really be going on. I want desperately to believe that my husband is being honest with me. Yet, on a deeper level, I'm also terrified to find out the truth. It's just so much easier, so much safer, to focus on my clients' issues instead of on mine.

That said, I'm delighted that Faith is making such progress, but I feel like I've failed Talia. I'm off my game and it's both angering and frustrating me.

My own termination anxiety regarding Talia was exacerbated by Carol Lerner's abrupt ending of her therapy sessions in the same week. Carol's insurance wouldn't cover more than fifteen sessions, and she didn't want to continue to pay for them on her own. Given Carol's income, and aware that she could afford the full freight, if necessary, I didn't extend to her the offer to continue our work on a sliding-scale basis. Now I'm second-guessing myself because I may have ultimately lost this client due to my own sense of greed.

Therapists have an uneasy relationship with money. On the one hand, we may see ourselves as healers who altruistically provide our services to whoever needs us, regardless of their ability to pay our fees. On the other hand, we're credentialed professionals with years of schooling and training under our belts, and we deserve to earn a proper living.

For the most part, my laundry room ladies, acquaintances with whom I work on a pro bono basis, could not afford an open-ended course of therapy, so I could hardly be accused of being in it for the money. And yet I feel guilty about losing Carol, who has a long way to go toward complete mental health and emotional stability.

With Talia, I feel the need to dig deeper into my creative well in order to discover a methodology that will work for her during her recuperation from knee surgery. She's got a lot of stuff to work though now, and I want to be able to help her. Although I never suffered an injury that forced me to rethink my career options, I did make the successful switch from dance to another field, and survived. Of course, in my case, the decision was more or less my own, but in some ways my body—those too-wide hips and weight problems that left me with an eating disorder—did make that decision for me. My empathetic understanding of Talia's situation is very strong; but at present, until I can find a workable technique that will bring her back into psychotherapy, I feel powerless to help her.

With Naomi and Claude, walking the blurry line of "Pal with Psych Ph.D." has become incredibly tricky. When a therapist makes the decision to actively intervene in a session, there's always a risk that things could backfire, which is exactly what ended up happening here. I alienated Naomi when she most needed to be included. As a result, she has withdrawn from active participation in the adoption proceedings to the extent that she can contribute to them. At least she's still attending their therapy sessions, so I suppose my candid thoughts haven't put her off entirely. Still, I'm unconvinced that I did the right thing by "putting in my oar." Instead of being didactic, I should probably have followed a traditional approach to psychotherapy.

Funny, how Claude and Naomi solicited my help with their adoption application, while at home it's like pulling teeth to get Molly to tackle her college applications. I wish I could help *her* more, but she's so resistant. Yet, if Molly were a client, I would push and prod her out of her comfort zone, so that she could grow. But knowing that there's no risk without the possibility of pain, I don't want to see my little girl hurting, even if she may *need* to leave that comfort zone in order to grow. My professional life and personal lives often bleed together. With Molly, I can't help but think as a mother, and not as a counselor.

It's going to be difficult for me to help my clients and my daughter with their respective paperwork: I have negative opinions about the efficacy of these documents in presenting what's positive and desirable and special about the applicants.

And in both situations, a child's future hangs in the balance.

PERMANENT PRESS

10

NAOMI AND CLAUDE

With an expectant look, Claude handed me the pale green envelope addressed to Ms. Susan Lederer and family written in a calligraphy that resembled Chinese brushwork.

"Read it," Naomi urged breathlessly. She scooted closer to Claude and grabbed her hand.

I slid the card from the envelope. " 'Your presence is requested at the union of Claude Li Ming Chan and Naomi Kelly Sciorra as they celebrate their love, at the Wesleyan Chapel, Fall Street, Seneca Falls, New York, on the thirty-first day of October . . .' My God, that's wonderful!" I said, trying not to tear up. "Congratulations! I'm so happy for both of you!"

"And if anyone has a gripe about this, they can pretend they're at a Halloween party," Naomi quipped.

"Look, we bought each other rings!" Claude said, and each of the women thrust her right hand toward me. "Yes, the right-hand diamond celebrates a woman's independence. And we're exercising ours by making as formal a commitment as we can to each other—by choosing to get married."

"She proposed to me," Naomi said, blinking back tears. "Claude actually got down on one knee and proposed to me."

I brought my hand to my heart. I was getting *ferklempt* after all. There's no way that even a therapist could remain unemotional about such a big, exciting change in her clients' lives. "What brought it on? Anything specific?"

Claude took Naomi's hand in hers. "For one thing, it was time. We've been together for years. For another thing, I wanted to find the most special way I could for Nay to know how important she is to me, and that, despite all this crap we're going through to try to get our little girl, that she's the treasure of my heart and I wanted her to know that in a way beyond words. Talk is cheap, you know! I wanted something official as well as something meaningful."

"I am so happy for both of you. And of course I'll be there."

"Road trip!" the partners chorused.

"I know it's short notice," Claude said apologetically. "Giving it to you only two weeks before, instead of six. But this was kind of a spur-of-the-moment decision."

"We would have asked you to be a bridesmaid, but we're not having any," Naomi told me.

"We figured we'd spare our friends the pastel polyester dresses," Claude added.

"So are you two wearing big white dresses?"

"I'm wearing white," Naomi said. "Claude's wearing a red dress; that's the Chinese traditional color for brides. She's got a cheongsam with the dragon and phoenix embroidered on it. It signifies good luck, and is supposed to chase away evil spirits. There's plenty of those in Washington," she added, "but they're not on the guest list."

"And all our flowers will be red and white," Claude said. "We're going to try to incorporate a few Chinese wedding traditions, actually. My grandmother—she's very traditional and conservative—doesn't know whether to be proud or appalled. She still doesn't quite get it that I'm living with a woman, and am so in love with her that I'm getting married, but that I'm not marrying a man! She keeps asking me what the groom's name is."

"You should hear *my* parents," Naomi said. "My mother made her peace with my sexuality years ago, but my father calls me *misere*. His misery. He always says to me, 'You wanna be a tough girl, how come you don't want to work with me at the hardware store?' "

"Would you believe that there are probably some straight people out there who think you're nuts?"

"For getting married? Fuck 'em!"

"No, Naomi," I said, "because the way the laws of the land currently stand, the only thing in gays' favor when it comes to the institution of marriage is that they get to avoid all the family bullshit that comes with wedding planning!"

"Well, there's always a downside to everything, I suppose," Claude said cheerfully. "Even equal rights."

I glanced down at the wedding invitation. "Seneca Falls. I like the significance."

Naomi beamed. "That's why we're having the big ceremony in New York, even though at this point we'll have to skip over to a judge's chambers in Massachusetts to do it up legally. But Claude and I love it that the Wesleyan Chapel in Seneca Falls is where the first women's rights convention in history was held."

"That's very cool!" I said. "Very cool."

"For us, it's a *civil* rights issue. We think same-sex unions—legally recognized ones—are as important to fight for as women's suffrage was a hundred years ago. And of course there was a time when blacks in America didn't have the vote either, and when interracial marriages were against the law. Look at all the states that had Jim Crow laws on their books for decades. And a lot of blood was shed to get all those laws changed and new ones enacted. But if our country was founded on the principles of 'liberty and justice for all,' and you believe that's more than empty rhetoric, it's the only way to go."

Claude nudged her partner in the ribs. "Get off the soapbox, Nay, you're preaching to the converted!"

"I want to hear all about the wedding plans," I told them, "but I'd also like to discuss the adoption situation, and how that's working for each of you, especially in light of the wedding."

"We still don't see eye-to-eye on it," Naomi admitted. "The bottom line for me is that, yes, I want a daughter, and I understand why Claude wants to get her from China, but I don't want to have to play games and get her dishonestly."

"And you, Claude?"

"It's not lost on me . . . the irony that Nay and I own a nightclub where *straight* women pay us money to *pretend* they're *gay* . . . that it's how we make our bread and butter. That it's how we would be able to afford to give our adopted daughter a really comfortable upbringing."

Eureka! "Naomi, what do you think of that?"

I'd never seen her eyes so wide. "Can you believe," she said slowly, "that that has never occurred to me before? It totally never entered my mind. And Claude has never brought that up until now."

"That's because it just hit me. It was an epiphany. I'm as struck by it as you are."

"And if I want to apply my own standards across the board, if your pretending that you're *straight* in order to get our daughter is an unacceptable hypocrisy to me, then our livelihood, which trades on sexual identity-bending pretense, really should be as well. And I can't conscience trashing the business Claude and I worked so hard to build."

"So does that mean that you're becoming more open to accepting Claude's signature on that heinous form attesting that she's a heterosexual, actively seeking a husband?"

Naomi gazed at the sparkler on her right ring finger. "As long as we can accept that none of us is condoning perjury, per se. Right?" Claude and I nodded.

"Of course right," Claude assured her.

"Actually, it's pretty funny—when you look at it the way I am this morning—right this minute, anyway." Naomi curled her diamond-bearing hand into a fist. "I'd like to see Claude 'actively seek a husband' when she's already got a wife!"

MERIEL

"You know if it isn't one ting, it's another wit' her," Meriel sighed.

"Have you thought about sitting down with Ms. Baum and talking about these issues?" I asked her.

"She tink because I speak wit' an ahkcent and work as a domestic dat I don't know how to have an intelligent discussion. She don't know dat I record de talking books for de sight-impaired people at my community center. It don't speak well for her kind, daht's all I can say."

"And what kind is that?" I prodded. I was taking the calculated risk of hearing something I would find unpleasant, given the similarity of my background to Amy's, but I had to get Meriel talking—at least to me—about the *root* of the problem she was having with Amy rather than about its manifestations, which we had discussed at length during prior sessions.

"What kind? Lawyers!" I must have looked visibly relieved because Meriel added, "Mrs. Susan, you tink I was talking about white Jewish women?" I tried to look enigmatic. "No-no, I hope you know me well enough for daht." I hoped I did too, but people can surprise you. "No, I talk about lawyers, who are supposed to be all about helping people. In French—I learn dis from Leon—de word for lawyer is *avocat*—same place we get our word 'advocate.' Mrs. Amy ahkt layk she's my enemy, not my advocate. Everyting I do nowadays, she find reason to complain about it. I tell you, I am at my wits' end wit' her. But I need de job, so I don't quit."

It would have been a violation of professional ethics to mention to Meriel that Amy had so much of her own *mishegas* going on right now that she was probably misplacing at least *some* of her ire, taking her frustration out on the help instead of on her husband.

"I know you want me to talk to her," Meriel continued, "to take de risk, to go out of de comfort zone—all daht stuff you talk about—but she don't want to discuss it wit' me. I tink when all is said and done, Mrs. Amy is a little afraid of me."

"In what way?"

"Afraid I get so ahngry daht I quit and leave her wit' nothing. But at de same time, she so rude sometimes daht she's practically pushing me out de door. Maybe she want me to leave, but make de leaving be my own idea so I don't complain to Al Sharpton or somebody daht she fire me for no good reason."

"So what's her beef with you these days? The carnival was weeks ago. It can't be that."

"Ohhh, William is getting ready to open his restaurant, and I been helping him out, trying out de recipes for de community— you know, ahsking friends and relations to try dem, see which are deyr favorites. I try to get everyting done fahst for Mrs. Amy so I can leave a little early to get back to Flatbush by seven or eight in de evening, so I can still help William. And some mornings I come in a little late because William want me to meet with de contractors too. He say de place need a woman's touch for de decoration, you know?" Meriel laughed. "William is good wit' de people and good wit' de food. He even bettah wit' de people dan wit' de cooking, if you ahsk me!" She leaned back against the sofa cushions and brought her hand to her face, to cover a blush. "But he *terrible* wit' de decor. Oh, my Lord, I can't help but bust out laughing just tinking about it. William say as long as de colors are Jamaican—de green and yellow and black—he don't care what de walls and the furniture look like. He pick de designs and show me so proudly and I go, 'Oh, my God! You making de place look like a high school gymnasium!' So Mrs. Amy doesn't layk it daht I spend de time wit' William on his restaurant and be all creative and excited and den I come into de city and she say I don't give her my best. I tell you, I'm doing de same job I always do for her. But she don't layk it daht I come in happy sometimes. She want me to be all beaten up inside like she is. You know de saying 'misery love company'? Daht's Mrs. Amy dese days. And I don't layk it one bit."

"Well . . . you seem to be enjoying getting the restaurant together so much, have you talked to William about there being a niche for you there?"

"You have a son, Mrs. Susan," Meriel said. "And in a few years' time he be telling you he don't want his mama making his decisions for him. He got to live his own life. I can help William wit' tings he have no big interest in, layk de restaurant decor, even choosing de best recipes to put on de menu, but Mama got to stay outta de kitchen, if you know what I mean!"

ME

"You know, it's always me who's doing the initiating these days," I murmured to Eli. When we'd made love that night, his mind seemed a million miles away. I know it's not uncommon to fantasize about someone else during intercourse, but when the fantasy is a good one, it usually results in added energy and spice, not the tepid tussle I'd just been a party to. "Are you feeling all right? You haven't had a checkup in years, you know. Maybe it wouldn't be a bad idea. At the very least a prostate—"

"I feel fine, Susie," Eli said evenly. "I'm totally healthy. There's nothing to worry about."

Nothing to worry about. Then why am I worrying? "Is it me? Is there something I'm doing—or not doing—that you wish I'd do—or not do?"

Eli smiled and caressed my cheek. "It's not you."

"Then if it's not you—and it's not me—" I bit the bullet. "Eli . . . ? Is there a third person in our bed?"

"Susie." My husband smiled weakly. "It's the book. The deadlines. I . . . I'm sorry . . . I just haven't been able to get myself to concentrate on anything else. You know I've never been the most focused person in the world; I really have to work at it. Call it immaturity, call it AADD, call it how I'm hard-wired, but I've been this way ever since you've known me. I know I haven't been pulling my weight around here lately, and I know you—and the kids—haven't thought Dad's been much fun lately. But I love you all very much. And . . . and . . . I don't know. Soon. Soon."

"What's that supposed to mean, though?" I asked gently.

Eli released an exasperated little sigh. "*Aghh.* See, you're always getting shrinky. I . . . I don't know what it means. I mean, it means what it means. Susie, you know I'm not the most verbal person in the world. I'm a *graphic* novelist, not a wordsmith, remember? I feel at a disadvantage when you're in the room. I . . . never feel like I can find the words I need to say. Or the words you want to hear."

I pursed my lips, trying to stifle my anger. "Then draw me a picture."

The phone rang shortly after two A.M. and startled me out of a sound sleep. Eli answered it and couldn't seem to make head or tail of the gist of the situation described by the urgent person on the other end of the phone.

"It's one of your clients, Susie," he said, rolling over and handing me the receiver. I sat up in bed, fearing every therapist's worst nightmare: that one of them has done something horribly self-destructive.

"Hello . . . ?" I said sleepily.

"Susan, it's Claude." Her voice, usually so calm, sounded panicked.

"Wh-What's the matter? Is everything all right? Are you okay? Is Naomi okay?"

"Yes . . . and no. Susan, we really need your help and you're the only person we could think of at this late date."

I wasn't fully comprehending. "Claude, what can I help you with at two in the morning?"

"We just got an e-mail from our caterer—well, it's the Jade Dragon, the local Chinese restaurant up in Seneca Falls. We were all set to have our wedding banquet there after the ceremony on Saturday . . . and they told us they have to cancel. That they can't be involved. Nay was sure that it had something to do with the fact that they realized they were going to be catering a gay wedding, but didn't want to put that in writing. And it's the Chinese way to be indirect, anyway. We don't confront things head-on. Think tai-chi, not boxing."

"I'm still not sure I know what you want me to help you with in the middle of the night."

"I'm so sorry for calling you now. It's totally inexcusable, I know. We freaked. Chalk it up to prewedding jitters. Planning jitters. We want this to come off so beautifully, and when we read the e-mail, the two of us kind of went into crisis mode. I apologize again for the ridiculous hour. And please tell Eli we're sorry too, for waking him up."

It had been the first night in a long time that Eli and I had gone to bed at the same hour, even made love, such as it had been, and despite the uncomfortable postcoital conversation. But there was no need to share that information with my client. Number one: it was personal. And number two: if I had, it would have launched her on a galactic guilt trip.

"So . . . I guess I called you for two reasons: one—to talk us down from the metaphorical ledge; and two—because you might be able to recommend another caterer. Someone who won't lose face by feeding two brides and seventy-five of their closest friends and relatives."

By now I was fully awake and almost alarmingly alert. "I have an idea," I told Claude, "but I can't make you any guarantees right this second. At 2:24 A.M., I mean. How do you feel about curried goat and jerk chicken?"

11

The weather gods favored Claude and Naomi with a brilliant Indian Summer day for their wedding. Not only was I looking forward to celebrating their nuptials, but the road trip gave the nuclear Lederer family a chance to spend the entire day together, something we hadn't done in weeks. Ian, sketchbook on his lap, wondered if any of the guests would arrive in costume, since it was in fact also Halloween. He didn't feel bad that he was missing a classmate's Halloween party. "Ma, I get dressed in costumes all the time for a living," he said, sounding terribly serious and grown-up. "Halloween for me is like Saint Patrick's Day for bartenders."

"What do you know about bartenders?" Molly shot back.

"Not as much as you do!" her kid brother retorted.

"Stop that, both of you! I'm about ready to turn this car around. I left tons of work in the city and I can't drive when you kids act like two-year-olds."

"Dad, you're *treating* us like two-year-olds," insisted Molly. "You've been doing it ever since we left Manhattan."

"Yeah," Ian agreed. "That 'I spy a cow' game? And counting out-of-state license plates? Puh-leese."

Molly favored us with the indelicate teen snort. "That's

'cause Dad draws comic books for a living. He thinks every-one's, like, twelve."

"Hey, I *am* twelve. So shut up, Molly."

"Shut up yourself."

"Kids!"

"Are we there yet? I need to pee."

"Ian, we just passed a rest stop five miles ago. Why didn't you say something then?"

"I didn't have to pee then."

Ahhh, the family car trip. Why had I been remembering them with such fond and rosy nostalgia?

Seneca Falls is a quaint little Finger Lakes town, full of Queen Anne gingerbread-style architecture, but it's not a place that's readily accessible unless you have a car. Having made the jour-ney, I realized that Claude and Naomi's guests would really have to want to share their special day in order for them to wake up at dawn and drive several hours upstate. Their presence would be as much of a statement as the wedding itself.

"See, Molly, if you go to Bennington, you'll have more or less the same topography, except of course for the canal. But the trees, even some of the houses, and the little churches . . . isn't it pretty during the fall? It even *smells* wonderful up here!"

"Can we not talk about this?" she grumbled. "Can we have *one day off* from talking about colleges?" She kicked at a pile of leaves in the parking lot.

"This church is pretty ugly," Molly whispered to me. "I thought it was going to be one of those New Englandy white clapboard ones with the steeple. Like . . . well, like Bennington."

"The restoration is pretty uninspiring," I agreed. "But look over there. Kind of stuffed in the middle. I guess that's what's left of the original nineteenth-century church."

"Taste, people, *taste!*" Molly moaned.

"Well, we're not here to critique the architecture. We're here to celebrate our friends' wedding. Do you see Meriel and William anywhere around?"

Whirling on her heels, Molly made a three sixty. "Wait, I think that's her."

Sure enough, Meriel was coming toward us, waving her arms and looking exceptionally striking in a print dress and matching head scarf. "I don't know where we supposed to set up de tent! And de woman with de flowers was here ahsking me questions about where to put dem because she tink I'm de caterer, and she cahn't find de brides, but I tell her I'm just pinch-hitting and I'm as much in de dark as she is." She pointed to an SUV. "William want to unload everyting, but he don't know where to put it."

By now Ian had wandered over and had two cents to offer as well. "I think they need a stage manager, Mom."

"And I have a feeling that's where you come in," Molly concurred.

I sent Ian to potter around with his father, while Molly trailed me into the chapel. The vestry was a scene of utter chaos. Both brides were running around in their bras and panties, acting like the proverbial decapitated chicken. "I can't find my other shoe!" Naomi exclaimed, limping around. "How far could it have gone?!"

"Oh, thank God you're here," Claude said, embracing me. "I think the chamber musicians got lost. They were supposed to be here a half hour ago. Did we invite anyone who knows how to play the organ? That seems to be the only thing we've got around here. Alice and Izzy are supposed to sing; Alice's boyfriend is bringing his guitar—he's a folksinger as well as a carpenter, you know—but I don't know if Dan knows anything classical. Nay, don't let all that bending over mess up your hair." Naomi's thick dark hair had been gathered into an elaborate French twist, with ringlets framing her face. It was the first time I'd seen her in full makeup.

"Okay, I need to start getting dressed," Claude muttered, half to herself. "Fuck!" she shrieked suddenly. "I just ripped my panty hose." She rummaged through the pockets of her garment bag. "Nay, do you have an extra pair? I knew I forgot something!"

"I do, but they wouldn't fit you," she replied, from halfway under a bench. "Hah! Got it!" She slid out, butt first, triumphantly clutching her white satin pump.

"I need a pair of hose," Claude said frantically. "I can't go bare-legged under a cheongsam. Granny's having enough fits as it is. This will kill her, and I won't be able to live with the guilt."

"Is there a drugstore or something around here?" I asked them.

"We passed one about two blocks away, around the corner to your left when you exit the chapel."

"Thanks, Naomi. Molly, make yourself useful." I opened my purse and handed her a five dollar bill from my wallet. "Pick up another pair of panty hose for Claude."

"Tall! Size tall. You're a lifesaver," Claude said gratefully, exhaling for the first time since we'd entered the vestry.

Molly shot out the door and I proceeded to ascertain where the food was supposed to be set up, then left the chapel in order to tell Meriel and William where to pitch the tent. While I was getting them on track, the photographer arrived, asked me if I was the mother of one of the brides—*I know I'm gray, but do I look that old?*—and I ushered him inside, first checking that Claude and Naomi were more or less fully dressed. They insisted that I stay to be part of the wedding photos.

"We couldn't have done this without you," Claude insisted.

When I stepped outside again, I noticed that the guests had started to arrive. Naomi and Claude, though somewhat calmer knowing that someone was in charge and that the caterer, florist, and photographer were aware of their marching orders—although the string quartet was still AWOL—were unsure whether they should greet their guests or follow tradition and remain out of sight until the walk down the aisle. Regardless of sexual orientation, when it comes to some things—the planning and execution of a wedding among them—life's little vicissitudes are just plain universal.

Alice and Izzy had arrived with Dan Carpenter, his acoustic guitar case in hand. "You don't have to feel sorry for me; I brought a date too," Izzy kidded, patting her swollen belly.

"Don't freak out, now, but you're a keeper," Alice told Dan, affectionately squeezing his arm.

"Why? Because I agreed to come to a wedding with you even though we've only been dating for a few weeks?" He winked at me as he set down the guitar and took Alice into his arms.

"Exactly!"

"You're right, he's a keeper," I agreed.

"You are a wonderful boyfriend and a very good sport," Alice murmured lovingly to Dan. "Just keep being this terrific and I'll never have to cry about you in front of Susan!"

"Threats! See, she's threatening me already," Dan teased.

"Ah, but that's a *good* thing. It means she's very comfortable around you," I assured him. I excused myself to assist a middle-aged Asian couple who were struggling to extricate an elderly woman from the backseat of their car and get her settled into a wheelchair.

"You must be Claude's family," I said, shaking the man's hand. "I'm Susan. A friend of theirs from the apartment building." Claude's parents, Lily and Stewart, greeted me graciously, but her grandmother scowled.

"Don't mind my mother-in-law; she doesn't hear so well," Mr. Chan told me quietly. "And when she heard that the food was not going to be Chinese, she was very upset with Claude."

It wasn't my place to divulge why the original caterer had backed out, so I simply smiled and acknowledged that life is indeed full of little disappointments, but they become unimportant in the long run when there is something to celebrate.

When I heard an argument about hardware, I assumed that it was being enacted by the battling Sciorras. Apparently Naomi's father had decided that some sort of elaborate tool set would be an appropriate wedding gift for his daughter and her life partner. "And what am I supposed to put on the card?" grumbled Mr. Sciorra. "To the bride and groom? Which one is which? To the bride and bride? To lesbo and lesbo?"

"Stop it, Silvio!" Mrs. Sciorra dug her manicured nails into her husband's dinner jacket. "I told you, you're gonna have to behave like a person today. Naomi's our *daughter,* for chrissakes. Get with the twenty-first century, will you! You act like you stepped off the boat at Ellis Island last week. No wonder our daughter ran away from this lifestyle. Gimme the card!" she said, grabbing it out of Silvio's hand. "You know what we're gonna write? Watch me, so you don't forget it and say something that's gonna embarrass the whole family this afternoon. See this?" She bent over the hood of the car, took a pen from her purse, and began to inscribe the greeting card. " 'To Naomi and Claude' . . . got that Silvio? They have names. You're gonna use 'em. *Naomi and Claude.* 'With prayers for their continued health and happiness and may they one day get God's blessing.' " She clicked the ballpoint and returned it to her handbag, then licked the envelope closed with a flourish. "Now gimme the present so I can stick the card under the ribbon so it don't fall out and get lost—though if it does, I'm sure they'll have no trouble figuring out who gave them a Skil set."

The ceremony itself, when all was said and done, went off without a hitch. The minister was a remarkable woman who gave a touching sermon about personal freedoms and choice and the resonance of the Wesleyan Chapel to this ceremony. I have to say that it was the most heartfelt wedding I'd ever attended. For Claude and Naomi's chosen lifestyle, marriage was not a rite of passage that was expected of them, or of course legally recognized throughout most of the country. Even in New York State their gesture was largely symbolic. My friends chose to stand up for their beliefs and make a public commitment to one another; and their guests, by their very presence (not to mention several hours on the highway) made the choice to support that decision. I was teary-eyed. Claude and Naomi walked down the aisle together, bearing matching bouquets of white roses and red carnations. White roses represented pure and spiritual love, said the minister, and the red carnations, an exceptionally hardy flower, symbolized the blood of Christ—and by extension referred to the fact that Claude and Naomi, by taking this very public step, were martyrs to the issue of same-sex marriage. Personally I found that a bit too militant for the occasion. Ruminating further on the bouquet subject, I figured that the women just liked the idea of having blooms that matched their gowns, and they hadn't a clue about the arcane language of flowers. I mean, who does?

The chamber musicians, a quartet of students from the Mannes School of Music in Upper Manhattan, did in fact arrive in the nick of time (they'd taken a wrong turn somewhere in the vicinity of Ithaca), and they were just terrific. Accompa-

nied by Dan's richly melodious guitar, Alice and Izzy harmo-
nized beautifully on a touching duet from the Broadway musical *Shenandoah*, called "We Make a Beautiful Pair." Ian became
a hit with his clever caricatures of the guests—including
Claude's grandmother—and earned the much-yearned-for ap-
probation of his artist father. And Molly's last minute panty
hose purchase had helped Claude save face with her grandmother, who sat through the ceremony with a look of complete
bewilderment on her face. Claude had told me that her grandmother speaks only a few words of English, even after living all
these years in America, so I doubt the old woman understood
much of what was going on. She did gaze approvingly, however,
at her granddaughter's traditional dress.

Alice, who was sitting just in front of me, was also visibly
moved by the ceremony. At one point she fumbled in her purse,
evidently looking for a tissue. I opened my bag, took out a
packet, tapped her on the shoulder and handed it to her.

"Thanks," she whispered, stifling a sniffle. She held up three
fingers. "That's the third time you've rescued me this way." I
gave her shoulder an affectionate squeeze as she withdrew the
top tissue from the pack—and handed it to Izzy, who was even
more emotionally affected. Alice leaned her head to rest it on
Dan's shoulder, while Izzy rested hers on Alice's. Upon Izzy's
audible sob, Alice, saving one tissue for herself, gave her friend
the entire package, pressing it into her hand. Izzy availed herself
of a couple, then stuck the packet in her purse. When she pulled
out her hand, she was clutching her cell phone.

"Excuse me, please," she whispered through a loud sniffle,
then tried to squeeze past Alice and Dan to get to the aisle,
where she did her best to unobtrusively leave the chapel.

"Is she going to be okay?" I whispered to Alice.

"I think she's really missing Dominick," Alice replied. "It's like that scene in *Woman of the Year* when Katharine Hepburn attends her aunt's wedding and it makes her realize how much she loves Spencer Tracy. I hate to miss this—it's rude of me—and the ceremony is so beautiful—but I'd better go check on her."

"They'll understand," I murmured sympathetically. I looked around, afraid we were drawing too much attention to ourselves. The minister had just asked everyone to rise and join in on "Lift Every Voice and Sing."

"This is probably a better time than most to slip out," Alice said softly, and scooched past Dan.

Ten seconds later Dan said, "I'd better check on Alice." He gave me a pained look. "I just hope that Claude and Naomi don't think their friends are deserting them in droves. It's actually *because* Alice and Izzy are so affected—in a positive way—that they had to step outside for a breather."

Claude and Naomi offered words of their own to one another before the official vows were taken and they exchanged rings. I wondered what the minister would say when it came down to the "I now pronounce you . . ." part of the ceremony. But she said, "I now pronounce you married," and the brides kissed, Mr. Sciorra visibly winced, Mrs. Sciorra smacked his arm with her program, and the Mannes quartet struck up the Mendelssohn recessional.

Outside the chapel, the brides were pelted with rice—Claude made a joke about how her family didn't understand why the guests were throwing away their dinner—and there were hugs and kisses all around. After I congratulated the brides, I made my way over to where Izzy was standing, her back to the crowd, still on the cell phone. She noticed me out of the corner of her eye and turned her tearstained face in my direction.

"Well can we at least talk about it, Dominick?" She waited for about fifteen seconds before replying. "I'm telling you, it makes you realize why people do it in the first place. All the *right* reasons, I mean. What? I can't hear you? . . . No, I'm in North Bumfuck, the connection's terrible . . . Well, there's nothing I can do about that now. What am I, AT&T? Yes . . . yes . . . we should have switched to Verizon . . . Okay. Well . . . we can talk about that when I get home too. Get back to Alice's I mean. No, it's gonna be late. We're something like five-plus hours out of the city and the reception hasn't even started yet. And I'll see you at Starbucks tomorrow at eighty-thirty . . . No, not that Starbucks, the other Starbucks. The one on the opposite corner, I mean. Next to the Gap. No, the other Gap. Dominick . . . What? I can't hear you anymore. This thing is breaking up again." She banged the cell phone against her palm, then brought it back to her ear. "What?" Izzy listened for a moment, then snapped the phone shut. "Fuck. The connection went dead."

"Well, the connection might have been breaking up, but it sounded—forgive me for overhearing—"

"You can't help but overhear when people have to yell into their cell phones. They probably overheard me in Buffalo."

"Anyway, I was saying that while the connection might have been breaking up, it sounded to me like you and Dominick might be getting back together."

"Bless you; you look so hopeful, Susan," Izzy said. "Well, it's a start," she added, shoving the phone into her purse. "At least he's willing to talk about it." She pointed to the church. "They really got me going in there. I mean, you were really reminded what commitment is all about. And love. And the risks you take if you want to love and be loved fully. And all that. Well, *I* was reminded anyway. I wish Dominick had been here. He would have bawled like a baby too, I bet. You know, there's just not a whole lot of love in this world," she said, starting to cry again. "Forgive me for being maudlin, but weddings always do that to me. And when you've got love, someone who loves you and someone to love back, even if you fight like hell sometimes, you realize what a precious commodity it is. Love, of course. Not fighting."

"I didn't think you meant fighting. But, speaking as a therapist for two seconds—there's often a blurred line between my personal and professional lives, so bear with me—speaking as a therapist, there are times when it's better to fight and get stuff out in the open than to pretend that everything is hunky-dory, and, in the interest of avoiding conflict or pain, not talking about what's really going on. Because then you're not being real. And that's no way to go through life, especially with your spouse! Speaking of which, I'm going to dance with Eli at this wedding if it kills him. He hates to dance in front of other people. But I think it's bad luck, or at least an insult to the bridal couple, not to dance at their wedding, so he'll have to shelve his self-consciousness for five minutes to honor Naomi and Claude."

I waited until Izzy pulled herself together, then we went under the tent to enjoy what I have to say might have been the hit of the day: the Jamaican wedding feast (with wedding cake and fortune cookies for dessert) concocted by Meriel and William on behalf of No Problem, William's fledgling Flatbush restaurant.

"This is fabulous," Alice said to me, munching on a jerk chicken drumstick. "How did Claude and Naomi get hooked up with them?"

I told her about the frantic two A.M. phone call from Claude. "They suddenly lost their caterer and asked me if I knew of anyone who could come in at the last minute, more or less."

"And you thought for a moment and said 'No Problem!'"
Alice posited, mimicking a Jamaican accent.

I took a sip of sorrel. This time it had been liberally laced
with rum, and nearly sent me spinning halfway across the dance
floor. "I wish I'd been that clever!"

12

FAITH

"Well, Stevo could give me no good reason why he won't, or can't, replace the washing machines," Faith said. "It's like Ten Little Indians. Now we're down to only two fully operating units. He took away the broken numbers two and four, leaving one and three still working tolerably well; but five apparently isn't draining the water after the rinse cycle, so no one will use it, of course; and six makes such an awful whirring sound during the spin cycle that you think it's in torment." She grinned mischievously at me. "I just wanted to get that in before you start telling me I'm avoiding again!"

"Touché! So what's really up this week?"

Faith settled back into the couch. Even in her body language she had come a long way from the cautious perching she used to do only a few months ago. And the fact that she was now comfortable undergoing therapy on what had been her own couch made me even more pleased with her progress.

"Well . . . I decided that it was finally time for me to sort through all of Ben's books and papers. After all, what am I going to do with shelf after shelf of medical textbooks and treatises, and I think one of the local medical schools, or at least the public library, could use them. If not, if they're too outdated, perhaps a theatre or film company could gut them and use the spines as props. I've read about that, you know. I e-mailed—yes, *e-mailed*—Columbia University, Ben's alma mater, to ask if they might want his papers. After all, he was highly respected in his field. They were very receptive, and are sending a grad student to look them over next week. He'll take what he thinks the university might like to archive, and leave the rest to me to either retain or discard."

I couldn't resist applauding. "Faith, this is fantastic! You have no idea how proud I am of you!"

"Oh, it was like a grand treasure hunt," she continued. "Thank you. I'm pleased as punch with myself, if you really want to know. After so many decades, one forgets what one owns, so it was quite a journey of discovery in a number of ways. Firstly, that I could tackle Ben's voluminous library without weeping, which felt more like a broad jump than baby steps, I'll have you know; and then to find all kinds of wonderful things that I had completely forgotten about." Faith tapped her head. "When your brain gets old, a lot begins to seep through the cracks."

"Tell me about some of the other stuff you found. What else you discovered," I urged her. "And how you felt about it."

Faith glanced down at her purse. "How I felt about it? Young. A girl again. Yes, I have to admit I felt young in some ways. My God, I unearthed items I hadn't seen since my college days, and suddenly there I was back at Smith, a shy freshman . . . too timid to speak up in poetry class. I think I never raised my hand in any of my classes until my second semester as a sophomore. I found something for Molly too," Faith added, her cat-that-swallowed-the-canary smile revealing a dimple I don't think I'd ever noticed before. "Do you happen to have a cell phone? On you, I mean."

I patted the pocket of my jumper. I always keep it on vibrate when I'm down here, in case Molly or Ian needs to reach me before they head off to school.

"Do you think Molly is still upstairs?" Faith asked. "I know we're in the middle of a session, but I don't mind the interruption. In fact I'm sure it would be worth it."

Reluctantly, I rang the apartment and summoned Molly to the laundry room.

"What's up?" she said, dropping her backpack on the center table with a tremendous thud. "I was almost halfway out the door."

"Faith has something for you."

Molly looked stupefied. "For *me?*"

Faith nodded and withdrew a slim volume from her handbag. "I understand you like to write," she told my daughter. "And your mother is turning me into a firm believer in risk-taking and moving on. So . . . I am taking the risk that you will enjoy this . . . and moving on in the sense that I have derived much pleasure in the past from this book, and from a brief acquaintanceship with its author . . . and feel it's time for another to reap its rewards." She handed the book to Molly, who looked at the cover, opened it up to inspect the flyleaf, and began to tremble.

"Oh. My. God."

I couldn't tell whether she was going to shout or break down in tears. "What? What is it?"

My sullen, surly teenage daughter had been transformed, at least for a few moments, into an utterly awestruck girl. I appreciated the change, however long it lasted. "Oh. My. God. Mom, look. Youhavetolookatthis." She handed me the book. "Where did you get it?" she asked Faith.

I read the inscription. " 'To my old classmate Faith. A Smith girl through and through and one I will never forget. 'To Virtue,

Knowledge' . . . and happiness always, Victoria Lucas, a.k.a Sylvia Plath.' "

"It's *The Bell Jar*, Mom. *The Bell Jar*. And Sylvia Plath *autographed* it! This *so* rocks!"

"Yes, I know, sweetheart. Faith, this is a tremendous gift. Oh, my God," I said to Molly, "don't you dare even consider selling this on eBay or I will have to kill you."

"Ma, are you crazy? I would never!" She hugged the book to her chest and a tear rolled past the right side of her nose. "Don't tell my mother, but this is the best present I ever got!" she said, embracing Faith. "I can't believe you *knew* Sylvia Plath. That is so awesome! Ohmigod, thank you *so* much! I can't wait to show this to Mr. Werner."

"Sweetheart, perhaps you should leave it at home and just tell Mr. Werner about it. It makes me nervous, bringing something so precious, so obviously special to you—not to mention, irreplaceable—up to school, and have it banging around in your knapsack and everything. Don't you think? We could photocopy the flyleaf on our all-in-one printer and you could show him that."

Molly sighed. "Okay. For once I agree with you. If this got wet or ripped, or ripped-off, I think I'd kill myself. Oops. See what Sylvia Plath'll get you! I've had her book for two minutes and already I'm thinking of suicide." She leaned in to Faith and gave her another kiss on the cheek, then threw her arms around me, grabbed her knapsack, and without another word left the laundry room like she'd just been shot out of a cannon.

"Amazing." I shook my head. "My daughter receives a gift that makes her mention suicide, and here I am thinking that it could be the best thing that ever happened to her!"

Faith grinned. "You are talking about the *book* of course. Being the best thing."

"Yes, the book. Of course, the book." I laughed. "Eli and I have been struggling for years to find the silver bullet, the 'open sesame,' the magic *something* that would jolt Molly into raptures. I was hoping that it actually existed. And apparently it does, as we have just witnessed. I just had to have faith, I suppose, that the answer would eventually reveal itself."

My client winked. "Yes, *that*—and isn't it funny how *Faith* had the answer!"

Progress Notes

Naomi Sciorra and Claude Chan: Things are more than back on track for this couple; I hadn't hoped for this much progress this fast. The partners decided to get married, affirming the importance of the commitment they share with one another. In the same session we revisited the issue of the adoption, and through a bit of active prodding, the partners discovered an irony in their lives as business owners that illuminated the issue even further, and served to crystallize key elements of the process for them. Feeling more emotionally secure after Claude's wedding proposal, followed by the epiphany they experienced in their session, Naomi was able to open herself up to alternative ways to view the thorniest issue (for her) of the adoption process. With a new eye on the humorous, or at least ironic, aspect of the situation, she made tremendous progress. Claude is visibly happier now that Naomi is happy; and her epiphany made the decision regarding the adoption papers a far less onerous one than it had previously seemed. Additionally, their public ceremony serves to further cement their partnership and provides them with an even more solid foundation on which to raise a child.

Meriel Delacour: At long last we are getting to what is at the core of Meriel's dissatisfaction, albeit still in a roundabout way. She lights up like a Macy's barge on the Fourth of July when she discusses her son's plans for his Jamaican restaurant. Despite her repeated avowals that this is his project and his alone, and that she needs to stay out of it as much as possible and let him do his own thing, it's evident how much joy she is deriving from her contributions—her input on the decor and recipe selection in particular. In our upcoming sessions, I plan to work deeper, confronting if need be, to encourage her to speak out regarding her own needs. Does she really yearn to be an active part of William's new venture? Is it *this* desire *specifically* that is at the root of her disaffectation within her current employment, or is it simply the urge to be doing *anything* that gives her job satisfaction and self-worth? Depending on her answer, I need to give her a gentle nudge onto that yellow brick road to wherever her Oz is.

Faith Nesbit: Faith's continued forward momentum continues to astonish me. I am unspeakably proud of her. After four and a half years, she is finally taking active steps to distribute or discard her late husband's medical books and papers, items that clearly have sentimental meaning to her, but which play no current role in her own life. To actually have those things removed from her apartment is tremendous. Faith's baby steps have become strides without any demonstrable loss of self-confidence. In many ways she would appear to be the model client; and in fact, clients like Faith give therapists faith (with a small *f*) in our own ability to make a difference. They reinforce our decision to enter this profession. I want to encourage Faith to keep up the good work, and make sure that she's not moving faster than she really feels comfortable going, in an effort to either please the therapist or to overreach—because if either of those is in play here, there exists the obvious danger of damaging backsliding and regressive behavior.

Me: I must admit that in many ways I'm a pretty happy camper these days; happier than I've been in quite some time. On the professional front, a number of my clients have made tremendous progress recently. In addition to exchanging vows, Claude and Naomi are currently on the same page now regarding the adoption issue; one couldn't ask for a better client than Faith; Alice seems to have a firmer handle on her career issues and looks radiant and happy with Dan Carpenter; Izzy is taking steps toward a reconciliation with her husband Dominick; and Meriel has finally opened up—truly blossomed—in terms of expressing what really rings her bells.

And, miracle of miracles, on the home front the same has happened to Molly. Faith's wildly generous gift to my daughter of her own author-autographed edition of *The Bell Jar* blew both of us away. Molly has taken to keeping it on the night table by her bed and reading it only when she's wearing an old pair of her grandmother's cotton gloves, the better to protect the book. In all her life I've never seen her treat a toy or a pet that well. Not that she's suddenly metamorphosed into a new person. That might be interesting, but actually unhealthy. No, she's still the same Molly, but she's Molly with a fire burning inside her about something. If I were Catholic, I'd light a candle to celebrate this most welcome sea change in her behavior.

The family had a delightful time up in Seneca Falls for Claude and Naomi's wedding. It was the first full family outing since Coney Island. And when Eli pulled me onto an empty dance floor, in front of seventy-five other guests, I thanked my lucky stars and planets for whatever had wrought that change in my husband, Mr. Too-shy-to-dance-in-front-of-anyone. Not only did he have the confidence to lead me out onto the floor, but he danced very well too! I don't know why he's been so reluctant all these years to strut his stuff. Yeah, there was that "ouchy" discussion in the bedroom a while back, but I have to trust Eli when he insists there's nothing wrong with *us*. In the more than two decades we've been together, counting our dating years, he's never given me any reason not to trust him, and it's true that he's never been a terribly verbal person. So I really have no right to fault him for not having those skills in his bag of tricks, and expect him to suddenly express himself with the agility of someone who is considerably more articulate. I have to remind myself that as frustrated as I may get over his disconnected behavior of the past few months, maybe I need to cut him some slack.

So, I have to say that things are *relatively* good right now. I'm in a better place, emotionally, than I've been in a long time, even though I've been hesitant to admit that things were less than perfect. One of the principles of psychotherapy is that if the client and the therapist each have hope that the client can be cured, the cure will indeed be made manifest. I held out hope that my woes were only temporary and that with patience and persistence things would improve eventually, and indeed they have.

Not only that, they can only get better.

DELICATES

13

ME

○
 ○ Then again, many people espouse the philosophy that
○ ○ things can only get worse before they get better. So when
 ○ the phone rang very late on a Saturday evening about a
month later, I feared once again that one of my clients had done
themselves some harm, and steeled myself to handle the crisis.

But I hadn't prepared myself for what had in fact transpired.
The initial conversation went something like this.

DISEMBODIED MALE VOICE
[moderate to heavy New York accent]
Susan Lederer?

ME
[hesitantly]
Yes . . . this is she . . .

VOICE
Mrs. Lederer, do you have a daughter named Molly? *[He rattles
off our address as well, for verification.]*

                         ME
                  [barely a whisper]
Oh my God.

                       VOICE
Oh, no, nothing to worry about Mrs. Lederer.

                         ME
                 [audible exhalation]
Whew. Who are you, by the way?

                       VOICE
Mrs. Lederer, this is Officer Lupinacci over at the twentieth precinct
on Eighty-third Street. We have your daughter Molly up here—

                         ME
What happened? Is she okay?

                      LUPINACCI
Physically, yes. There was an incident earlier this evening in
which your daughter was involved.

                         ME
               [audibly panicking again]
Holy shit . . .

                      LUPINACCI
She's unharmed, Mrs. Lederer.

                         ME
You said . . . you said the incident was "earlier this evening."
[Getting a bit angry now, despite my better judgment.] Why did it

take this long for someone to phone me? Isn't everyone entitled to make one phone call after they get arrested, or does that only happen on TV? Didn't Molly have her cell phone with her?

LUPINACCI

Well . . . Mrs. Lederer, your daughter's cell phone was confiscated. It's being held as evidence.

ME

Evidence?? And isn't there still such a thing as a pay phone?!

LUPINACCI

Mrs. Lederer, we'd like you to come up to the Two-oh so that your daughter can be remanded into parental custody.

ME

Of course. Right. Of course. [*Words desert me.*] I'll grab a cab. Please tell Molly that I love her and I'll be there as soon as I can.

I hung up the phone and immediately called Eli, who was at his studio working on *Gia*, but I got the answering machine. I punched up his cell number and it went through to his voice mail. "Guess who's got to handle this alone," I muttered angrily as I threw on a pair of jeans and a sweatshirt. Perhaps I should have looked more, I don't know, *maternal*, but they were the nearest garments to hand, and I didn't have the presence of mind to worry about which outfit might convince Officer Lupinacci that I'm a good parent. *Honest, Officer, I swear it. Just ask my other kid*—who was sound asleep until I woke him up to explain that Mommy needed to go out for a little while to pick up his sister.

CUT TO:

INT. POLICE PRECINCT. NIGHT.

[A frantic mother overtips cab driver in her urgency to attend to more pressing matters. She races into the precinct as though, well, as though she's about to rescue her daughter who is in dire danger.]

So, that's the scenario. I asked two different people behind two different information desks—one in uniform and one a civilian—where to find Officer Lupinacci, and was directed to two different doors, one of which turned out to be the men's room, where the janitor kindly pointed me in the right direction.

Molly was being detained in a small office cluttered with paperwork and littered with coffee mugs and the aluminum foil and plastic detritus of a day's worth of takeout and delivery. It was not the monklike interrogation room that you see on *Law & Order.* My daughter was pale, and looked very scared. Dark circles of exhaustion under her eyes made her look like she was nearly thirty. Torn between chewing her out for ending up here in the first place and weeping from relief that she was apparently unharmed, I just threw my arms around her, inadvertently whacking her in the back with my purse.

"You're fine, aren't you, baby?" I asked her, peering into her eyes. Although I only gave them a cursory examination, she didn't look like she'd been drinking or doing drugs. Thank God for that, anyway.

"Yeah, I'm okay."

I registered Molly's involuntary flinch. "They didn't . . . hurt you . . . or . . . touch . . . you in any bad way, did they?" I whispered to her. I glanced back at Officer Lupinacci, whose expression was significantly more parental than I ever would have anticipated.

"No, I'm fine, Ma. They even took the cuffs off once we came in here," she added, indicating this room.

I turned on the cop. "You cuffed my daughter?! What for?"

"Standard procedure, ma'am, when we apprehend a shoplifter. Once we determined that she was a minor who presented no threat of bodily harm to either herself or anyone else, we removed the restraints."

"Shoplifting? Molly, if you needed money, you've got an ATM card. Or you could have phoned home, and we would have found a way to get it to you. What did you need to shoplift for?"

"I think we'd better start from the beginning," the officer told me. "Your daughter was caught shoplifting from Zabar's—"

"Zabar's!!? What did you do? Try to steal tomorrow's brunch?"

"Sort of," Molly said sheepishly. "But it was for my Bennington application."

"I'm completely confused," I confessed.

Officer Lupinacci flipped open his notebook. Reading from it, he informed me, "Your daughter used her cell phone to film herself shoplifting a package of smoked fish, a quarter-pound plastic container of vegetable cream cheese, and a chocolate bar with almonds."

"What, no bagels?" I fumed sarcastically.

"Everybody knows that H&H has better ones and that they'll be fresher if you get them Sunday morning rather than Saturday night."

"Now you're a comedian?" I snapped.

"*You* made the first bagel comment."

I threw my hands in the air. "So where do we stand?" I asked the policeman. "And what was this stunt all about?" I demanded of Molly. "What's this about the Bennington application?"

A heavyset gentleman in jeans and a plaid shirt was ushered into our room and nodded curtly to the cop.

"I swear it's all just part of my college application. I've been phone-filming myself doing slacker stuff like cutting class, playing in video arcades, and now shoplifting, as part of my supplemental materials to Bennington, illustrating what happens to a teenager when she runs amok; and that a sound college education, offered from institutions like Bennington—well, specifically Bennington—can save an at-risk young woman like me from turning into an example of what's wrong with our society. They can uplift her instead and mold her into a model citizen representing what's best about the future of America. You know . . ." She bracketed her words as though we were watching them unspool on a giant screen above our heads. *"Save another promising creative mind from ending up like* this."

"Do you believe any of this?" Lupinacci said to me.

"Knowing my daughter as I do, yes, I'm inclined to," I replied. "Will you un-impound her cell phone, because it might back up her story. And who's this man?" I asked, looking at the stranger in the room.

The stranger extended his hand to me. "Bob Akins. I'm the Saturday night manager over at Zabar's."

"Look . . . do you mind dropping the charges? Molly's a minor, she's never done anything like this before and I'm certain she never will again. I'm sure this was all just a stunt that got out of hand; she was making a movie, and it just looked a little too real for comfort. Getting into college is so competitive these days that I suppose some kids are tempted to do anything—however misguided—that they feel might give themselves an edge." I looked at Mr. Akins. "I can understand that you had to do your job and call the police. But we've discovered it was more or less a mix-up and we've straightened it out, now, haven't we? You don't really want to drag this through court, do you? How much money was the merchandise worth, after all?"

Officer Lupinacci referred to his notebook. "Twenty-two dollars and twenty-seven cents. But there's tax on the chocolate bar . . . so it's a little more than that."

"Let us reimburse you," I offered, "and just call it a night. I'm sure you don't want the publicity," I said to Mr. Akins, "and you, officer, don't want the paperwork. Twenty-two dollars and twenty-seven cents? Call it an even twenty-two fifty. Molly, please pay Mr. Akins."

My daughter mumbled something that I couldn't hear, so she crooked her finger and drew me closer. "I don't have any money on me," she whispered.

"What? How many times have your father and I told you never to leave the house without—"

"That was part of the *thing*," Molly whined. "I wanted to know what it would really be like to get arrested for shoplifting and everything. To make it really real. Not to just get out of it by paying if I got caught. And so I didn't bring any money with me on purpose."

I wanted to kill her, but she was flesh and blood, so my allegiances were clear. I took twenty-five dollars from my wallet and handed it to Mr. Akins. "I'm asking you as a mother: can we please just put a period on this little incident. I'm sure that my daughter has learned a lesson from all of this, if the frightened look on her face when I walked in the door was any indication."

Mr. Akins pocketed my cash and handed me back $2.50. "Of course, what she might have been scared of was *you*," he quipped.

"Do you have teenagers?" I asked him plaintively.

He grinned. "I have fifteen-year-old twins. That's why I accepted your offer."

"Are we good to go?" I asked Officer Lupinacci. He nodded, then explained how Molly could redeem her phone. As we headed for the personal property room, the cop stopped us with his voice.

"Hey! I just gotta question, Mrs. Lederer."

"Shoot. Oops, I didn't mean that, obviously. I was trying to say 'go ahead.' What's your question, officer?"

"I just wanna know what it is you do for a living. Your profession. Just curious is all."

"I'm a shrink."

He shook his head in bemused stupefaction. "It figures."

Outside the station, I hailed a cab. "If you think there won't be any fallout from this little episode, you are grievously mistaken," I warned Molly. "When your father finds out that—"

Molly held up her hand to silence me. "You know, Ma, you're always telling your clients to think things through for themselves, not to rely on others to solve their problems, not to be *co-dependent*. And whenever something happens at home, you're always waiting for Dad to weigh in on it before you make a move. And half the time he's not even *around*. At least not lately."

That stung. And she did have a point. "That's because there are two authority figures in our household and we've agreed to share the responsibility for everything." *Even though* I *usually end up with the lion's share of it.* "Don't try to make this about something else, Molly. I'm on to you. You're trying to shift the focus away from yourself, and that's not going to work."

Sure enough, when we returned home, Eli—who claimed to have arrived there not ten minutes after I'd left, but was sure I had everything under control and thought it made more sense for him to stay home with Ian—had something to say about the matter. Rather than rail and scream at our daughter for turning out to be an irresponsible hoodlum, however, he decided to put Molly on trial, offering her the opportunity to defend herself. Molly demanded a juror of her peers, but since it was well past midnight, I voted against reawakening Ian. Sigmund seemed willing to listen as long as he had a bone to gnaw on, and like many jurors, ended up being more preoccupied with the demands of his stomach than with the proceedings.

To support her contention that she staged—or should I say filmed—the shoplifting incident as part of a streaming video she was making to supplement her college application materials, Molly screened the work-in-progress for us and offered her partially completed college application as further evidence. She also informed us that she was submitting her diary—the original and not a photocopy—as further evidence of her wasted life, a prime example of a perfectly viable human being who has been content until now to take up time and space.

"I think the diary will totally blow them away," Molly told us. "I mean, won't they think it's awesome that someone would be so vulnerable—maybe even so stupid—to let total strangers know their innermost thoughts that they wouldn't even share with their best friends?!"

"Ever watch reality TV?" Eli was skeptical about this contention. "Are you sure you haven't kept two sets of books?" he asked our daughter.

"*Ucgh!* Dad, that is so rude!"

Eli smiled at her. "Your mother and I have learned to take nothing at face value in this life. And deviousness is a behavior that is not entirely unknown to you."

"Okay, if you don't believe me, search my room! I swear, I *promise* you, there's only one diary."

"We're getting derailed here," I said. "Molly, you committed a crime. A real one. And there are going to be real consequences. You're just damn lucky—we all are—that the Zabar's people didn't insist on pressing charges. Your allowance couldn't exactly cover legal fees."

"I got the scare of my young life; isn't that enough?"

Eli shook his head. "No holiday parties this month. You can forget about the ski trip during Christmas break, and don't even think about getting any presents."

"It goes beyond the Christmas and Chanukah parties," I added. "New Year's Eve is cancelled for you too. And you're grounded indefinitely as of this moment."

"I don't think the sentence is harsh enough," Eli said. "And we forgot to get the juror's verdict." We looked over at Sigmund, who was busy with his porterhouse steak bone.

A malevolent smile crossed my lips. "Molly, you're in charge of walking the dog, and being responsible for cleaning up after his accidents in the apartment too. Also indefinitely."

"Maaaaaaaaaaaaaa," she moaned. "That one is really unfair."

"Tough shit," I said.

"What *she* said," Eli echoed.

We hadn't tag-teamed a punishment in a long time, Eli and I. It felt good; just like the old days. I felt like we were truly a couple again, presenting a solid front in the face of adversity. I'd almost forgotten that he hadn't been home to deal with the issue when the shit first hit the fan. "Do you think we should assign some community service as well?" I suggested.

"Where are prosecuted juvenile shoplifters sent?" Eli wondered aloud.

"There must be some kind of program that they're compelled to attend. Or maybe a halfway house. I'll phone Officer Lupinacci on Monday and ask him about it. I'm sure places like that can always use volunteers. Particularly during the holiday season."

Molly glared at both of us. "You two are so mean!"

We reminded her that we were benevolence personified compared with New York City's juvenile justice system, and sent her off to bed.

I raised my hand to Eli for a high-five. "Good work, pard'ner. I've missed that!" I wrapped my arms around him and leaned forward for a kiss. He turned his head, leaving my lips to make contact with his cheek.

"You too, pard'ner." He kissed my forehead.

Oh.

Do I say something . . . or let it go, and not make such a big deal about it?

"Eli . . . I really missed *you* tonight. Take a break from the book and let your imagination replenish itself. Focusing *too much* on something can sometimes cause as much anxiety as not being able to devote enough time to it. Can't you spend one Saturday night with your wife every so often? I miss romance, Eli. Even if it's just a bowl of popcorn in front of a late night screwball comedy on TCM."

"Speaking of missing things," Eli said, emitting a frustrated little sucking sound out of the side of his mouth, "I can't seem to find my lucky boxers. You know, the aqua-colored ones with Betty Boop on them. I'm still kind of at an impasse with the *Gia* book, and whenever I feel creatively blocked, I put on my lucky boxers, and sooner rather than later, the muse reappears."

"I haven't a clue, Eli. I haven't seen them lately. Or, not that I'm aware of, anyway."

"I can't find one of my Mickey socks either. The navy *Sorcerer's Apprentice* ones. And you're the laundry maven, so I thought I'd ask. I was sure you'd know."

"Well, Eli, I don't know," I sighed, aware that he'd ignored my remarks about his neglecting me and giving short shrift to our love life. "And if it's that big a deal, you can do the laundry yourself from now on so that you can account for every garment. If that's too much responsibility on your shoulders, you can go back to the store where you got the first set of Bettys and buy yourself another pair or two. Ditto for the Disney socks."

"You're really edgy tonight, Susie," said my husband, in an immediate attempt at mollification. I knew he wouldn't like what I said about his taking over the household laundry duties. Eli stepped behind me and massaged my shoulders. I was hoping for a neck nuzzle, but didn't want to appear too needy.

"Well, you're not the one who had to leave the apartment at midnight to collect our firstborn child from the local police precinct. And you're not the one who reasoned our daughter's way out of prosecution for her misdeed. I swear, I'll never look at cream cheese and lox the same way again." I leaned my head back against Eli's chest and looked up at him. "Let's go to bed. We'll deal with the rest of life's little problems in the cool, clear light of day." I held out my hand to lead the way.

"Don't forget about my lucky boxers. And my sock."

I flicked the light switch in the hallway. "How could I?" I sighed.

14

FAITH

"You will never in a million years believe what I'm about to tell you," Faith told me the following morning. She was positively giddy. Gone for the moment was the ordinarily composed woman-of-a-certain age.

I grinned at her. "Try me."

"Well . . . remember a couple of weeks ago when I asked you if you wanted to join me for that holiday jazz concert up at the 92nd Street Y?"

I nodded. "Sorry I couldn't make it. Ian had something at school that evening."

"I can't say I blame you for not joining me; after all, your children must come first; but you missed a magnificent concert. In fact . . . it was so wonderful, so . . . so invigorating and jubilant . . . that I did something I have never done before in my seventy-two years. Are you ready?"

"Absolutely! Hit me, baby."

"Oh-ho, you know the jazz terms! Very snappy. Well, Susan, just like a stagestruck schoolgirl, I waited for the musicians to come out after the performance. One in particular, a pianist, just knocked my socks from here to Cincinnati. Elijah Loving, his name is. Brilliant musician. Just brilliant. He brought tears to my eyes. So I had to tell him so. There was just no way around it. I couldn't leave the auditorium and head for the bus stop without telling this Mr. Loving how much his performance had affected me. I was so nervous, I tell you, Susan, I couldn't believe I'd gotten up the gumption. So I waited . . . and I told him . . . and then guess what happened next?"

"I can't guess," I replied, unwilling to play along. "I'd rather you told me."

"He invited me for coffee!" Faith blushed from the apples of her cheeks to her hairline.

"No!" I exclaimed happily.

"Yes!"

We double-high-fived each other.

"Wow! This is amazing news!"

Faith beamed. "The first time in my entire life since I was a college coed that I ever went out on a date with a man. You know once I met Ben, there was never another man for me. Ever. Well, until the other night."

Talk about finally moving on. I wanted to hug her.

"Susan, I found myself so taken with him. Positively *smitten.*"

"You mean smitten with his musicianship, or smitten-smitten?"

Faith fanned herself with her hand. "Both, actually. But I know what you're really asking. And, yes, *smitten*-smitten. And there's more. More that you'll never believe."

I laughed. "Okay. Try me."

Faith leaned toward me and dropped her voice to a pajama-party conspiratorial whisper. "He's only forty-eight!" A younger man! I stifled my impulse to squeal. After all, the session was still a professional situation. "And . . . he's"—her voice grew even softer—"an *African-American.*"

This revelation was completely unexpected. Just a few months ago, if someone were to ask me whether I believed Faith Nesbit harbored some racial prejudices, I would have had to uncomfortably admit that I did in fact think that might be the case.

"And another wonderful thing about Elijah," Faith said, primping a little, "he loves the color purple."

I was momentarily perplexed by this bit of news. "The book or the movie?"

"Wh . . . ? Oh, no, silly! My fashion sense, of course. Funny, I hadn't thought about the other two possibilities until you just mentioned them. So I want you to know this, in case you fear that I'm backsliding; I just might be wearing more of my violet clothes in the coming days, and leave the light blue and rust-colored garments in the closet for the nonce." Faith tipped me a wink. "I invited Elijah to join me at the opera next week. Isn't it wonderful? He appreciates Donizetti as much as he admires Dizzy Gillespie. Oh . . . and he's as great a Hoagy Carmichael fan as I am! More than that, he's a collector. He asked me to come up and see his Hoagy memorabilia," she added with a wink. "And you know 'Stardust' used to be 'our song' when Ben and I were married. It was our first dance at our wedding, in fact. *And now the purple dusk of twilight time . . .*" she sang softly. "Purple dusk . . . *mnh* . . . when I first heard 'Stardust' as a girl, I fell in love with the song and wore dusky purple clothing from then on."

Faith had experienced another breakthrough in this session; she had not launched herself on a single unrelated tangent in forty-five minutes. As I walked over to unlock the room, I debated whether to mention this, and decided it might be more effective for our work if I didn't raise the subject.

MALA SONIA STRIKES AGAIN

When I opened the door, Mala Sonia was standing before me, decked out in a yellow ruffled blouse, skintight jeans, and a pair of ostentatiously glitzy evening sandals that could have come from one of those fancy European designers or else been a knockoff from Payless; I wouldn't have known the difference. Her hand was poised in midair as if she had been preparing to knock. She looked pained. "I need to speak with you," she said, lowering her voice when she saw Faith sitting on the couch. "Privately, if possible. I have had powerful vision that I must give you a reading." I stepped aside and Mala Sonia entered the laundry room. "I wake up in the middle of the night and feel something very important going on." She brought her hand to her heart and fingered the ostentatious crucifix that dangled between her heavy breasts. "I feel in here something that concerns you. I toss and turn until this morning wondering whether I should speak to you about these bad feelings, because I know you are an unbeliever." Mala Sonia wrung her hands in consternation, the consummate actress.

"If by 'unbeliever' you mean that I wouldn't conduct my life based upon a tarot reading any more than I would from my daily horoscope in the newspaper, then I suppose you're right. If you think I don't believe in God, you're wrong."

"Okay, then, I'll ask you another way. You believe in such a thing as women's intuition?"

"Well . . . yes. Absolutely," I admitted.

"Well, I have had an intuition, let us say. Let *me* say, I mean. An intuition that something is very important and I must give you a reading. You will not be sorry, I promise."

I hesitated. I didn't need to be down at the women's health

center until that afternoon, so I wasn't in a rush. Still, I had plenty of constructive uses for the time, like writing up progress notes or vacuuming the apartment. "I'm not paying you twenty dollars," I told her curtly.

"I'm not asking."

That was a surprise. "And Faith stays—if she wants to." We both turned to look at Faith. I suppose I wanted a witness. For what, I couldn't even say. "Would you? Could you?" I asked her.

"It would be my pleasure. Where do you want me to sit?"

Mala Sonia and I both pointed to the couch. "Stay there," said the Gypsy. She removed a candle from her purse, the kind you'd find in a fish restaurant: nestled in a thick red goblet covered with plastic netting. "Overhead lights no good for reading today. I want to tell you something first about the cards," said Mala Sonia earnestly. "Something you may not know. Maybe it will make you more of a believer in their strength. Sit." She motioned to one of the ratty dinette chairs, and I dragged it to the center table. Mala Sonia removed the tarot deck from her purse and spread the cards faceup on the table in a disorderly mess. "You see that there are four suits, just like in a deck of playing cards, yes?" I nodded, curious as to where she was headed. After all, I encourage my clients to take risks and broaden their horizons, and I would be a hypocrite if I was myself unwilling to go where I prodded them.

"Four suits: Pentacles or Coins, Cups, Swords, and Wands. Fifty-six of those cards: the Minor Arcana. With numbers and face cards for royalty just like in poker deck, yes?" Yes, I nodded again. "Then we have twenty-two cards with Roman numerals. We have, for instance, the Lovers, the Devil, the Magician, the Fool, and so forth. Yes? These cards are called the Major Arcana. And this is where I think you, as a psychologist, will recognize that there is something more than mumbo-jumbo, as you like to say, in the tarot. Many people believe that the twenty-two Major Arcana cards correspond to Carl Jung's archetypes."

I did in fact find that information intriguing. Human beings actually do tend to fit or force, even stereotype, individuals or entities into an archetype: Jung termed it a "preconscious psychic disposition." And although I am not a Jungian therapist any more than I am a Freudian one (preferring to employ a "Chinese menu" of methodology depending on the client and their presenting complaints), I certainly give credence to Carl Jung.

Okay, part of me was still inclined to believe that this tarot stuff was total b.s., but the explorer in me, the risk-taker, sought to open myself to the intersection of Gypsy lore with the tenets of one of the largest-looming and most seminal voices in the realm of psychotherapy. Jung describes a Shadow Archetype, where we project our dark side onto others and interpret them as enemies or as exotic presences in our lives that both repel and fascinate us. Have I been projecting this shadow onto Mala Sonia?

"Here is more information for a skeptical person, or for a person of science who likes to know the sources of things. Tarot is even older than playing cards. Every card from tarot deck is a piece of a story. The placement of a card, whether right-side up or upside down—which is also called reversed or inverted— changes its meaning. The placement of a card, meaning which other cards it is next to, can affect its meaning as well. Here is also information for you: in any reading, an abundance of Minor Arcana cards can mean that the story they tell applies to the short term. So if the story contains unpleasing elements, you can rest happier knowing that your situation will change in not too much time. If more cards from the Major Arcana instead, the reading will be stronger; more archetypes means situation will continue to exist for some time into the future."

Mala Sonia began to gather the jumbled cards into an orderly stack, to the jangling accompaniment of her numerous bangle bracelets. She had certainly dressed the part of the Gypsy this morning. "And I tell you another thing that will interest you, Susan, as an unbeliever, as a woman who thinks tarot is nothing but occult hocus pocus: one hundred and fifty years ago there was a Jewish man who linked the numbers on the Major Arcana—your archetype cards—to the letters in the Hebrew alphabet. Interesting, no?"

"No," I echoed. "I mean, yes. It is interesting." Clearly, it was very important for Mala Sonia to sell tarot's legitimacy, appealing to me as a woman of science and as a Jew, and she was working inordinately hard to get me to buy it, figuratively speaking.

"I do the ten-card reading for you," Mala Sonia said, lighting the candle. "Full Celtic Cross." She switched off the overhead fluorescents and locked the door. "Not the twenty-dollar six-card reading. Don't worry," she added, assessing my dubious expression, "I told you no charge. This I must do. For *me*—to obey the vision I had last night—as much as for *you*. Are you comfortable?"

I felt very nervous, for some reason. Very anxious. "As comfortable as I can be under the circumstances, I suppose."

"Now," said Mala Sonia, "my vision told me that something has been troubling you, but that you are not able to put a finger on what it is; so you can't begin to deal with the problem because it has no face for you, no name. It is a feeling you have inside that something is somehow wrong."

"Are you asking my question for me?" I said. "I'm very puzzled here. I thought *I'm* the one who is supposed to ask *you* the question."

"In your therapy sessions you don't always work exactly the

same way with every client, yes?" I accepted the truth of her statement. "Think of this as the same thing. So if it makes you feel better to be the one asking the question, ask me why you feel out of balance in your life, out of sorts; saying that you have felt that way for some time now, but can't explain why, and you want to know what is the trouble in your life and will you over-come it?"

I sighed. "Okay, Mala Sonia. I want to know what has been disturbing me lately, and knowing what it is, once it has been identified for me, can I overcome it?"

"Very good question!" Mala Sonia smiled. "You are good stu-dent." She shuffled and cut the cards, then dealt ten of them from the top of the deck, rather than asking me to select them from a fanned spread as she had done with Amy's and Alice's readings. She glanced at the entire layout, then for several mo-ments examined the cards individually, as if absorbing each one's relevance to the whole. I tried to analyze her facial ex-pressions. At times she appeared studious, then reflective, then anxious, and at one point I thought I saw a flicker or two of fear. Naturally, this did not put me at ease, particularly since I felt that I was being force-fed this reading.

"I will explain as we go, bearing in mind your question."

"Your question, really," I added, correcting her.

"*The* question. The question that comes to me in my vision last night, that keeps me awake and troubled with such bad feelings. The question that surrounds your aura."

The ten-card configuration consisted of a cross within a cross and four cards arranged in a vertical line to its right. Mala Sonia tapped the lower card of the inner cross. "See this? Card one: the Empress. First card represents your present position; who you are or who you have been up till now, and which is the basis of your situation. A Major Arcana card. So, Susan, we imagine you right now as her."

"Okay . . ."

"And *who* is the Empress? She is archetype of the nurturing female. She is Woman. She is Wife. She is Mother. She is Marriage. Think of Demeter in the Greek mythology, yes? This card in this position would direct us like a road map to your home life as the center of the dark trouble surrounding you. The Empress can also represent the motivating force behind a successful partnership. So we are looking at you, Susan, *in your home*, as the motivating force in your relationship with your husband, with your children. In your life, the personal and the professional often become blended, because you conduct your therapy sessions in the same building as your home, so we can also say that each of your clients is a partner, and as their therapist you are the motivating force behind these marriages as well. You are the one encouraging them to succeed; not the other way around. You are with me so far, yes?"

"Yes," I said, immediately trying to analyze how the symbols reflected by the Empress card applied to me. Damn, I was sucked into buying into this tarot gimmick already. I was angry with myself for being so gullible.

"I think we are really looking at home, rather than work, as the core here. While work is related, you will agree that signs really indicate that home and hearth is where we must look for source of your troubled aura."

"If you say so," I sighed.

Mala Sonia tapped the horizontally laid card in the center cross. "Card number two indicates where you are now and the immediate influences of your situation on who and where you are. We have here the Page of Cups. Where you are now? Here is answer," she said, poking the card more forcefully. "You are a reflective and loyal person, Susan. You like to be of service to others, helping them achieve a specific goal, and you are also a very trustworthy person too. So this is good."

"This is eerie," I said, already congratulating myself for embodying the best traits of a therapist, as represented by the Page of Cups. Was I the same way as a wife and mother, I wondered, since that was the sphere we were dealing with? I've tried to raise my children with the goal of becoming good citizens with strong values. I am certainly a loyal wife; infidelity has never once been on my radar screen.

"Ready for third card?" I nodded and Mala Sonia pointed to the Magician, the card placed directly above the inner cross. "Card number three represents your goal or your destiny, as well as your hopes or fears. Another Major Arcana card, the Magician. A very powerful card. The Magician embodies the positive traits of self-reliance, willpower, and self-confidence, as well as spontaneity and dexterity. But he can also connote trickery and sleight of hand; so you are fearing that perhaps you are in some ways fooling people that you are competent and all-wise and in control, when in fact you are pulling the wool over their eyes."

She made me begin to wonder whether I was just going through the superficial motions of being a good wife and mother, saving the Magician's positive traits for my clients. Or perhaps I feared I was kidding *them* in some ways too. Coming across to them as the all-powerful, mentally healthy, and emotionally stable one with all the answers, when in fact I am just as dysfunctional as they are. "I'm not sure I understand how these things relate to my *destiny*," I said to Mala Sonia. I could have kicked myself for getting so quickly caught in her web; she was quite the seductress.

"The way I interpret what cards say, you must use your greatest powers of self-reliance, as well as your gifts of ingenuity and dexterity, to see you through to a resolution. Your self-confidence—also represented by the Magician—will aid you on your journey, as long as you are strong enough to maintain it. The Magician emphasizes change: something new. Imagine him pulling the rabbit out of a hat or lifting up a bright red scarf to reveal a dove. It is 'Presto! Abra-cadabra!' So part of your destiny is a big and surprising change."

"You're talking about a big and surprising change on the home front, right?"

"The domestic sphere. Home and hearth. Yes. Do you have any questions?"

I shook my head. "Not yet."

"So, Susan, now we come to card number four. The card in the fourth position represents the foundation of the situation in your distant past, as well as the way the situation existed in your recent past. This card also represents long-term blocks or influences. Though its effect may still be felt now—in your present life and also perhaps your very near future—its influence is passing and moving out of importance in your life. So we are referring to something that has been a huge part of your home life for several years in a very important way, and which *remains* a major fixture, but which is in the process of transiting out of your life."

Mala Sonia shook her head dolefully. "This will be very difficult for you to hear, but your fourth card, Major Arcana card Roman numeral three—the Emperor—represents stability; it represents father; it represents husband."

I allowed Mala Sonia's words to sink in, resuming my analysis of the interpretation as it might pertain to the facts of my life. Okay, maybe I was getting too carried away with all this, because my thoughts were tumbling down, down, down, to a dark and ugly place. The unthinkable pushed its way to the forefront of my mind, until I regurgitated the words like poison.

"Mala Sonia, are you trying to tell me that Eli is having an affair?"

15

Mala Sonia flinched. "You know I just interpret cards," she insisted, with trepidation in her voice.

"But is . . . is what I just said your interpretation?" I wasn't at all sure that I wanted to hear her reply.

"You are an intuitive woman, Susan. You make your living analyzing people's personal situations and interpreting them . . . as do I."

Well, that was indirect. Clearly she didn't want to come down on one side or another. Do Gypsy "psychics" ever get sued for malpractice when a prediction or reading turns out to be phony? I do acknowledge, from my own work, that analyzing an issue is like looking through a prism; there are more ways than one to approach and interpret it.

"I tell you a little more about who is the Emperor, Susan. The Emperor, of course, is head of his household. He is enthusiastic; he is creative. He can love fun, which makes him an irresistible man. But he can also act like baby. He can also feel trapped by his responsibilities, which can make him bored and restless, even discontent."

This too-apt description of Eli was feeding my worst fears. "Let's just get on with the reading," I said shakily, trying to mask my anxiety by assuming what I hoped was a clinically curious countenance. Somehow I was sure that Mala Sonia was able to create doubts in my mind and then prey insidiously upon them with the same "radar" that draws sharks to blood. If she sensed weakness, she would undoubtedly exploit it.

Mala Sonia pointed to the card placed just below the center cross. "We are up to card number five, yes? Fifth card signifies recent past events in your life and the forces either for or against you. Whatever card is in this position plays a major role in determining the outcome of the reading."

"And why is that?" *Curiosity killed the cat, Susan.*

"Card represents the core or crux of all the preceding events that pertain to your question. What we have here is first Minor Arcana card in your spread: the Nine of Pentacles. This card too, when we apply it to the sphere of the home, indicates safety, material well-being, and a sheltered environment. In this card we see a woman tending her garden. She is not an adventuress. She is more of a cautious explorer, as well as a nurturer, and through her accomplishments her garden has blossomed. She has been dwelling in comfort and safety."

"Dwelling in comfort and safety *until now*, you mean," I interrupted. I felt my body growing tense. "You said this card stands for everything that has preceded my question—which is supposed to have something to do with trouble at home or in my marriage."

"Yes, you are right," Mala Sonia said glumly. "Until now. Until now—or up until recent past—everything has been, like the garden, rosy. Now? Not so good, I hate to tell you. Which brings us to the sixth card. This position represents your near future and its influence. This card indicates how you have emerged from your recent past, as well as any new factors that have come into being. Your sixth card is the Two of Pentacles; so what you have before you—I feel terrible to say to you, but this is what the card indicates—is difficult situations arising, new troubles, embarrassment, worry, and a change which must be faced with equanimity. You will have a lot to juggle up ahead. Including with your financial situation."

"Are we still talking about my home life here? My marriage?"

"Whole reading is about the same Big Question. We have never changed the subject. What is troubling you so deeply and where is its source? That is question on the table. From looking at your very first card, the Empress, we have concluded that the source is your home and not your job. Your family and not your clients."

I pointed first to the Nine of Pentacles and then to the Two of Pentacles. "So, let's say we are in fact referring to my marriage. You're telling me that it used to be stable and rosy, but something has happened; Eli—the Emperor, I mean—is bored and restless, and there's a lot of strife and upheaval to be dealt with up ahead, which I can only imagine is somehow related to the discontented Emperor."

Mala Sonia kept a poker face. "Strife and upheaval is a good way to interpret—but remember your destiny, your Magician card. You will be able to use your strengths of willpower and self-confidence to see you through the upcoming storm."

Small compensation, I was thinking; then realized I would probably encourage one of my clients to do the same thing in a parallel situation.

"We have card number seven now. This card has often been interpreted as representing you, the questioner. It helps illuminate also how the near future will evolve for you. The card that comes up in the seventh position reveals the way in which you've responded to the near future and how or in what way your future is evolving."

I gasped and pointed to the card. "That's *Death!*" Assuming this reading was shaping up to represent a portrait of Eli's infidelity and the resulting fallout, visions of him butchering me in our bed—or the other way around—danced across my brain. God, my head was in one of his lurid comic books. This wasn't pretty.

Mala Sonia held up her hand as if to assuage my darkest fear. "Death is not always what you think it is."

Yeah, Anna. Sometimes a cigar is just a cigar, to paraphrase Freud.

"The Death card—another one from the Major Arcana—can indicate a transformation, a clearing away of the old to make way for the new. So you see, it can mean the end of one thing so that another can begin, bearing in mind that the card also can represent an alteration in your life as you know it; an abrupt change, or loss of financial security."

Swell. Fuck him. So, we're going to get divorced when all is said and done? Is that what's in my near future? I'll demand alimony and child support, if I have to fight him for it. I'll get the judge to saddle him with the kids' college tuition!

Shit! I was jumping to conclusions; overanalyzing. I was hating myself. This was ridiculous. What was I doing here wasting my time, and Faith's—the innocent witness to all this Gypsy folderol—by listening to Mala Sonia's prattle? I suddenly realized what all this was about. It was Mala Sonia's little joke on me, nasty payback for my nay-saying during her attempts to suck money out of my laundry room therapy clients. She was pissing on my psyche. That's what this was. But I decided to let her finish the reading. We only had three more cards to go.

Mala Sonia rapidly blinked her eyes, and I spied a tear running down her cheek, drawing a fault line through her makeup. "Are you crying?" I asked incredulously.

"No. False eyelash has come unglued. I must fix later." She peeled it from her lid and placed it on the table, where it lay, curly and inert, morbidly resembling a dead centipede. "We continue, yes?" Mala Sonia said. Funny, she didn't look either as pleased or as malevolent as I had thought she might, since she was giving me such an unpleasant drubbing. "I add something about the Death card, so that you don't feel so bad," she said to me. "Death card can mean that you must be brought very low before you can be raised up. Think of Our Lord and His resurrection." At which point she fervently crossed herself—backward.

"Your eighth card is another Minor Arcana card: the Three of Cups. Three of Cups indicates a resolution of a problem, a conclusion. There will be solace and healing, and a compromise will be reached. Number eight position in the ten-card spread refers to the environmental factors regarding your situation, a new turn of events, and the effect of others on you. So we are looking at the Three of Cups to represent new developments or unexpected changes that will alter your course or shed new light on existing situations. Are you with me?" I pursed my lips and nodded. "Good. This particular card also puts a spotlight on friendship among women. So we will see that your friendships with women will both enable you and encourage you to reach a resolution regarding your situation. They may provide you with the solace and healing that you will need to help you get through your difficulties. On this card, three women carry cups that are overflowing with abundance, symbolizing happiness and togetherness. Three of Cups is a card of celebration, of parties and gatherings where the guests or the members of a family come together to celebrate something new. A renewal, even."

Well, that left the door open for some hope on the horizon. But hadn't Mala Sonia told Alice that she too would experience a resolution to her question during a time of celebration and renewal? I was beginning to wonder about stock answers. Maybe Mala Sonia really told everyone the same thing, with slight variations on the theme, depending on what the client wanted to know. For Alice, a single woman, it was job and career-related. For the wives and mothers—Amy and me—it was all about hearth and home and husband.

Mala Sonia tapped the next card: the High Priestess. "She is the ninth card, representing your inner emotions and how your surroundings will affect you, and also how you will think and behave in times to come. So, yes, Major Arcana card number two—the High Priestess—symbolizes wisdom and sound judgment. You will be able to handle the problems facing you with serene knowledge and with common sense. If you look closely at the card, you will see that she bears a scroll with the word 'Tora' on it. While some interpret this word as an anagram for 'tarot,' for me that is a complicated and silly explanation of its meaning. 'Tora' is much closer to Jewish 'torah'—the law—so can be also a Hebrew connection here. This card—ninth one— also describes the questioner. The High Priestess—you at the moment—is a practical person and an analytical one—"

"Well, that's true enough," I said, despite my recent notion that this reading was born only out of Mala Sonia's desire to prove to me that her tarot interpretations were as valid as psychoanalysis when it came to assessing a troublesome issue presented by the client, and giving that client the tools to handle and overcome it.

Mala Sonia shifted in her chair and adjusted her breasts. Her push-up bra was working overtime. "Now, finally, we come to the last card. This is your outcome: the summation of everything. Once again, we have a Major Arcana card. We have Justice. So the outcome of your situation will seek to achieve balance and harmony, provide everyone with fairness and their just reward. It can also refer in the more literal sense to a court case and to adjustments in marriage or a partnership."

"Like divorce court," I muttered.

"There is always more than one way to interpret anything in life. Am I right?" Mala Sonia didn't wait for an answer. "What the Justice card is also symbolizing is the need for you to balance things out."

I immediately began to interpret that as the need to find a better balance between my work and my home lives. Did I give more of myself to my clients than I did to my own family? For fifty uninterrupted minutes a week, each client received my undivided attention, while they revealed their most personal secrets and we tackled their most deep-seated neuroses. Did I give the same kind of attention to Ian? To Molly? To Eli? In a word, no. Where at work I had a single focus, at home I considered myself the consummate multitasker. I oversaw homework while I stirred the soup, checked on the chicken, and conversed with my mother over the cordless phone. My family had to content themselves with receiving pieces of me, while my clients were awarded the whole. Ian, model child that he is, once asked plaintively if he had to make an appointment to tell me about the kids who were teasing him at school for being a "faggot" because he wore puffy shirts and makeup in *Les Misérables*. And since Ian is not a complainer by nature, in fact is the relative who presents the least amount of trouble, I should have listened even more closely to what it was he was really saying. No wonder Eli had become remote, Molly's acting out had manifested itself in criminality—if that isn't a cry for attention, what is?— and Ian felt shortchanged.

Maybe this whole reading, were I to take it seriously, was all about my home life suffering because of my disproportionate attention to my career. After a long day's listening to clients, I wanted to—needed to—chill out and let someone else do the heavy lifting for a few hours, but I lacked that luxury. When I got home, I was still expected to be the caretaker; yet by dinnertime there wasn't much left of me, to be honest. I was fried and my family was stuck receiving second best.

But . . . this new interpretation of mine didn't seem entirely on the money either, for some reason. Funny, how many people's first instincts always veer toward the worst, rather than the best scenario. Psychologists are not immune from this doomsday behavior.

"You have learned many hard things from the cards. I am sorry to acknowledge that my vision was correct: that something very big was indeed hanging over you. Let me give you a summation of reading," Mala Sonia said. "In the beginning I told you about Major and Minor Arcana cards in terms of long-term and short-term duration of the situation surrounding the question." She waved her arms over the cards. "Six Major Arcana cards out of ten suggests to me that situation could be long-term, but," she said, shrugging her shoulders, "it's close enough to fifty-fifty, so it could really go either way. You don't look too happy, Susan."

"Well, my future doesn't seem bright enough for me to need shades," I said, in a feeble attempt at lighthearted humor. "If, as so many of these cards suggest . . . and I hate myself for even thinking this . . . but if . . . let's say you're telling me—the reading does indicate—that Eli is cheating on me . . ." I lowered my voice to a whisper. "I think I want to know something more. I think I want to know who the woman is."

Mala Sonia grew tight-lipped. "I am not sure you do. Maybe it's not a good thing. *Si khohaimo may patshivalo sar o tshatshimo.* There are lies more believable than the truth."

"I think I want to know."

The Gyspy frowned and fretted. "All right, I give you final card. One card to answer ultimate question: who is your husband's mystery woman?" She palmed the top card off the deck and flipped it over.

"*What?*" I asked, trying to decipher her expression. "What is it? *Who* is it?" I couldn't believe I wanted to know this, but it's part of my training. We always risk pain as we face our issues and fears and then take the necessary steps or make the behavioral modifications to overcome them; but it is easier to face the known rather than the unknown. In fact, how can you surmount your issues if you can't even identify them?

"The final card is the Queen of Pentacles."

"And who is she? What does she mean, I mean? Signify?"

"How interesting. This is your only card in the reversed position in the entire reading. The Queen of Pentacles is a dark lady. She is an earthy person. Perhaps not bright in terms of intelligence or education, but she has great depth of feeling and is a vibrant personality too. In reversed position, also known as ill-dignified position, she can be an untrusting person, maybe even a vicious one, who is suspicious of what she cannot understand or what is new to her, and . . . who . . . ."

Mala Sonia seemed to have a difficult time getting the words out. "Who . . . is unable to see beyond material possessions, so she is enjoying what is nothing but a false prosperity. She can also symbolize neglected responsibilities. The suit of Pentacles also represents the domestic sphere, so the Queen of Pentacles can be someone close to your home."

Mala Sonia took my hands in hers—holding me so tightly that her rings began to cut into my skin—and looked deeply into my eyes. Hers glittered in the amber candlelight, but I couldn't fully analyze what I saw there. It could have been triumph or it could have been the start of tears. Or neither of the above, frankly. Years of observing Mala Sonia's behavior had convinced me that everything she did or said, each inflection, every gesture, was both calculated and choreographed. She was simply a full-time performer. I'd have a field day with her as a client. Getting her to be "real" would be a Herculean task.

"Final card," she said quietly. "Yes. I hope you have learned what you needed to." Then she blew out the candle and left the laundry room, leaving me sitting in the dark.

"Susan?" Faith whispered. Neither of us moved. "Are you all right?" When I didn't respond right away, she rose and turned on the light, then came over to the table and seated herself in Mala Sonia's chair. "*Ehrmh!* It's still warm from her tush," she commented, then gently laid her hand on my arm. "How're you doing?"

"Fine. I'm fine. Now that you turned on the light. I feel like someone who's gone for the ride in the haunted mansion and got very scared while it lasted, but once I exited the tunnel into the light, all my fears were left behind on the rickety little cart. I'm just experiencing the usual wobble in the legs that you get when you step out onto solid ground."

"Are you certain?" Faith asked sympathetically. "I have to say, that was quite intense."

"Did you believe any of it?"

"I'm a rather pragmatic sort, Susan."

"Was that a yes?"

"I think it's a lot like psychotherapy. If you believe that something works for you, then it will work. It you demonstrate no faith in the methodology, then it's going to be powerless."

"Very astute, Faith!" A little dose of my own medicine might have been just what I needed at that moment. Now . . . the next big question was . . . did I believe Faith . . . or Mala Sonia?

16

ME

Lucky for me, the rest of the day became unexpectedly busy, so I didn't have a spare moment to waste obsessing over Mala Sonia's psychic reading. I did, however, spend the rest of the day making a conscious effort to be Supermom, so I certainly had internalized at least some of the Gypsy's message.

Ian was going to be the seventh-grade star of Fieldston's annual Christmas-Chanukah-Kwanzaa pageant, and needed drilling on his lines after school. Molly was in the homestretch with her college applications, which were due on January first. She did in fact invest some extra effort on her Bennington application. She hadn't been kidding about her "a slacker mind is a terrible thing to waste" campaign. Her cell phone "movie" was a pretty masterful production. It was clever, edgy, offbeat, and totally Molly; though I wasn't very pleased during the "screening" when I saw the haunts she had frequented in order to make her point. And to my utter astonishment, she had elected to write the "toads" essay after all. I'm not sure whether it was what the Bennington admissions committee had been thinking

of when they devised the assignment, but Molly had written a
story called "The Ambivalent Amphibians" in which a princess
is presented with an array of suitors—all toads.

*She'd heard the old wives' tale that by kissing a toad, it would
turn the warty creature into a handsome prince, so she bought into
the cliché and started smooching. Lo and behold, the old wives had
been right! Each toad turned into a handsome prince. Some were
more handsome, more charming, and more accomplished than others, but they all shared a single trait: every time the princess began
talking to them about marriage and commitment and little
princelings all decked out in adorable velvet suits and feathered
caps—just like miniature versions of their father—and what a
wonderful wedding they would have with a seventy-five piece or-
chestra and elaborate floral centerpieces and a Viennese table that
would rival that of even the most prominent Jewish American
Princesses, and a gown made out of cloth-of-gold, and how wonderful it would be if they spent their Sunday afternoons antiquing together, or maybe even furniture- or tapestry-shopping, instead of
staring stupidly at the TV, watching the NFL or Nascar, the toad-
princes would hop like mad for the hills.*

*The princess was quite puzzled. She removed her pointy hennin
so she could scratch her head. Why was it, she wondered, that each
one of the toad-princes had exactly the same reaction to her endless
rhapsodizing about domestic bliss? While in many ways the toad-
princes didn't resemble one another in the least, being tall or short,
muscular or wiry, dark or fair, athletic or creative—not to mention
the fact that some were better kissers than others—they shared this
common trait. When she quietly sat with them side by side; or
silently strolled with them through the kingdom's deep and verdant
woods or along its many beautiful powdery beaches; or while she
and the toad-princes were engaging in a bit of nookie, where only
nonverbal expressions of contentment were exchanged; or indeed*

*when the princess was inclined to compliment them on one of their
many favorable attributes, or indulge them by ardently rooting for
their favorite sports teams, the toad-princes were the very models of
modern, major chivalry. But every time, without fail, that the toad-
princes heard the princess raise a subject that had anything what-
soever to do with commitment, or heard her wax lyrical imagining
what their coat of arms might look like once their two households
were connubially conjoined, the toads bolted, even though they acknowledged that the nookie with the princess had indeed been very,
very good.*

*Why did each of these toad-princes respond so positively to her
cheers of "Go, Knights!" but experienced a fight-or-flight (invariably
flight, actually) response when she tried to tally aloud the exact
number of times that they would wish one another a good night
during the long and happy years of their marriage? The answer
soon became as clear as the well water in which the princess
washed her flowing hair. Evidently, the toad-princes hadn't liked
what they'd heard.*

*The princess thus arrived at the unhappy conclusion that given
the selective nature of their behavior in her presence, toads had the
capacity to hear. She then tested her theory on the toad-princes who
subsequently made her acquaintance; and to her great dismay, her
hypothesis proved correct each and every time.*

"Molly, this is brilliant!"

"I hope the Bennington people weren't expecting science on
this one. I did say on my application that I want to study creative writing."

"Well, this is creative problem-solving, so if I were them, I'd
be delighted by the way you tackled the assignment. You found
a way to play to your strengths, and provided what I'm quite
certain is an unexpected response to their question."

Molly grinned. "Yeah . . . well. Could you see me poking

around in a terrarium or something?! Not! I had to do the toads, though—by default. I didn't even understand the first essay question, and the third one was so boring. And these people do claim to encourage individuality, right?"

And what had been the catalyst for this newfound diligence? Sylvia Plath. After devouring *The Bell Jar,* Molly Googled the poet, and learning a little more about her life, found a role model in the teenage Plath's constant striving for perfection, particularly in academics. Molly's grades had shot up (amazing what happens when one applies oneself!) during the second half of the fall semester. She was now pulling down A's and A-minuses in everything but math and science, where her test scores were nearly miraculous (for her) solid Bs.

"And don't worry, I won't stick my head in the oven," she assured me. "Just because I admire her doesn't mean I also want to be fucked-up like her. Or that I'm going to marry an adulterer! *Duh!*"

Duh. Gee. Nice to know she was still Molly under all that scholastic achievement. I was so pleased with her accomplishments, though, that I lifted one of her shoplifting punishments. She was no longer on incontinent dog duty.

I hadn't neglected Eli either, although I'd been unable to locate his lucky boxers and Mickey Mouse sock. I'd mentioned the missing undergarments to Faith when she asked me right after Mala Sonia's reading if I had noticed any strange behavior on his part. I wanted to play the hero, so that evening, after I left the women's health center, I braved crush upon crush of holiday shoppers, visiting four stores before I found another pair of Betty Boops. They weren't quite the same as the aqua-colored missing pair (the new ones were green with Betty dressed in a red and white Santa minidress and stocking cap), but it was the best I could do. Heedless of calorie, cholesterol, and carb counts I cooked Eli's favorite dinner, listened to him gripe about his long day at the drafting table, and massaged his aching shoulders, before I began to vent about my day in the dark and narrow trenches of shrinkdom. When he shrugged off my advances in the boudoir, pleading fatigue, I decided not to push it and waited instead for him to make the first move.

It had been like Santa's Dysfunctional Workshop at the women's health center as they were gearing up for their annual office Christmas party. I got to the sign-up sheet late and found that all the easy responsibilities, like paper goods or candy, had already been taken. So I was stuck with either cookies or music, both of which are never guaranteed to please everyone. With the cookies, there are the store-bought devotees and the homemade ones, neither of which can agree on a choice. Some people hate ginger, others hate peppermint, some can't tolerate nuts. Music isn't much easier. Too much "Christmas music" is either too denominational or too depressing. Statistics show that many people commit suicide over the December holidays, and I didn't want to be responsible for anyone's overdose of sentiment.

Still, cookies are a one-time thing, while CDs are forever. As far as the office party was concerned, if I did it right, I'd only have to do it once. I scribbled my name next to "Music."

When I got home, I noticed that someone from the building management had strung some colored lights and tinsel in the lobby, and erected the shabby faux fir, decking it with dimestore ornaments. Taking a quick peep in the basement, I saw that they had neglected the laundry room, as usual. I thought it could use a large dollop of holiday cheer. After dinner, I went back downstairs and covered the door with wrapping paper, so it resembled an enormous present. I ringed the washers with twinkly white lights, which didn't create an obstacle to doing the laundry, since for the past several days only one unit was working. We were now down to a single washing machine from half a dozen. Stevo appeared to have completely abrogated his superintendential responsibilities. He was no longer even offering the tenants false hope that new washers would be forthcoming.

Crowds had been gathering in the laundry room, and more than one fight erupted over whose turn it was for the washing machine. Last week, in an effort to ensure a fair and balanced washday (since no one else had taken the initiative to make order out of chaos), I posted a blank schedule where the tenant (or their housekeeper) could pencil in their name and apartment number next to a time slot, but it went largely unheeded. At the best of times, it resembled a coffee klatsch down there; at the worst of times, it was like the first day of the Barney's Warehouse sale.

The day after Mala Sonia had given me the psychic reading was Christmas Eve. It was a madhouse in the laundry room; everyone seemed to have extra loads.

As Sigmund had not given *me* a break from his sporadic incontinence, I had a laundry emergency, dashing downstairs that afternoon only to find the washing machine in mid-cycle. It was clearly one of those days I've described previously: where if someone was absent when the red light went out, their stuff would get "evicted" and dumped on one of the tables in a damp heap by the next person in line for the machine.

Claude and Talia—who no longer needed her crutches, but did rely on a cane—were already waiting. Meriel came down with a bunch of things to wash for Eric and Amy, but had to keep running back and forth from their apartment to the laundry room, since Amy didn't want her to waste the entire work-day waiting for the washing machine. Alice and Izzy—who, well into her third trimester, was still negotiating her reconciliation with her husband, popped their heads in and were ready to give up when they saw how many people were ahead of them. Faith had a load of purple clothes to be laundered, and she was up next. If the nearest Laundromat weren't over a quarter mile away, it certainly would have been a more viable option. And at the rate the snow was falling, we were practically guaranteed a white Christmas.

Although they'd been discouraged at first by the lengthy wait, Alice and Izzy suggested that we look at the bright side and turn the gathering into a festive occasion, so they went back up to Alice's apartment to fetch homemade holiday cookies, which they brought downstairs to feed the masses.

The red light went off, and we all stared at the machine. "After you," Claude said to Faith.

Faith hesitated. "You know, I've never done this. It just doesn't seem right."

"Bite the bullet, Faith," Alice encouraged her. "C'mon, we're all waiting."

"Whose is it?" Izzy asked, pointing to the washing machine.

"I tink it belongs to Mala Sonia," said Meriel. "She was in here when I first came down. She wanted to do more den one load, but I tell her daht everyone waiting, and she should do one and go back to de end of de line. So, she load her bigger load, de colors, and say she come back to do her white tings later."

"I know you say I should be bold, Susan . . ."

"Hop to it, Faith," Talia teased. "Don't make me hobble over there and do it for you." She pointed to the small table. "Dump 'em. Believe me, she'd do the same to any of us."

Faith set up her cart beside the washing machine, then lifted the lid and began to remove Mala Sonia's colorful array of garments, including the ruffled yellow blouse the Gypsy had been wearing when she gave me the psychic reading. She placed them in an unceremonious though remarkably tidy heap on the table.

Faith suddenly paled, and standing with her back to the clothes-covered table, beckoned to Claude. "Sweetheart, would you mind helping me with something?" Claude quizzically regarded the older woman. "No, I mean it," Faith added anxiously. When Claude was too slow to respond, Faith said, "I think I need some assistance. I must have wrenched my back when I bent over the washing machine to pull out the clothes."

"Oh, my God! I'll help you," I offered.

"No! No! Claude is . . . younger. And . . . and *taller*. If I collapse, she'll be able to catch me *much* more easily. You just sit tight, Susan."

Claude approached Faith, who drew her close and furtively whispered something in her ear.

Claude stifled a gasp, then nodded and turned to Talia, who was seated on one of the dinette chairs with her bum leg stretched out in front of her. "Talia, weren't you telling me about this new equipment you got from your physical therapist? I was just thinking that Susan . . . being . . . being a therapist of a different sort . . . might be interested in seeing it. And as long as you both have a bit of a wait before you can do your wash, you might want to take her up to your apartment and show her. While . . . while I help Faith get rid of her back spasm."

"*What?* Y'know, I have no idea what you're talking about, Claude."

Claude crooked her finger at Talia, and the dancer slid herself away from the table and limped over. Faith draped her arm over Talia's shoulder and whispered to her.

Talia winced. "Actually . . . that wouldn't be a bad idea, y'know? Meriel . . . ? I can show Susan the equipment, but I may need . . . uh . . . would you just come *over* here for a sec!"

So Meriel joined the knot of whispering women by the table.

"Okay, something's obviously going on," Alice said, and rose from the couch.

"Wait! Me too," Izzy demanded. "Pull. I can't get up like I used to." Alice heaved her extremely pregnant friend to her feet. I was very pointedly left out, sitting all by myself at the other end of the room like the kid who never gets picked for kickball.

The women appeared very upset. It was driving me nuts the way each of them kept looking from one to the other and then back to me with undeniable pity.

Then Alice, whose theatrically trained voice sometimes became unintentionally louder than she desired, said, in what amounted to a stage whisper, "Yes, but is it *our* place to *tell* her?"

"Okay ladies!" I planted my feet and stood up, arms akimbo. "I'm not the kind of person who enjoys being left out of the loop. 'Tell her' what?"

I was met with a half-dozen horribly pained expressions. Alice bit her lip so hard that she made herself cry. Meriel wrapped a comforting arm around her shoulder. Faith reached out her hand and Claude clasped it in commiseration. Talia's nose was growing red from trying not to weep, and Izzy handed her a tissue.

The cluster parted, exposing Mala Sonia's moist pile of laundry. I still didn't understand what the consternation was all about, so I came over to join them.

"It's a very delicate situation. We wanted to protect you," Faith whispered gently.

"From what?"

My clients exchanged anxious glances. Then Alice began to

disentangle and separate the garments until each one became clearly visible. Faith gingerly lifted up a pair of aqua-colored Betty Boop boxers and a single navy sock depicting Mickey Mouse in a dunce cap and gown—the Sorcerer's Apprentice. She pressed the items into my hand. "I think you told me that you were looking for these."

"We are so sorry, Susan," said Alice. "*So*, so sorry," she reiterated, and the women enveloped me into a hug.

Progress Notes

Faith Nesbit: This client's progress continues to be a marvel. The baby step she took in purchasing concert subscriptions some months ago became a giant leap when she screwed her courage to the sticking place and introduced herself to one of the musicians following a performance. The man is also a generation younger and of another ethnicity, and Faith seems very pleased with her ability to move on—not just from her old behavioral patterns of living for her late husband—but in the way her risk-taking has enabled her to broaden her horizons both socially and romantically. I do want to continue to take Faith's pulse, so to speak, closely monitoring her in subsequent sessions, in order to be certain that she's not moving too fast. Her rapid progress, while it delights me, also gives rise to my one concern: Faith has accelerated so quickly that I want to be sure she's not headed for a train wreck.

Me: And speaking of train wrecks . . . I was deliriously happy that Molly seems to have gotten herself on track, supporting my contention that she was perfectly capable of fine work, as long as she discovered something to be passionate about.

However . . . it would appear that my marriage has become derailed. I confess that in many ways I didn't see it coming, and yet on some far deeper level, I'd suspected it for a while. Was I in denial about Eli's remoteness of late? He had insisted that it had everything to do with his *Gia the Gypsy* book. Irony of ironies, he was actually telling the truth. I can't believe I didn't—couldn't—wouldn't see it. I tell my clients to pay attention to all the signs around them, and listen to what's *not* being said too; and yet I failed to do the same when it came to my own life. It's like the cobbler's kids who go barefoot and the dentist's kids with rotten teeth. Now I realize that Eli's late nights . . . if . . . well, there's no other explanation for his missing underwear turning up in Mala Sonia's wash. I may have been slow to catch on (okay, on a conscious level I didn't catch on at all, GODDAMNIT!!!!!!). I'm so angry at Eli, and perhaps even angrier with myself. Once I was faced with the cold hard truth (or the damp facts), there really is only one conclusion to be drawn.

Mala Sonia had been trying to tell me something in that so-called psychic reading. Reflecting on the way things had transpired that morning . . . she hadn't let me choose the cards at random the way she had done with Amy and Alice; instead, she dealt them from the deck herself . . . and I realize now that she might very well have manipulated the entire thing, using sleight-of-hand tricks when she laid out the cards in order for them to spell out what she wanted me to know.

The reading was in fact her admission of adultery. What an unusual thing to do—not just the method, obviously, but to confess it in the first place! Perhaps Mala Sonia had been feeling guilty about it, but didn't know how to raise the subject with me, or how—even whether—she should reveal the truth to her rival. Had she been trying to spare my feelings or slaughter me? Oddly enough, some of the cards as she interpreted them contained rays of hope. For me, I mean.

Like a therapist, she helped illuminate the issues for the client without handing them the answer. And like a therapist, Mala Sonia allowed the client to work out the resolution or outcome of the issue herself.

Why didn't I wonder where Eli was learning all that Romany?

And it wasn't as if our sex life had dried up completely. Thinking about it, it was pretty de rigueur for many couples approaching twenty years together. Yeah, I wanted more than

Eli was often in the mood to give, but that's not uncommon either.

I . . . I can't write any more words right now. I feel like there's been a death in the family . . . and I need time to grieve before I can begin to heal. I have nothing more to say. I'm numb. I think I'm going to be sick.

KNITS

17

Right after Christmas, I sat down with Anna, my supervisor down at the women's health center, and told her that my marriage had come unraveled. The revelation had been a sucker punch to the solar plexus, I said. And where had I been while it was happening? Asleep at the watch; in denial, perhaps; taking what seemed like a good life for granted that it was a great one. Anna asked me if I wanted to talk to someone about it, and offered to make a recommendation. I sounded like some of my clients when I expressed the desire to see an analyst who was licensed to prescribe sedatives.

Anna asked me if I wanted a referral for a couples counselor. When I got home, I broached the subject with Eli, who said that he didn't think that was necessary.

"And why is that?" I asked, every nerve in my body clutching and tensing and pulsing.

"I really don't think it's going to help. I want to see how things go with Mala Sonia. That's where I want to be right now."

"And what about your kids? You're ready to walk out on your kids over this?"

"I'll be right across the street."

"You'll *what?*"

"Stevo's gone. Mala Sonia told him about us the same day she tried to tell you. He left their apartment that night and didn't come back. She says she doesn't know where he is. Mala Sonia and the kids can't live there if the super's quit, but her cousin is the super of number thirty-seven across the street and there's a vacant apartment over there that we can take. A rent-controlled tenant just died."

"Did I really just hear you say that you are moving in with the super's wife?!" If there was ever a person who did not deserve to have a rent-stabilized apartment on the Upper West Side fall into his adulterous lap, it's Eli. Not only is he rubbing his affair in his family's face, he's probably tickled pink at the wages of sin.

Eli looked like a lost little boy. I had neither patience nor pity for his predicament. "Your suitcase is on the top shelf of the linen closet."

I'd tried to hold it together, for the sake of Molly and Ian. I didn't want them to see their mother turning into a screaming harpy, ruining the holidays for everyone. As it was, things were very strange up in apartment 5C. Eli kept coming and going, moving his stuff out of our place and down the street on rolling dollies. Through it all, as ridiculous as it seemed, we tried to maintain a semblance of normalcy for the children. And although they felt betrayed and confused, our kids hadn't entirely abandoned their priorities. Molly wanted to know if she could have her dad's home office as a bedroom. Ian fought her on the subject, claiming that she'd be going off to college soon anyway, and she didn't need to hog the bigger room. His tiny bedroom was what would have been a maid's room back when the building was built. So he did have a valid point about switching rooms. Once he hit his growth spurt, his limbs would be practically touching the walls.

I retreated emotionally. The apartment became my cocoon and I grew very quiet, speaking to Eli only when absolutely necessary. I preferred to be alone with my thoughts. The kids tiptoed around me as though I were a victim of shell shock. In a way, I was.

Where I fell apart was on the couch. The analyst's couch, I mean. Figuratively speaking. Anna had given me three names: two women and a man. I preferred to work with a woman, given the nature of my major issue. One of Anna's recommendations I knew by virtue of reputation, so I phoned her first. She had absolutely no openings in her schedule for the foreseeable future. On to option two: the other woman. Her voice mail indicated that she would be out of the office (probably on St. Barth, guessing what she usually charged her clients) until February first. I couldn't wait more than a month. So I called the third referral, a shrink named Alvin Lee, who slotted me in. We had our first appointment on January second.

I had wondered what Dr. Lee would look like. His surname was a common one: he could have just as easily been black, white, or Chinese. Turns out, he was Chinese, and much younger than I had expected. His office, located in one of the grand prewar apartment buildings on West End Avenue, was paneled in blond wood and crawling with family photos and expensive Asian antiques. His three degrees from Harvard had pride of place on the wall behind his desk. His clients didn't recline, actually; they sat on an original Eames chair that was probably insured for more than it would have cost to feed a family of four for a year. I felt very intimidated. Now that I was about to take the hot seat, I had an even greater understanding of how my laundry room clients felt, being put at ease by the spectacularly low-key atmosphere down in the basement where the scent of soap and fabric softener were often as effective as aromatherapy.

"How are you doing this morning?" Dr. Lee asked, smiling pleasantly and shaking my hand.

"As well as can be expected," I sighed, "having spent the last couple of days being unable to shower!" Dr. Lee gave me a quizzical look. "The boiler in our apartment building fritzed out on New Year's Eve, so we've had no heat or hot water since then. My husband is having an affair with the super's wife, and when he found out about it—the super, I mean—he disappeared. So no one's minding the store. The tenants are up in arms, completely livid. They're practically ready to take up torches and pitchforks—"

"Mrs. Lederer, I asked how *you* are doing?" Dr. Lee gently said, motioning me to the Eames chair. "Not the tenants. Though I'm sure they have reason to be upset about the loss of services."

"Loss of services," I echoed mockingly. "Do you know that's what they call 'no sex' in lawsuits? One spouse gets injured or has an accident and is unable to make love, or can't do it the way they used to, so the uninjured spouse puts in a legal claim for 'loss of services.' "

Dr. Lee rolled his desk chair onto the Oriental carpet and seated himself, favoring me with another of his kindly, though I thought somewhat condescending, smiles. "You're being a bit evasive, you know."

Good God . . . I say the same thing to *my* clients. I hadn't been in therapy since I was a doctoral candidate, when it was part of my training. Funny, how you sometimes forget that people walk funny when the shoe is on the other foot.

"I feel . . . I feel . . . Angry. Bereft. Betrayed. Blindsided. Confused. Duped." Was Dr. Lee smiling at my pain? What was up with this guy?

"Do you realize that you listed your feelings in alphabetical order?" he said to me, folding his hands in his lap.

I blinked a few times. "No, I hadn't realized that. I was too busy feeling angry, confused, *whatever* it was I just said."

"You told me over the phone that your husband had no wish to attend couples therapy."

"Yes. Eli doesn't see the point. He thinks he's in love with this woman and wants to give it a shot."

"So have you been able to have a dialogue with him at all during the past few days?"

I shook my head. "I've been giving him the silent treatment, mostly. I'm afraid that if I say what I'm feeling, it'll all come out in some incoherent rant and I'll sound like a banshee and it'll end up reinforcing the decision he already seems to have made."

"Mrs. Lederer . . . let's do a little role-playing. What would you say to your husband if he were in the room right now? This room is like a safe house. You know that, of course. You can let all your emotions go, uncensored, without fear of embarrassment or censure. Allow yourself to work out your anger and your thoughts in here, so that when you eventually do approach your husband, you will do so from a more confident emotional place. Go ahead," urged Dr. Lee gently. "Use me. You know what to do."

I looked the baby-faced Asian analyst in the eye and envisioned Eli: pale skin punctuated by dark circles under his eyes from all those late nights at the drafting table—or not—ever-so-slightly receding hairline, runner's build. "Why, Eli?" I said, immediately bursting into tears. "How could you throw away more than twenty years of our lives together? Do they suddenly count for nothing to you? Are they bullshit? When did you become so dissatisfied with our marriage? With me? Why did you never talk to me about what the hell was going through your head? You said you 'couldn't help it.' That you'd approached Mala Sonia to help you with your *Gia* book research and after a while one thing led to another . . . that you 'couldn't help' yourselves. Of course you could! That's what being an adult is all about, Eli. *Boundaries.* Common sense. Restraint. Actions have consequences; every kid who's ever been punished knows *that!* So now you want to 'try it' with Mala Sonia, to see what you really have. And what about the collateral damage from your little domestic experiment? Did you even consider how it might affect me? And how your actions could damage your relationship with Ian and Molly? Or weren't you thinking that far ahead? You just went on and did whatever the fuck you wanted, like a self-indulgent little boy. You're a brat, Eli, d'y'know that? You're a *brat*. All these years I thought I'd been married to a man who was more in touch with his inner child than many; but in fact there was no man there at all, just an overgrown boy with secondary sex characteristics! And what if things don't turn out so well with Mala Sonia after all? What if her kids end up despising you as much as your own flesh and blood does at the moment? You're even allergic to ferrets! Are you planning to come crawling back to your family, red-eyed and wheezing, expecting us to take you in again and forgive you? It's not that easy. Eli . . . ? Do you even love your kids? Do you love *me?*"

Dr. Lee allowed me to vent for the remainder of our session. When, out of the corner of my eye, I caught him surreptitiously glancing at the clock, I collapsed my head into my lap, totally spent, utterly exhausted from my tirade.

"I'm sorry, but we're going to have to stop now," he said softly. "I'd like to see you next week at the same time."

Rising on wobbly legs, I took out my checkbook, but Dr. Lee refused payment, insisting that our first session was a professional courtesy. I left his office unsure as to whether I felt any better and whether Dr. Lee was the right person for the job. He was credentialed up the ying-yang, no question about his background and training; but I think analysis is a little like marriage. Finding the right therapist is as important and individual a decision as choosing the right spouse. After all, it's the therapist who'll see you at your most vulnerable and unguarded and to whom you'll confess your deepest secrets and confide your darkest fears. And when I stepped out onto West End Avenue, I wasn't convinced that I'd made the best match in either case.

When I got home, the answering machine was blinking urgently. I admit that I'd hoped it was Eli, abjectly begging to come back across the street and be reconciled to the bosom of his family, so I could decide whether to embrace or eviscerate him. It wasn't. The message was from Talia Shaw. She asked me if it was all right if she resumed her therapy sessions with me.

I didn't return her call right away. Nor did I return it the next day, or the day after that, or even the following week. I felt like a hypocrite and a fraud. How could I possibly have been—and still be—or ever be—of use to my clients, when I couldn't even help myself? I've been an analyst for years, but now I had absolutely no desire to sit in a chair all day and hear about other people's problems, absorb their neuroses, encourage them to find healthy solutions to their issues: ones that didn't involve acting-out and impulsive or self-destructive behavior. Even "retail therapy" can turn into a nightmare when a client has no impulse control and maxes out her credit cards, sending herself into spiraling debt because in her despair she had convinced herself that she just had to have something—a sweater, an evening gown, a fur coat, a motorcycle—in every color, and then everything would be all better. Maybe all my empathetic understanding, which I had always considered one of my therapeutic strengths, had turned me into a dysfunctional sponge, a walking petri dish of toxicity that had somehow managed to poison my own domain.

During the past few days I had come to realize that there was more going on than my feelings about Eli's infidelity and the collapse of our life together. As a therapist, I was burned out. I had nothing more to give my clients. I'd allowed my own ship to end up on the rocks; how *dare* I pilot other captains? What chutzpah I had!

I needed a break; maybe even for forever.

But giving up was something I routinely discouraged my clients from indulging in. Adjusting their attitude, overcoming and throwing off bad behavior, yes; throwing in the towel, no. Yet I was running on fumes. Maybe I'd been that way for a while, which is why I sometimes felt I had so little to give my family (no matter how hard I tried to give them everything I had left) after a long day sitting across from the couch.

The Catch-22 was that even though I needed to take a breather, I really couldn't give up my practice. It looked like I'd be heading for divorce court. No matter what the settlement, given Eli's income it couldn't possibly cover one kid with six more years of private school ahead, and another one bound for college in a few months. I didn't have the luxury of quitting. And as long as I was going to continue my salaried sessions down at the women's health center, I had a moral obligation not to abandon my pro bono laundry room clients either.

18

TALIA

"Look!" Talia brandished her cane. "I almost don't need it anymore." She ambled over to the sofa and seated herself, positioning her back against the armrest with her injured leg stretched across the length of the couch.

"You know, it might be hard for you to get up from there, if you want to move around during your session."

"That's okay. I don't know how much moving I'll be doing. I've gotten very Zen over the past few months of having to sit still a lot. Now I can see dances in my head; the inside of my forehead is like a giant movie screen, y'know? And there's all this choreography going on inside my brain. And I can picture *myself* moving through space too. So I can, like, see myself dance while I'm sitting here."

"Have you ever considered a future as a choreographer?"

At least I didn't get the same kind of reaction that I'd received months ago when I suggested that Talia consider teaching. "Maybe . . ." she said thoughtfully. "But I'm not willing to let myself believe that my dance career is over, just because of this ACL crap. You taught me something, Susan. It wasn't anything you said, specifically. It was more like leading by example, y'know? When dancers learn a new piece, the choreographer, or his assistant—or if the choreographer is dead, there's usually a person who is like the official recorder and teacher of their ballets . . . anyway, the piece is always demonstrated for us, right there in the studio. The choreographer, or whoever, shows us the steps and the attitudes and we follow their example and then make it our own—I mean putting our own expression into it, of course—not doing our own steps or anything."

"So how did I lead by example?"

Talia looked at me as though I were utterly dense. "Because *you* didn't give up! You didn't call it quits even when what you thought was the worst thing that ever happened to you happened. Well—you did call it quits, but you didn't give up. You came back down here after a while, even though it was probably a really hard decision to make after telling us that you were too burned out to continue our therapy sessions. It couldn't have been easy listening to nut jobs—speaking for myself only—all day. Y'know, I know I'm not the easiest person in the world. I'm vain and I complain a lot, and I see the glass half empty most of the time, and if all your other clients are like me, no wonder you needed a break! And maybe . . . maybe it's really good for you too, that you've come back, because, if you think about it, while you sit there listening to all of us go on and on about our problems, you might even realize that you're not nearly as messed up as we are. Which should make you feel better about *yourself*."

I laughed. "It doesn't quite work that way, Talia. I can't even say that I wish it *did*. Because if it did, if my clients aren't making progress toward healthier behavior, it would mean that I'm not doing my job *after* all. I appreciate the sentiment, though."

"I told you I'm not very good with words," Talia said, giving me a goofy smile. "But I'm getting better. I'm actually saying stuff now, y'know? A few months ago, if I'd been unable to dance during our sessions, I would have sat here like a lump. So I guess the ACL injury had a weird benefit. I've had to use other parts of my body in order to express myself."

"So now that you've discovered the power of words, how do you feel about using some of them to talk about what's been up with you since we last spoke officially."

"Ohhhh . . . I'm not sure I can talk about *important* stuff! You're asking an awful lot of me right off the bat, y'know." We both burst out laughing. "Have you ever heard of the Miller Clinic?" I shook my head. "Oh. Well, never mind, I shouldn't have expected you to. It's just a place that specializes in P.T. for injured dancers. I've been rehabbing my knee down there and going back to a modified version of my Pilates exercises, and my physical therapist is a dancer who ruptured a tendon years ago and was never exactly the same since, but she totally got into Pilates—teaching it, I mean—and found that it was really rewarding. She even started liking teaching better than dancing because she was seeing right up close that she was having an effect on people; her students became sort of like an audience. So . . . I dunno . . . maybe it's something I should think about. I'm definitely not going to stop dancing. But this injury has made me think about my future—after dancing. Y'know, I've realized for a while now it's not going to be that far away. Oops. Excuse me."

Talia awkwardly got to her feet and made as mad a dash as she could for the little bathroom. I heard her wretching through the partially open door. She returned to the couch wiping her mouth with a damp paper towel and looking very pale.

"I want to talk about that," I said calmly.

"What?"

I pointed to the bathroom. "Talia, an eating disorder is a very—"

"Is that what you think I have?" She looked shocked.

"Well, in the past when you've run into the bathroom, I wondered whether you were purging yourself with diuretics. I have to say that the signs do point to—"

"It's not! I promise you. Why does everyone assume that just because a skinny dancer pees a lot or throws up that she's got bulimia or something? You've never met my mom, but she's always been as thin as a whippet—until the alcohol started to add weight. I—this is going to sound really stupid—"

"Try me."

"I . . . have a low potassium thing. So I'm supposed to take supplements and eat a lot of foods that are full of it, y'know? Like bananas. But I hate bananas. The doctor told me that I could drink a glass of grape juice every morning instead—the real thing, not like 'grape *drink*,' y'know? So I do. And I really like grape juice. But for some reason, whenever I drink it, which is first thing in the morning, it makes me throw up."

"Talia . . . ?"

"What?"

"Do you drink the grape juice on an empty stomach every morning?" She pondered the question and nodded. "Well, if what you're telling me is true—that all this throwing up is purely due to an adverse reaction to drinking grape juice on an empty stomach—then you might want to consider eating a bit of solid food with it."

Talia made a face. "I can't eat breakfast. I can't even think about eating until about ten in the morning."

I regarded her skeptically. "I really hope that you're telling me the truth, Talia. I've been through it. So, believe me, I understand how painful and embarrassing it can be. And how horribly self-destructive it is to your body. I want you to know that we can talk about it in here. And we'll get you some help. Okay?"

"I know what you're saying, Susan, but I swear to you, if anything, I have a food allergy, not an eating disorder."

"Just giving you food for thought."

Talia tugged at her ponytail elastic and her dark hair came tumbling down over her shoulders. "Ahhhhh," she murmured happily, vigorously shaking her head. "And another thing . . . you have *no* idea how good it feels not to have my hair pulled into a tight bun all the time. I never realized why I always seemed to be walking around with a headache until my ACL popped and I didn't have any reason to stick all those bobby pins in my head every day!"

"So . . . to go back to what you were saying before the hair subject . . . you're becoming the ant and not the grasshopper . . . planning for the future instead of living for the moment. Which isn't the same as living *in* the moment, by the way. You *should* live *in* the moment. And it sounds like you're thinking about training to become a Pilates instructor down the line. What about teaching dance? Have you reconsidered that?"

"I can't say I've changed my mind there." Talia frowned. "Y'know, 'Those who can't do, teach.' "

"I know you seem to put a lot of store by that adage. But you just said you were considering teaching Pilates. What am I missing here?"

" 'Those who can't do, teach' applies to those who are teaching in the professions they trained to do, or used to do—not to people who teach something else entirely," Talia said emphatically. "I know you want to get me to move out of my 'comfort zone' so I can be open to change and all that . . ." She twirled a lock of hair around her index finger. "I'm just not ready to be pushed too *far*, okay?"

AMY

"I'm too exhausted to vent today," she said, sinking onto the sofa. She stretched her body along its length and flopped an arm over her eyes. "I think I'd get better use out of our time if I just *slept* for fifty minutes."

Amy did look pretty haggard. And unusually unkempt, as if she had just thrown on whatever clothes were closest to hand and hadn't even bothered to run a comb through her hair. I got up and switched off the lights. "Tell you what, Amy: I'll let you lie there in the dark, but I think it would be a good idea for you to share what's been going on lately. You've cancelled the last couple of sessions, and I've got to say, you don't even look like yourself today."

Amy groaned. "Everyone knows the expression 'Be careful what you wish for,' right? Remember Mala Sonia's so-called psychic reading?"

"Which one?" I grumbled.

"Oh, right." Amy sat up. "My God, Susan, I am so sorry. I heard about the reading she gave you. And what happened. Is it possible that she's really got a psychic gift? I mean, everything she said to me came true too."

"Maybe she just got lucky." I didn't add that in my case I thought Mala Sonia had manipulated the cards.

"You were in the room with me when she did the reading; you're my witness."

"Why do you say that Mala Sonia's prediction turned out to be true?"

Amy sighed deeply and lay back down on the couch. "Months ago, I had it out with Eric about pulling his weight in the parenting department. He said I was probably suffering from postpartum syndrome. I called him a Neanderthal and threatened to strangle him. After Mala Sonia's reading, I raised the subject again. 'You're a partner now,' I reminded him. 'You're one of the people at Newter & Spade who gets to *set* the rules.' And I more or less gave him an ultimatum: if his idea of parental responsibility was just paying the bills, I told him he could do it from his own apartment and I'd be happy to collect his alimony and child support payments. So he finally found a way to rearrange his schedule—his calendar was pretty light in December, anyway—in order to spend time at home taking care of Isaac. And when Isaac went down for his nap, Eric would be able to do his work at home so he wouldn't get too far behind schedule. It sounded great in theory. In practice, it was a whole other story. I've begun to wonder whether men really do lack nurturing skills, or whether Eric is trying to do a lousy job so I can throw up my hands and say 'Yeah, you were right. I'm much better at this than you are. Go back to the office.' I had been hoping that with Eric at home *I* could work out an arrangement with Newter & Spade and go back to work, at least part-time. I've missed my career so much. So Eric's been home for a few weeks, and the house is in complete turmoil. Isaac screams like a lunatic whenever his father tries to lift him out of his crib and only gets calm when I hold him. You can't blame the baby, I suppose; he hardly ever sees his father, so he didn't trust the funny-smelling stranger who wanted to touch him. I thought the more Eric got to know his son, the more Isaac would respond to him. But so far it hasn't worked out that way. Of course, Eric seems so uncertain when he holds him that Isaac probably thinks he's going to get dropped on his head. So I said to Eric that maybe it would be a good idea if he took care of other things, like the grocery shopping and the cooking, while I took care of the baby, and at least I still wouldn't be doing *everything.*"

"And how is that working out for you?" I asked her.

"Oy vayyyyyyyyyyyyyyyyyyyyyyyyyy!"

"That doesn't sound like a ringing endorsement."

"He's inept! He practically burns boiled water! You think I'm kidding, but I asked him to make me a cup of tea, and he left the kettle on the burner for so long that all the water evaporated out the spout and it ended up charring the bottom of the kettle. He just *forgot* that he'd put the water up. A simple grocery list is beyond him—this is a man with an advanced degree from one of the top schools in the country. I can't take it any more. And Newter & Spade keeps giving me the runaround, so I feel like *I'm* wasting even more time and space not being able to bring in any income. Being a partner, Eric's annual take is calculated on a percentage basis, and since he hasn't been there over the past few weeks, he says there's been a call to change the equation so that he gets less of a share than the other partners who are in the office full-time. It's a nightmare!"

"What do you think you've learned from this?"

"Honestly? That you can never rely on anyone but yourself. In the long run, if you want something done right, and done to your satisfaction, you can't delegate. Everything Eric has done, as far as the baby and the domestic chores are concerned, I've had to either undo or redo. And don't let anyone ever try to convince you that men are tougher than women. At the first sign of crisis, they run! The first day Eric was home, Isaac spit up on him and Eric just lost it! My husband started to blame the baby, complained that his clothes were ruined—who told him to burp the baby in a Zegna shirt?—and he just stood there looking helpless. When Isaac got fussy in his bath, Eric just yelled for me to come into the room and take over. He utterly gave up. Susan, this is a man who makes a living representing corporate polluters, and he can't even wipe up his son's vomit."

"Well, with both you and Eric at home during the day, is there a way that you can reassign Meriel's duties so that she can help Eric handle his new baby-related responsibilities while you remain relieved of at least some of the burden of feeling like you're still doing everything?"

"That's a whole 'nother issue," Amy fretted. "Meriel is underfoot all the time, or so it seems. I mean we have a fairly good-sized apartment, but with Eric home now, everything seems so disrupted. Everywhere one of us turns, there's Meriel. And it's becoming a too-many-cooks situation. It doesn't make sense to keep her on; on the other hand, I can't stand housework and have no time for it. If Eric were *competent* at it, we could let Meriel go—or at least furlough her for a while. But he's not, and he doesn't seem to want to be, and I think that if I give Meriel her walking papers, things will end up going from bad to worse. Besides, I hear so many horror stories from my friends about their housekeepers or au pairs, that I'm afraid to fire her. And if Eric returns to Newter & Spade full-time, we'll be back to needing someone almost every day anyway. God knows she's not the most reliable person in the world, but at the risk of sounding like a cliché, it's so hard to get good help nowadays."

MERIEL

"I don't know how much longer I'll be coming down here." There was resignation in Meriel's voice. "I read de writing on de wall. You know upstairs wit' Mrs. Amy and Mr. Eric, I am caught between de rock and de hard place. It seem layk she is standing over me wit' everyting I do for dem, and I cahn't work daht way. De oder day I am dusting all her knickknacks and I feel her standing behind me. I get so tense I drop what I am dusting on de carpet. Good ting it was no'ting breakable. But I bend down to pick it up and I am trembling all over. I need to have de job—de books I record on tape is only volunteer work—but dis is not a good way for me to live."

Meriel buried her face in her hands. Rather than ask her a question or offer a suggestion, I patiently waited for her to resume speaking.

"You know . . . maybe I should quit de job. I have a feeling daht Mrs. Amy want to get rid of me, so maybe de leaving should be my idea instead. On de other hand, you know I need de job. Dey always say don't trow away de old couch until you have bought de new one."

I was wondering if there was an adage or cliché that had been left unexpressed by my clients during the past week. "It's understandable that you'd feel more confident if you were the one choosing to leave your job, rather than waiting to get let go . . . assuming you think a dismissal really is forthcoming."

"I told you, I see de writing on the wall. She and Mr. Eric are not happy wit' de current situation. And Mr. Eric is not ahkting layk de man in de family. So Mrs. Amy have to be de big decision-maker for bot' of dem. You know who I feel sorry for? Daht baby. She fuss over him all de time but say such bad tings about being a mother because she tink he too little to understand because he don't talk yet. I don't know about you, Mrs. Susan, but I tink babies understand a lot more than people tink dey do. I'm glad you are back doing de terapy, because Isaac going to need you in a few years!"

ME

 "Guess who I just saw down by the mailboxes?" Molly practically galloped into the apartment. "Naomi and Claude! They just got the letter from the adoption agency in Georgia that the paperwork went through. They're going to get their Chinese daughter!"

"That's fantastic!"

"Alice was in the lobby too, and when she heard the news she said she felt like a fairy godmother, because she'd notarized their papers. She said she was glad that all the years she'd worked as a legal assistant didn't end up a total waste of her life after all."

We high-fived just as the phone rang. It was Claude and Naomi. "I know . . . Molly just told me . . ." I laughed at Claude's response. "Sorry, she 'spoiled it' by getting to me before you did . . . I'm thrilled . . . honestly, I couldn't be happier for you . . . congratulations!"

"They're leaving for China in a couple of weeks," I said to Molly after I hung up the phone. "First they visit their baby's province . . . I think she's from Sichuan; then they head to the city of Guan Cho, which is where all the expecting parents stay while they're waiting for their respective daughters to be delivered to them. So they'll be gone for two to three weeks. Naomi found a viable way to accompany Claude too. She's going to tell anyone who asks that she's going to be the baby's nanny."

"They are going to be such wonderful moms, don't you think?" I nodded. "People can be so blind about it," Molly added. "Think of all the straight women who totally fuck up in the motherhood department." She opened the refrigerator and stood in front of it for several moments trying to figure out what she wanted to snack on.

"Why don't you have some of Faith's Scotch broth?"

"Nuh-uh. Too heavy. Besides, I'm not that hungry."

"Fine; but how many times have I told you not to leave the refrigerator door open. Now that you know what's in there, you can decide what to eat with the door closed."

Molly ignored my suggestion. "You aren't, though, Mom. A fuck-up. *Dad's* an asshole, but you're a really good parent." Molly finally opted for an orange and we sat down together at the dinette table.

"Use a napkin, Molly. Thanks. For getting the napkin and for the compliment. You know, I don't want you and Ian to choose sides; your father over me. We're both still your parents."

"Too late for that," Molly said, dumping the orange peel into the paper napkin. "It's not like we *chose* to choose between you and Dad. It's *obvious*. He followed his dick and walked out on us—"

"Molly, he's still your father! Don't talk about him like that. Show a *little* respect, at least."

"Why? Did he show *you* any respect? Did he show Ian and me any respect? You're always asking me if I learned anything about ethics at the Ethical Culture schools . . . well, yeah, I did, okay? For one thing, you have to *earn* respect; you don't get it automatically. Even if you're a relative. And *Dad's* ethics are for shit, by the way. I bet that if I were one of your clients you'd tell me that my anger is valid and I have a right to vent it, and not go '*Whoa-oh*, he's *still* your *father*,' " Molly added mockingly. "I'm mad at him for pissing on you. So, yeah, I can't help but choose sides, because Dad acted like a total baby, doing what he felt was good for him, regardless of how it affected other people. He, like, ran away with the woman who was his comic book heroine. Is there anything more sophomoric than that?! I mean, he should get a *grip!* And I'm mad at him for pissing on me and my brother too. You can't tell me I'm not allowed to be mad for my *own* sake, even if you're being shrinky. And another thing: if he decides to come crawling back with his dick between his legs—"

"Molly! What did I just say?!"

"Mo-om," my daughter intoned, with the same inflection reserved for *duh-uh,* "okay, forget the second part of what I said. But if Dad decides to come crawling back—blah blah blah— then I think we should put it to a family vote. He should have to make his case to all three of us. And right now, my projected polls say . . . *ehnh!* Dad loses! Because he gets a no vote from me, and he hasn't exactly been a real hands-on dad to Ian—I mean they never did father-son stuff like shooting hoops or going to baseball games—so Ian probably will just side with me. You've always had a career and you've always taken good care of me and Ian, even if we—well, okay, *me*—have been a handful sometimes."

Chewing thoughtfully, Molly offered me a slice of orange. *"Ermh,"* she munched, "it's too bad I mailed in my college applications already, because I just thought of something I could have added."

"Which is?" *I* was merely grateful and astonished that she had completed them and mailed them in on time.

"Well, I just wondered whether it would have given me a bit of an extra edge if I'd told them I come from a broken home."

The following Saturday afternoon I asked Molly if she was planning to accompany me to the baby shower.

"Claude and Naomi didn't get their kid already, did they?"

"No. They haven't even left for China yet. *Izzy's* baby shower. Alice's friend."

"Oh, yeah, I forgot. I didn't get her anything," Molly replied dubiously. "Was I supposed to?"

"You can share my gift. I had The Body Shop make up a whole basket of great-smelling stuff she can pamper herself with. Alice has been knitting up a storm for months now. She's made baby sweaters, a blanket, booties, a cap . . . she's brought her knitting to our therapy sessions so she doesn't lose any time. She's worried she won't get all the projects finished in time."

"When's Izzy due?"

"Two weeks; February fourteenth."

"Yikes, that's soon. A Valentine's baby. Does she know what it is yet?"

I nodded. "When she had the amnio, she asked. She told me she wasn't good at secrets."

"And . . . ?"

"Girl. And I think she plans to name her Valentina."

"That rocks! Awesome!"

"Yeah," I said reaching out to clasp her hand, "girls can be pretty awesome."

Progress Notes

Talia Shaw: I am pleased, first of all, that Talia has resumed her therapy; and secondly, that she has become much less resistant to the idea of change. It's a much healthier mental outlook that can only serve her well as her body continues to heal. It's important for her to begin looking at the long-range forecast and having some options in the event that her knee injury inhibits her from performing at her prior high level. Her eye on the future has also boosted her self-esteem; the client is no longer complaining that her "life is over." I remain concerned, however, about the real possibility that Talia continues to suffer from an eating disorder. She vehemently denies this, and offered me an explanation, but I want to monitor the situation more closely in subsequent sessions. If there really is a problem, I intend to encourage her to obtain special counseling.

Amy Baum: Amy is to be commended for taking control of her dominant issue, rather than letting it continue to control her. After months of venting her frustration with her domestic situation, she took the risk of confronting her husband and demanding his co-parental participation. Unfortunately, things appear to have backfired on her in a big way. But rather than allow her to accept it as the manifestations of an accurate "psychic prediction," thereby absolving herself of personal responsibilities, we need to focus on active problem-solving. Client, though a high-functioning individual in her career, has a very high-strung personality and immediately panics when things are not running smoothly in her home life. Her first response is to give up on the situations that are creating the most profound frustration and to want to run toward the place where she feels safest: the office, in her case. It's a common behavioral pattern; our instincts invariably tell us to flee a difficult and anxiety-provoking milieu and seek our favorite shelter, which is often the place where we feel the most respected and appreciated. Nevertheless, in our subsequent sessions I will have to encourage the client to work methodically and patiently in order to restore her mental and emotional equilibrium, which will then translate into her ability to resolve her domestic crisis.

Meriel Delacour: The client's pragmatism is serving her well. Meriel is fully aware that her job as a domestic is in jeopardy, and is not in denial regarding the possible outcome of her employment situation. I want to work with Meriel in future sessions to come up with, and then further develop, a game plan for her future. She has already taken a big step toward taking control of it by thinking of resigning her job, instead of leaving all the power in the hands of her employer. However, using Meriel's analogy about the old couch/new couch, we need to focus on how she will continue to support herself financially if she moves on, and I do not tend to encourage my clients to take a big jump without a safety net beneath them. They may look very free in flight, but the results—mentally, emotionally, and financially—can be catastrophic.

Me: I needed to take a break from counseling. And I think I needed to come back to it too. Perhaps I needed to be needed, since my husband of twenty years clearly no longer needs me. My clients do. My children do. Returning to the chair opposite the couch illuminated for me just how much progress my clients have been making, which I can interpret as an indication that I have indeed been able to help them; I've made a positive difference in their lives. And knowing that I can and do make a difference is one of my greatest rewards.

On the home front . . . while Dr. Lee and I just grazed the tip of the iceberg in terms of my owning my anger at Eli and being able to take control of a part of my life that is spinning dizzily out of orbit, at least I don't feel like a hypocrite. Despite all my fears of inability or unwillingness to put into practice in my own life what I preach to my clients, I did not play "ostrich." I'm not now in denial about the deterioration of my marriage and I am not trying to run from the consequences. Okay, I'm not convinced that I'm seeing the right analyst for me, but I knew I couldn't go it alone; I did need to talk to a professional.

I've learned a lot from the events of the past few weeks. I've learned that my clients are grateful for my presence in their lives and the ongoing counseling I can provide them. I've learned that my children, particularly Molly, are strong kids even though they've been blindsided and betrayed by one of their parents. Molly was right: she *should be* allowed to be very angry at her father. What I won't allow her to do, however, is to become self-destructive. Thanks to Faith and Sylvia Plath, my daughter is coming into her own; though I was thrilled to hear from Molly's lips that she believes I've been a good mom . . . because there have been plenty of occasions over the years—*particularly* where Molly has been concerned—that I've had my doubts! And I've learned that I can in fact take control of my life (or begin to pick up the pieces), even after the worst has happened. And . . . as I type this, I have to acknowledge that Eli's departure is not the absolute worst thing that could happen. I have my health; my children have theirs. And so do my parents. We all have roofs over our heads and enough to eat. My children are being afforded the best that our educational system has to offer. We live in a society that (on paper, anyway) permits us to express ourselves freely. And every day I am privileged to spend time in the company of strong, fascinating women who broaden my own horizons.

So maybe Mala Sonia was right when she "predicted" that I would be able to slog through the hell of my disintegrating marriage with the support of my women friends. Although my laundry room clients are hesitant to cross the boundaries between our professional and our personal relationships, I am keenly aware of their . . . well, their love, I guess. Without expressing it in so many words, they've let me know that they're here if I need them. They are *my* safety net.

RINSE

19

ALICE

"I apologize for being totally bleary-eyed," Alice said, ensconcing herself in a corner of the couch. "When Gram started getting really affected by her Alzheimer's, she used to tell me that there were ghosts who lived on her air conditioner outside her bedroom window and they would moan and knock against the window next to it trying to get into the apartment to steal her soul. I had *no* idea what she was talking about; just that what she kept telling me was both deeply disturbing and deeply disturbed. I mean, *ghosts?* C'mon! But then I gave Izzy my bedroom and moved my stuff into Gram's room—the role-playing you had me do way-back-when really enabled me to finally categorize and chronicle and clean up Gram's things. I had no choice when it was clear that Izzy wasn't just going to be a houseguest for a week or two. So I moved into Gram's room. It has a very odd shape; there's really only one wall where you can put a queen-sized bed without turning the rest of the room into an obstacle course. So my bed had to go right near the window. And I've recently figured out who the 'ghosts' are." I waited for the other shoe to drop. "Pigeons! Every morning, the same damn pigeon alights on the air conditioner and begins cooing. I swear to God, it's like the urban version of a cock crowing in the morning. And now that I'm no longer working an office job, I really have no need to get out of bed at seven A.M. But he's there, like clockwork—except for *this* morning, when he decided to put in an appearance at 4:17. Do you have any idea how *loud* a single male pigeon's mating call is? It's like a low gargle that becomes increasingly higher pitched the longer they sustain it. And it's making me *crazy!* I dive under the pillow. I yank the covers over my head. And I can still hear this fucking pigeon just as loud. It's like a torture out of Edgar Allan Poe! I get up and bang on the window, but these birds have chutzpah. It doesn't scare them; they just look at me as though they're fully justified to invade my sleep and camp out on my windowsill; it's like they're saying, 'You lookin' at *me?*'

"Back when Stevo was around—oh, sorry, I probably shouldn't have brought up his name. If I hit a nerve, I really apologize for that."

"I'll be all right," I assured her, "this isn't my therapy session."

"But still, I feel like shit for even unintentionally raising the subject. Are you sure?"

"I'm sure." I put on my resilient face. "Scout's honor."

"All right . . . well, I'd complained to Stevo about the pigeons and asked what he could do about it. Naturally, he did nothing. He said he'd 'get to it,' but of course, he never did. I thought birds flew south for the winter, but I guess on the Upper West Side pigeons consider it a migration when they come down from 125th Street.

"They're having *sex* on my air conditioner too. The other morning there were three birds there, and I think they were going for a *ménage à trois oiseaux* or something. You should have heard all the noise, and feathers flying, and scrabbling of little pink pointy pigeon feet on the air conditioner . . . and the *noise* . . . I guess that's where we get the word 'squabbling.' I'm being awakened by fucking pigeons fucking! Dan thinks it's funny—"

"Oh-ho!" I grinned. "So how *is* your love life these days?"

Alice rolled her eyes. "A bit like one of those dreadful reality TV shows where they throw a bunch of people in a house and audiences are expected to get a kick out of watching them interact. It's been hard with Izzy there for so many months. Plus, we've had an infant there for the past couple of weeks, because all of Izzy's baby stuff was at my place, since none of us knew how long she'd end up living with me. So it was kind of a major prophylactic, actually," Alice added with a blush. "But . . . soon it'll be over," she sighed, "I mean having Izzy as a roommate. Moving day is Saturday. You saw how blown away Dominick was in the hospital when he got to hold Valentina?! He was weeping and going on and on so much about the miracle of birth, you'd think Izzy was the first woman ever to become a mother. Usually, when couples are having problems, they think having a baby will solve them, and it never does. It usually does the opposite, in fact, and creates even more problems. But Valentina's birth ended up being the clincher for Izzy and Dominick's reconciliation. You know they'd been talking about getting back together, and Izzy asked Dominick to read a whole stack of baby and pregnancy books, which, wonder of wonders, he really read. And he told Izzy that she was still a pain in the ass, but now he understood a bit more about the biology of the whole pregnancy-motherhood thing; and then again he realized he wasn't exactly God's gift to anything and sometimes he couldn't believe she'd stayed married to him for as long as she did—he was always running off with his motorcycle buddies and coming home—or not—at all hours—he really tested the limits of their relationship sometimes.

"So, now Izzy—and Valentina—are moving back home, and we can get all the baby stuff out of my living room. Dan's kind of thrilled about that, I have to say. In order to make room for the crib, we'd moved aside Gram's antique settee that he'd worked his ass off to restore, so now it will have pride of place again. He suggested that we celebrate by making love on it, but I'm not sure he's up—so to speak—for another major repair job: somehow I have a notion that it wasn't built for active nookie." Alice laughed. "We can always go the old-fashioned route in the bedroom and compete with the pigeons!"

"Sounds to me like you're getting your house in order in more ways than one," I said. "Now, what's up with your acting career these days? I remember you told me that the Actors Equity tribunal decided in your favor."

"Gosh, we're really wringing the most we can out of every one of my issues today! My head is spinning!" Alice adjusted her position on the sofa. "Right. The union sided with me, which, to be honest, I hadn't expected; but my happiness was kind of short-lived."

"What do you mean?"

She expelled a puff of air. "Well . . . I got to keep my job in *Grandma Finnegan's Wake*, but Bitsy Burton—I told you about her; she's the actress who originated the role I was playing—continued to make things pretty miserable for me. She also hired an intellectual property attorney and took the producers to court, claiming that she had rights in the development of the character of Fionulla Finnegan; and if she wasn't going to continue to play the role, she wanted financial compensation for her creative input during the production's developmental process. The producers got scared, looking at bad P.R. as well as huge legal bills, so they called me in and said they were going to have to let me go and let Bitsy play Fionulla from now on. They said it was their most viable option in terms of resolving their dispute with Bitsy. So I got canned, and we all agreed that I just wasn't appropriate for the other role Bitsy had been playing while I was doing Fionulla—the part of cousin Megan, the unsexy psychologist—sorry, again," she added, blushing and stealing a glance at my purely functional ensemble, if you could call my denim jumper and red cotton turtleneck an "ensemble."

"Still, I was really worried that the *Grandma Finnegan* producers would dispute my claim for unemployment benefits, and I would have to end up crawling back to my Uncle Earwax's law office. Well, his real name is Uncle Erwin, Erwin Balzer, but anyway, I would rather have slit my wrists than gone back to being a legal secretary—"

"Alice, don't even joke about suicide."

"I wouldn't *really* slit my wrists—you know that . . . ? Don't you? I was just . . . I was just indulging in hyperbole. Don't worry, I may be a bit neurotic, but I'm not mentally unstable. So, anyway, I came to the conclusion that since I'd gotten fired as an actress, I deserved to collect unemployment as an actress, and I should continue to look for acting jobs, as opposed to office jobs. I mean that's not who I am anymore. I AM A LEGITIMATELY UNEMPLOYED ACTRESS! YAHOO!" Alice yelled. "I AM *NOT* AN UNEMPLOYED LEGAL SECRETARY! I *do* see the humor in all of this, you realize, Susan. So I'm going out on as many auditions as I can, given that I still don't have an agent. Later today I'm going to send my head shot and résumé to the casting director at an advertising agency. They're doing an international ad campaign for a dust rag. Don't laugh! It's like the Swiffer. It's called 'Snatch.' "

"Isn't that a little, well, dirty?"

"Not in England, apparently, which is where they're launching the product. What's a snatch over here is a fanny over there. Which creates a whole *other* set of problems, linguistically speaking, when you think about it."

"Not that I don't want you to get the job, but why are they looking for an American to be the spokesperson for an English product?"

"I think they *want* people to get the dirty little joke. At least subliminally. The Brits seem to love that kind of humor."

"Well, break a leg at the mailbox!"

Alice grinned. "Thanks! Just don't tell me to break a . . . never mind!"

ME

"Welcome to No Problem. Table for five?" Meriel asked as Molly, Ian, Faith, her date—renowned jazz pianist Elijah Loving—and I entered William Robertson's Jamaican restaurant. It was a Saturday night early in March; after a blustery few weeks the weather was beginning to show signs that spring was indeed just around the corner and we could move the shearlings into storage.

Meriel had been playing hostess at her son's restaurant when she wasn't working for Amy and Eric. "So, how do you like my decorating?"

The walls were a bright lemon yellow, trimmed in black. Chic paper lanterns in Jamaica's official colors hung from the ceiling. Yellow and green madras plaid cloths graced the tables. "I want de red restaurant guide to call us 'casual and classy,' " Meriel told us. "William didn't see de need for de tablecloths, but I didn't want de place to look like a fast food restaurant or a cafeteria. So he listen to Mama because he know Mama's right. And you notice de music . . . ? De reggae not so loud daht people can't hear demselves talk." She seated us and told us that her son would come out from the kitchen to greet us as soon as he had the chance. I felt a bit sorry for them because it was prime time on a Saturday night and the place was doing only a modest business; it wasn't exactly hopping, as Meriel and William had hoped. The odds of success in the restaurant business are so iffy, and I really wanted them to have as good a shot at it as possible.

There appeared to be more trouble in paradise than I might have guessed. From where we sat, I could hear Meriel criticizing her son's recipes for having too little of this or too much of that or the portions not being large enough, or that they were too generous; she even found fault in his presentations. With few patrons to seat, she had nothing but time at her disposal, and she couldn't help entering the kitchen to "supervise." I watched her either moving or removing a garnish, or decorating a plate with little squiggles of sauce she squeezed out of unlabeled plastic bottles in order to give it "a dash of elegance." William, naturally, was not taking kindly to his mother's interference, and I felt sure that this night was just like all other nights of the year since he'd opened No Problem to the public.

Molly was trying to get a rise out the rest of us (just as she had done when she pierced her navel and subsequent body parts) by ordering the oxtail stew. She only picked at it when it arrived, which Meriel chalked up to the recipe not tasting exactly the way it really should. I wanted to tell her that there was probably nothing wrong with William's cooking; Molly was just finding that exiting her epicurean comfort zone was riskier than she'd thought, and that oxtail stew was no doubt a bit of an acquired taste for her palate. Faith raved about her jerk chicken entrée, although Meriel kept whispering in her ear that she wished William would use *her* recipe instead of insisting on cooking up his own.

Ian wanted to know if the dishes did "taste the way they were supposed to," and figured Elijah might provide the answer.

"I can't tell you, my man," Elijah said, shaking his head. "I grew up in North Carolina. Ask me anything you want about pulled pork but I'm no connoisseur of jerk chicken! I'm a pecan pie expert, not a black fruit cake one. I'll tell you this: it all sure tastes good to me!"

"Faith, your boyfriend rocks!" Molly whispered.

"So, how did you enjoy everyting?" Meriel asked graciously as we insisted on paying the check. If they'd been doing a land-office business I might have accepted their offer of a complimentary meal, but under the circumstances, it didn't seem like the right thing to do.

"Everything was delicious," I answered, speaking for the table.

"And we wish you and William all the luck in the world," Faith added.

Meriel looked around the room. Only four of the sixteen tables were occupied. "Tank you," she sighed, then leaned over the table and whispered, "I hate to tink we gonna need it!"

Progress Notes

Alice Finnegan: Since she first began her therapy with me, Alice has had to deal with so many major issues that occasionally I felt we were neglecting some of them, or giving them short shrift, because there just wasn't enough time within a given session to accord each issue an equal degree of attention. To Alice's immense credit, she has kept these plates spinning with remarkable dexterity, and has not allowed setbacks to paralyze her or send her into a panic. In times of crisis, she's resisted the urge to act-out or indulge in self-destructive behavior. With her career, especially, she allowed herself to be pushed way out of her comfort zone and took the calculated risk that she would be all right. Rather than revert to old (and damaging) behavior by returning to the safe and familiar (though toxic) territory of her uncle's law office after she lost her job in *Grandma Finnegan's Wake,* she accepted and embraced her unemployment situation, using it as an opportunity to grow her career as an actress. Taking in her friend Izzy as a roommate ended up being emotionally and mentally beneficial in ways that Alice had never imagined. Having a dear friend around all the time reminded Alice that she was still lovable and appreciated, even though her grandmother had passed away; and I believe Izzy's constant presence helped Alice avoid the loneliness and depression that can come with grieving. Izzy's presence also compelled Alice to slow down in her blossoming relationship with Dan Carpenter. Restrictions on privacy within her apartment had a way of ensuring that Alice didn't rush into anything. Her relationship with Dan had the chance to unfold on its own time, which gave it a more stable foundation, and also lessened Alice's chances of getting emotionally disappointed, or even hurt, by pushing for too much too soon. In future sessions we'll work toward solidifying her self-confidence and patience so that they become second nature and she isn't tempted to revert to old behavior now that she no longer has all those metaphorical plates in the air.

Me: *I* should take a leaf from Alice Finnegan's book. When the universe asked her to cope with so many big changes simultaneously, she discovered that she was able to navigate through them in an emotionally healthy way. If there's one thing I've learned over the years, in case after case, it's that we are much more resilient than we believe ourselves to be. I'm referring primarily, of course, to people like my laundry room ladies, not to people who are clinical—who require medication in order to stabilize the chemicals in their brains.

Something else I've been thinking about . . . the parent-child paradigm. No matter how old your child gets, you still think that as his or her parent you're still entitled to be the boss. William Robertson is in his thirties, and Meriel still wants to run the show, even in his place of business. William is still trying to please his mother while asserting his right to independence. Molly and Ian will be the same way, of course. And, Lord knows, my mother is the same way with me. Just because I'm considered an expert in the field of human behavior by virtue of my profession, it doesn't mean that the four of us are off the hook.

So, how do we keep the parent-child relationship healthy and stable, especially in the face of upheaval within the family: a death or a divorce?

Ask me again in a few months' time. I'm still learning.

FINAL SPIN

2⃝

MERIEL

"You are looking at a happy woman," Meriel announced when we next met. "I am going to give Mrs. Amy my two weeks' notice at de end of de day today."

"That's wonderful! Have you decided what you're going to do next?"

"You are looking at de proud new chef of No Problem Jamaican restaurant in Flatbush, Brooklyn, New York!"

"Goodness! I thought you'd wanted to stay out of William's kitchen."

"You nevah know how tings might change. After we been open awhile and we see daht business is not getting bettah, we wonder why No Problem is not catching on; so we taste-tested all de recipes for de last month, his and mine, and people like my cooking bettah dahn William's. I told you he good, but Mama bettah!" She laughed. "So William see where de bread is buttered and he now going to be de owner-mahnager. He be greeting de customers in de front, and you know, he love people so much daht it's bettah for him to be out front and centah dan back in de kitchen hidden away. Wit' William out front and

Mama in de kitchen, he got a money-makah for sure! You be reading all about us soon in de red restaurant guidebooks. Next week on Sahturday night is de grand reopening, and I want to invite you and de children to be our guests. I tink even Mrs. Amy and Mr. Eric might want to come. And you tell Mrs. Faith daht we gonna have more jerk chicken on de menu dahn she can carry in a wheelbarrow, so she come along too! And tell her to bring her handsome boyfriend."

"I'm going to miss you as a client," I told her. "You're a very special lady."

Meriel laughed at me. "Oh, don't tink you gonna get rid of me so fast. I might need to talk to a specialist from time to time, you know, and just because dey might be terapists a little bit closer to home, don't mean dey as good as *you*."

ME

We were now nearly a month into spring and I had thought it would be lovely to gather together all of my laundry room clients for some sort of celebration. They had come so far over the past several months, and in doing so, had brought tremendous value to my life when it seemed to be going the way of Stevo's washing machines.

The Passover seder was Amy's idea, actually. "Do you have anywhere to go for the seders?" she asked me. "It's such a family ritual, as well as a communal one; you shouldn't be alone."

"Well, the kids and I were planning to do a mini-seder on the first night. They've been through it so often that it's no longer as much fun for them, even though they do enjoy the ritualistic aspects of the celebration. That's the sort of stuff that makes all of us feel warm and fuzzy and grateful to be alive to see another year; and that God willing, we still live in a country where Jews have the freedom to openly worship. But Molly and Ian have always kind of liked to fast-forward through all the prayers and the parables and get to the dinner as quickly as possible. You know, Four Questions, Four Sons, get through the juicy stuff about Joseph and Pharaoh and the ten plagues, sing 'Dayenu,' and then hurry up and part the Red Sea so we can eat!"

"That's more or less the right order." Amy laughed. "So you don't do it in Hebrew, I take it."

"None of us know any," I confessed. "As I once told Alice, we Lederers are 'Christmas tree Jews.' We're pretty assimilated. Does phonetically reading the transliterations count? Ian's very good at that."

"I guess there's two camps," Amy chuckled. "The speed-reading 'Fed Ex commercial' version, and the one that seems to do its best to mimic those forty years in the Sinai. In our family, the seders go on forever. We do Hebrew, English, then everybody's kid gets to read the Four Questions—it's democratic, but interminable—and every branch of the family knows their own version of the songs, plus a few new ones every year. By the time you get to the macaroons and 'Chad Gad Ya'—you remember, the story of the goat who was bought for two zuzim—you really know why they say that Jews understand the concept of suffering better than most any other group. Although, I'm telling you, I can't wait until Isaac is old enough to recite the Four Questions, so I can get my revenge on my smug sisters who are so proud of their little Shoshie and Ben and Dinah and Jordan!!"

She'd made me laugh. "I'm not entirely sure that using your young son as an instrument of revenge upon your sisters, nieces, and nephews, is a healthy desire, you know!"

"Okay, then. Pretend I was making a joke. That said," Amy added, "why don't you invite all of your laundry ladies to celebrate the second seder with you? After all, with the subject of our freedom from the bondage of slavery, Passover is about rebirth and renewal, in a way. We should make it a women-only feast night, if that's all right with everyone. I'll be your first RSVP. In fact, I'll even leave Isaac with my mother. Or let Eric take him to *his* mother's house." Amy clapped her hands with a schoolgirl's gleeful enthusiasm. "Oh, my *God*, it feels good to *organize* something again!"

She thought it would be more fun if the seder was conducted in the laundry room, instead of up in my apartment, and suggested that in order to make it even easier on me, each guest could be responsible for one of the dishes: a Passover potluck. Everyone would need to bring a chair, since there were only two or three of them that "lived" in the laundry room, and the couch was too low to be a viable option, although, as Amy pointed out, it would certainly give a couple of us the chance to "*really* recline at the table."

Amy also insisted that I be the one to lead the seder, despite my comparative lack of experience and education when it came to my own cultural heritage. "You know much more about this than I do," I protested. "Eli was always the leader in our house, and even then, it was a pretty truncated version of the celebration. I told you, we more or less skimmed the Haggadah."

"Excuse me," Amy said, hands on her hips, "but I have a therapist who is always encouraging her clients—gently but forcefully, if that's possible, but you know what I mean—to get outside their 'comfort zones' and take risks. And hey," she added, softening and draping one arm over my shoulder, "we're all here to catch you if you fall."

So late in the afternoon before the second seder, Faith used her shopping cart to schlep her mother's antique silver flatware and damask table linens into the laundry room. With the skill and efficiency of Emily Post, she set out place settings for ten on the long table in the center of the room. I noticed that she was no longer wearing her wedding ring. Faith apologized for buying gefilte fish instead of making the appetizer from scratch, but I assured her that I would have done the same thing.

Amy made sure that plenty of the traditional kosher wine had been chilled, but had also purchased a more sophisticated alternative—although I happen to love the popsicle-sweet and sweetly nostalgic Manischewitz. It's "comfort booze." Amy had also made a trip to the local bookstore and bought an edition of the Passover Haggadah that presented the story of the Israelites' exodus from Egypt in a way that our multicultural guest list would surely enjoy. It contained concise and entertaining explanations of the traditions, included sheet music with all of the songs, and was peppered with famous authors' pithy quotes about freedom. She'd also purchased the matzoh and provided the silver goblet to be used as Elijah's cup. The cup would be filled at the beginning of the meal and remain on the table as an offering to the Old Testament prophet, who, according to Passover tradition, paid a symbolic postmeal visit to every Jewish home. Molly wondered aloud, and with some asperity, whether he'd know to find us in the basement.

I took charge of the key items on the menu, roasting the turkey with my mother's matzoh stuffing recipe and creating all the emblematic fixings for the seder plate that would rest on the center of the table—the roasted egg, bitter herbs, and so forth, with the exception of the roasted lamb shankbone, which Meriel offered to provide. Molly was in school that day, so I had to assume her responsibilities as well. She's always loved to chop the apples and nuts for the *charoses*, which represents the mortar the Israelite slaves used in the building of the pharaohs' pyramids. She also enjoys taking out her frustrations on the chopped liver, which makes a good hors d'oeuvre on matzoh crackers.

Alice cooked two of her Gram's favorite recipes: chicken soup with matzoh balls, and stewed carrot and prune *tsimmes*, which is so sweet for a vegetable dish that it's almost like cheating.

Once Talia heard that there was going to be music as part of the seder meal, she schlepped her portable synthesizer down to the laundry room. She was walking on her own now. In fact, she was so anxious to show me how well she had healed that she began doing *fouettés*. "Look Ma, no popping!" she crowed ecstatically each time she whipped her bum knee off her pirouettes.

"Macaroons are pretty big in Italian households too," Naomi said, arranging the contents of an enormous cookie tin on a lovely red lacquer tray. "Claude and I made these from scratch, though. It's just egg whites and coconut; no flour. We know the Passover rules. It's hard to grow up in New York City and not have at least one Jewish friend! When Claude and I first got together, we used to go to separate seders because we each had our own circle of friends, of course. And, you know, one thing I love about this city is that no one looks at a Chinese woman funny when she's standing around with a group of people talking about where they're spending Passover and she says she's going up to a friend's house in Westchester for the seder. Or when a woman whose last name is Sciorra says she's headed out to Long Island to be with her Jewish friends."

Knowing that we had two-thirds of a book to read before we'd get around to the meal, I set the dinner hour for six P.M., figuring we'd first enjoy some hors d'oeuvres (gefilte fish and chopped liver on matzoh crackers) to tide us over.

Meriel arrived carrying a casserole and was cordially greeted by Amy, who had hired a young Irish woman named Siobhan to replace her. There wasn't a trace of animosity between them, which really warmed my heart.

"Here is your shankbone, Mrs. Susan," she said, handing me a carefully wrapped package. "And for Mrs. Amy, I bring a present for Hector." She gave Amy a machine-knit dog sweater patterned after the Jamaican flag. "In de casserole is my curried goat. You said I should bring someting from *my* culture to de seder, and I find out from de Internet daht goat is kosher—in case someone observes de dietary laws tonight—and I don't want to insult anyone. Den I realize that some of de Jewish patriarchs in de Old Testament were goatherds and shepherds, so what else dey gonna eat?" Meriel placed the casserole on the side table.

Claude entered the laundry room carrying their new baby. "Oh, she's beautiful," I gasped.

"Meet Jin," she said. "That means 'gold' in Chinese. And our little girl is more precious than gold to us. Jin Sciorra-Chan, meet Susan." Jin immediately grasped my finger and brought it to her rosebud mouth.

I found myself whispering. I have no idea why women tend to do that around babies. "How old is she?"

"Seven months. She was born in the middle of October. She's a little Libra girl; a seeker of harmony. And well-balanced. So we're hoping she never needs therapy!"

"She was born in the year of the Rooster, though," Naomi added, "which is supposed to mean that she loves attention and spending a lot of money on clothing."

Claude gave their baby a kiss. "Is it okay if Jin sits on my lap during the seder? If she gets fussy, I'll just take her outside the room and walk her up and down by the elevator."

"Jin is very welcome," I assured her. "And it wouldn't be the first time a seder participant wasn't shy about exhibiting her short attention span!"

"Hey, you guys! Is there room at the inn for one more? Oops, wrong holiday." Izzy poked her head in the door. "It's one of Valentina's first times out since we came home from the hospital, but we wouldn't have missed this for the world. Don't worry, she doesn't eat much," Izzy joked. "I wish she would, though. Are there any rules about breast-feeding at the seder table?"

"I don't know whether to think that's cool or gross," Molly said.

Claude rushed over to introduce them to Jin. "Seven months," I heard her tell Izzy.

"Two," Izzy replied, gazing lovingly at her infant daughter. "We don't have the world's longest attention span, though, Susan; it's one of the things we got from our daddy," she added, shrugging. "But what're ya gonna do? So if she gets antsy—"

"That's funny," Claude told her, "*we* just went through the same little speech." She lifted Jin above her head and made her go *"Zoom!"* back into her arms. Jin was in raptures. I can't remember when I'd seen a little kid so animated. She absolutely glowed. Her infectious giggle and radiant smile would melt the polar ice cap.

"She loves playing 'airplane,' " Claude said. "Probably because she spent so many hours on one in order to get here. She can do this interminably. *I* get tired long before she does."

"Good thing she's got another mommy to take over! Here; my turn." Naomi reached for their daughter.

As soon as Alice arrived downstairs, her cell phone rang. "Oh, God, you guys, I am so sorry," she exclaimed. "This is horribly rude. We shouldn't be talking on our cell phones during the seder. But I've been waiting for a call all day. Hello?"

"Don't worry, the seder hasn't officially started yet," I said.

"Ohmigod! Ohmi*god! Ohmigod!*" Alice yelled into the phone. "Wait, I can't hear you." She dashed out of the room like a circus clown shot out of a cannon.

"Gee, do you think it's good news?" I asked the other women.

A few moments later Alice returned to the laundry room. She was so excited that her entire body was trembling. "Well, don't keep us all in suspense!"

She whispered something in Izzy's ear, received an "Ohmigod!!" from her, and then murmured something to her friend about "saving it" until we got to the part of the Passover seder where the first of the Four Questions is asked: *Why is this night different from all other nights of the year?*

"Well, in that case," I said, "since I'm eager to hear your news—shall we all be seated?"

Amy immediately realized that she'd forgotten something, apologized profusely, and ran back up to her apartment, returning with a graceful goblet, a more feminine version of the Elijah's cup she'd already provided.

"Is that a Miriam's cup?" Naomi asked. Amy nodded, impressed that Naomi had heard of one. Naomi shrugged. "I've been to a lot of feminist seders."

Faith looked intrigued. "What is a Miriam's cup?"

Amy explained its significance. "It's not part of the old tradition; there's nothing in the Haggadah—those books in front of you that tell the story of Passover. Naomi's right about the 'feminist' influence, though. It's a 'new tradition,' if that's not an oxymoron, that began a few decades ago, and it's meant to kind of accord equal time to the women who are the ones who prepared the seder meal and who, through times of trouble as well as those of prosperity, hold the family together. It honors the contribution of our foremothers, biblically and in real life, and is a toast to our own ongoing contributions as well."

"I really liked what you said about it being the women who hold the family together in the bad times as well as the good ones," Molly said, using Faith's mother's damask napkin to dab her eye. "I know it's a little *Fiddler on the Roof*-y, but that is *so* true!"

"Where are the fathers and sons tonight?" Faith wanted to know.

"My William be back in de kitchen. One night only! I tell him. Just like de song. I be back tomorrow so don't chase away de clientele!"

"Ian went to his best friend's house for the second seder," I said. "Talk about show tunes—the kid's father is a Broadway composer, and he's written original music for all the old Passover songs."

"That's *so* Upper West Side," Alice quipped.

Izzy clapped her hand to her heart. "Can you imagine! I bet the meal is practically like an audition. I wonder if you can get rejected from a seder."

"I have to say, before we officially get started, that I love the fact that we are doing this," Faith said. "I haven't been a member of a sorority in several decades, so it's been a long time since I spent an evening in the company of so many women, but I'm suddenly reminded this evening that something wonderful happens when women come together. There's strength and power and beauty and mystery—in our diversity as well as in our common bonds—and when we gather specifically to celebrate a religious ritual or tradition, to me that power is expanded multifold. It is, as I suppose Molly would say, although we don't quite mean it in exactly the same way: 'awesome.' "

"That's a beautiful way to begin the seder, Faith," I said. "I'm very touched by your words." There were murmurs of assent from the rest of the table. "And since I have zero experience in leading one of these celebrations, I'm giving everyone fair warning: it may all be downhill from here."

"Don't men usually lead seders?" Talia asked me.

"It's the custom for the head of the household to lead it," Amy said. "And the people who devised that tradition assumed it would be a man, as it once was, and often still is. My father still leads our family seders. And Susan told me that Eli used to until . . . until he decided that he no longer wished to be the head of their household. Which—" Amy said, extending her arm as though she were presenting me to an audience, "gives Susan full and proper license to conduct her seder. Our seder."

I asked my guests to open their Haggadah—it was Naomi who turned the book in Talia's hands, explaining that it's read back-to-front, like all Hebrew texts, even though our version was in English. I asked Alice to read the book's introduction, which explained the significance of the Passover seder.

" 'The story of the exodus of the Jews from Egypt is told and retold so that we give it meaning, context, and continuity for our children and our children's children,' " Alice read. "And isn't it cool," she added, departing from the text, "that we've got two of our 'daughters' here tonight for whom this is a totally new experience."

"Oh, God, you're making me cry. That's *so* unfair," Molly told her.

"You're making me cry too," said Izzy. "Now I've got Valentina's head all wet. The poor kid probably thinks it's raining."

The blessings over the fruit of the vine and the fruit of the earth were made, and all the emblems identified: the roasted shankbone, representing the sacrificial lamb; the *charoses*, for the mortar; bitter herbs for the bitter life of slavery endured by the Israelites under the pharaohs; a dish of saltwater to represent tears; the roasted egg, a symbol of life; and the unleavened matzoh—representing the bread of affliction.

And then it was time for the section of the Haggadah that is either every kid's worst nightmare or greatest chance to show off. Traditionally, the Four Questions—which openly ask what the whole seder ritual is all about and why the heck do we feast like this when we never do it on any other night of the year—are read (or chanted if the kid reads Hebrew and knows the tune) by the youngest son. Many modern Jews have reinterpreted the rules to mean "youngest child." As Amy had mentioned, *every* kid in her extended family got a shot at them. "Since neither Valentina nor Jin can read this year—"

"Just wait'll next year," Claude quipped.

We all laughed. "I'll expect her to know it in Hebrew too," I shot back. "Molly, it's all yours."

"I am *so* too old for this."

"You're the youngest child who can read. Get over it. One day, you'll have kids of your own and you'll wonder how you got 'old' so fast, and you'll miss being young enough to read the Four Questions."

"Are you really talking about *you*, Mom?"

"Read, kiddo. Your leader has spoken."

Molly sighed, then began the litany immediately recognized by Jews all over the world: "*Ma-nish ta-nah, ha-lai-lah ha-zeh?* Thank God for transliteration. Why is this night different from all other nights of the year?"

I help up my hand to stop her. "Okay. We'll pick up the rest of the questions and all the answers—at least the traditional answers—in a minute. We've all had a remarkable past several months, for better or for worse but one reason we're here this evening, beyond the significance of the seder, is to celebrate our achievements regarding the 'better,' and our ability to overcome the 'worst.' Now, I know that *Alice* has something to disclose that has made tonight different from all other nights of the year for *her*."

Alice beamed. "The phone call I was waiting for all day? That's the one I got just when I walked in the door. It was from the casting director at Seraphim Swallow Avanti. And . . . I booked the Snatch job!"

"What?" chorused Claude and Naomi.

"It's like Swiffer, only British. I'm going to England next week to shoot the commercials *and* the print ads! I'm going to be their Snatch Girl!" She received a hearty round of applause from the table.

"And you were worried I couldn't keep a secret for more than ten minutes," Izzy joked, leaning over to give her best friend a kiss on the cheek. "You go, girl!"

Alice looked at her watch. "It wasn't much *more* than ten minutes, you know! Anyway, that's why this night is different from all other nights of the year for me."

"Let's go around the table and give everyone a chance to do this," Molly suggested. I liked the idea and asked Meriel if there was something that made this night different for her.

"Oh, I had no idea daht we were going to do someting layk dis," she said, a bit flustered. "I need to get my purse, first. Let someone else go ahead of me."

Claude and Naomi agreed that the presence of their daughter Jin, especially after such a protracted and contentious adoption process, made the night special. Izzy referred to Valentina's presence, then added that although it hadn't happened that evening, her complete reconciliation with her husband Dominick was "nothing short of a minor miracle, all things considered. Not only that . . . I have something I want to ask my pal here . . . because Dominick and I are finally beginning to get our act together to plan Valentina's baptism." Turning to Alice, she asked, "Will you be Valentina's godmother?" By way of a reply, Alice burst into tears.

"Okay, I'm ready now," Meriel said, taking a newspaper clipping from her handbag. She unfolded the paper and announced, "Dis is just from de local Brooklyn paper—it's not de *New York Times*—but listen to dis: 'A newcomer to Flatbush, No Problem, run by de mother-son team of Meriel Delacour and William Robertson, wit' Roberston out front and "Mama in de kitchen," offers authentic and delicious Jamaican fare in a casual, yet classy setting. You cahn't go wrong no matter what you order, but don't be too chicken to try de curried goat and de oxtail stew, and deyr jerk chicken is a standout.' " Faith raised her wineglass to her. " 'For dessert, we recommend de black fruit cake, a dense confection daht will stick to your ribs, and if you're too young to imbibe one of de Jamaican beers on de menu, order de sorrel, a spicy-sweet beverage similar to ginger beer. For two dollars more, de proprietors will also spike de sorrel wit' a shot of rum. Reservations are getting hard to come by, so book well in advance if you want to hear de cheery words "No Problem" when you get dehm on the phone.' "

"A toast to Meriel!" Faith proposed, and we all raised our glasses.

"Bravissima, Meriel," Amy said. "I may have to start saying 'I knew you when!' "

As Meriel carefully restored her precious rave review to her handbag, I asked Amy what made this night different for her from all other nights of the year.

She laughed. "On all other nights of the year," she began, echoing the next sentence of the Haggadah's Four Questions, "my husband Eric is working late and leaving me the entire responsibility of taking care of our son Isaac. But on this night he has taken our son to his mother's house for the seder without ever giving me a single word of complaint about it. He took Isaac's extra didies and his bottle and his four favorite squishy toys—Isaac's toys, not Eric's—and headed across town without once fussing about wearing an Armani suit and tie while juggling a squirming baby and a huge quilted diaper bag with pictures of Grover all over it."

We toasted Amy and I turned to Talia.

"Can I dance it?" she asked.

The guests exchanged glances. "Why not?" I replied.

Talia rose and began to twirl about the room in her flowing chiffon tunic and skirt. "Well, I said I was never going to teach dance, because of that whole 'those who can't *do*' adage—y'know? It's not like I'm quitting dance—believe me, they're going to have to carry me off the State Theater's stage in a wheelbarrow—but I have a friend who runs a community center in Spanish Harlem, up near Mount Sinai Hospital. So I'm going to teach dance classes part-time in the afternoons at the community center; and once a week, I'll conduct a class in the hospital's pediatric orthopedic wards. I'll be working with kids who are recovering from an operation, teaching them dance moves and exercises that they can use in their rehab. Twice a year, my fully recovered kids are going to return to the hospital to give a dance concert for the kids who are recuperating at the time. I haven't started yet; we just settled the details today. It's not about the money, obviously. Susan knows what I mean when I say I'm being the ant and not the grasshopper. And I'm really looking forward to giving back, as they say."

"Hooray for you!" Izzy exclaimed. Valentina began to fret. "Oops. I think I just woke her up. Does being a mother ever teach you to be less loud?" she asked the table.

I grinned and looked at Molly. "Just the opposite, I'm afraid. A lot of the time, anyway." Molly gave me a dirty look and I decided to disengage and offer Faith the chance to tell us what made this night different from all other nights of the year for her.

"Oh . . . I'm not ready to say anything yet. I mean this night *is* different from all other nights of the year for me, but we're having such a beautiful celebration . . . I don't want to ruin everyone's appetite after we've all worked so hard to make such a special meal . . ."

Her words spread a pall over the entire room. Given Faith's age, although illness can strike anyone at any time, I feared the worst. I leaned over and whispered, "You're not . . . sick . . . or anything, are you?"

"Oh, no, I've never been better," Faith assured me. "But you know me . . . one toe in at a time; baby steps. I'm just not ready to share my news yet. I'll do it after dinner; I promise."

"Then it's my turn," Molly said. By this time she was unable to suppress her gloating.

"Molly, I've known you all your life. And I have a feeling you orchestrated this entire share-fest because you had something to announce."

"O-*kay*, o-*kay*. You're right, Mom. As always. No, not as *always*. As *often*. You were too busy cooking today to go downstairs to the mailbox, so I picked up the mail when I got home. And as everyone with a child who applied to college knows, the colleges mail out the regular decision letters on April fifteenth. Which means that any day after that, there might be a little present in the mailbox. A nice fat one or a depressing thin one. And, Mom, you'll be happy to know that your daughter is not a total slacker, goof-off, fuck-up, failure . . ."

And before I had the chance to interrupt with, "I never said you were," Molly added . . .

"She is going to be a Bennington freshman in September."

"Aaaaaaaaaaccghhh!" I jumped up from my chair to embrace her, knocking over my red wine in the process.

"Don't worry," Faith said, catching my look of horror. "Believe it or not, the tablecloth is machine-washable."

"Molly, I am so proud of you! Congratulations, sweetheart!"

Molly grinned. "Thought I might not be able to pull it off, didn't you?"

"I always knew you could do it, once you applied yourself."

"And I owe a big debt of thanks to Faith," Molly said, breaking our embrace to give Faith a hug as well. "You and Sylvia Plath. She'll never know she saved my life."

"That's a bit of hyperbole, don't you think?" Faith asked jovially.

"I'm going to become a creative writer; I'm allowed to indulge in hyperbole."

Molly received her props from the table and insisted it was now *my* turn.

"My daughter got accepted to college today. That's enough to make this night different from all other nights of the year. And I am surrounded by an amazing group of women who, particularly over the past several weeks, have supported me and been patient with me and have absolutely changed my life for the better. Knowing each one of you is a gift to my soul."

"Awwwwwwwwwwwwhhhhh," they chorused.

"Now! People always complain that the seders drag on forever, so I think we should get back to the Haggadah."

Molly finished the Four Questions and I hid the afikomen, the portion of the matzoh that would be ransomed after the meal by the children at the table—meaning Molly again, as she was the only one who could walk. I didn't want to hide the afikomen anywhere else in the basement, so we played a bit fast and loose with tradition and the women covered their eyes while I concealed the contents of the turquoise linen napkin.

I called upon each of the women to take turns reading from the Haggadah, embodying the different personalities of the story's four sons who are taught the meaning of Passover. Faith was the wise son; Molly the belligerent, "wicked" one; Talia the doubter; and Izzy the utterly clueless one—a part I probably should have reserved for myself. "Thanks a whole lot!" Izzy said when I assigned her role.

"Don't worry; that's why it's called 'acting,'" Alice assured her with a chuckle.

When we got to the retelling of the Book of Exodus and the tyrannical Pharaoh who kicked Moses and company out of Egypt, Molly glanced at her watch. "They usually lock the laundry room at eight o'clock. Do you think that new super they hired will come in here like Pharaoh and kick us out of Egypt?"

"We're not making any noise," said Naomi. "Well—not *much* noise."

Claude nodded her head. "The door's already closed; I'm sure we're not disturbing anyone."

"Oh my God," Alice gasped. Nine adult heads turned to stare at her. "I just remembered something! Susan, you're my witness. Remember when Mala Sonia gave me that reading all those months ago? She told me in chapter and verse all these horrible things that were going to happen with my acting career. And everything she said came true. Stuff fell apart almost exactly the way she predicted it would. But this is the kicker, get this: Mala Sonia did foretell that everything would turn out all right for me, but it was going to take time. She said I would finally find success—specifically in my acting career—during a holiday time when there would be joy and feasting." Alice opened her arms. "Well, I just got the call today to be the Snatch Girl and they're *paying* me to travel to England! And look!" she continued excitedly. "Here we are! If a seder isn't about feasting and celebration, what is?"

Amy winced. "Everything Mala Sonia said about my domestic situation panned out too. But she told me that the outcome would involve much pain and cruelty."

"Perhaps it was wishful thinking," Alice quipped. "By the way, I don't hate you. I wanted to, though. I did hate Eric. But I'm long over that. And I envied you for a while—before I looked at the bigger picture from a lot of angles. Falling in love with Dan sure helped me get past it fast," she chuckled. "Good luck with Eric. I want to say 'you deserve him,' but you'll probably take it the wrong way."

"Or not," Amy shot back. "I wanted to hate you too. Sometimes I wondered whether Eric was ever thinking about you as 'the one that got away.' But in the long run, it really isn't helpful—or healthy—to live your life with your head in a negative place that might have nothing to do with the truth of the situation—anyone's situation. Am I right, Susan?"

I laughed. "Not bad; but don't quit your day job, Amy."

"Thanks. Thanks a whole hell of a lot!"

"Everything Mala Sonia told *me* came true too," I said, admitting this for the first time in front of all of them. "The bad and the good. She 'predicted' that I would be able to transcend and triumph over my personal adversity with the love and support of my women friends."

"Yeah, Mom, but you told me that you thought Mala Sonia was palming cards and manipulated your reading so she could confess her own crime in the only way she knew how. You've had the love and support of your women friends all along. Always. You just didn't think about it until now."

"Bingo, Molly!" Alice agreed. "You had the power to get back to Kansas all along," she lilted, in a dead-on imitation of Glinda the Good Witch.

"Now can we *puh-lease* get through the next twenty pages and the ten plagues so we can eat? I'm starving over here."

Molly grabbed her Haggadah and, picking up where we had left off, began to read aloud.

The meal itself was a huge hit. Of course there was a bit of running around involved, because there was no way to keep everything warm down in the laundry room, though Naomi joked that we could have locked the food in Tupperware and sent it to spin on the dryers' "low" cycle. So Alice had to dash back to her apartment to fetch the soup and *tsimmes*, and Molly and I had to head up to our place to fetch the turkey and its fixings. "It's all right; we're working off the calories as we eat. A very effective exercise regimen," I posited.

After dinner, Molly had to find the hidden afikomen or by tradition the seder couldn't continue and—nontraditionally— no one would get dessert. It took her all of about five seconds to locate it.

"You are so predictable, Ma," she said, as she carefully lifted the turquoise napkin out of the well of the only working washing machine. By tradition she also got to ransom it from the seder leader, and was angling for big-ticket items, like her own car while she was up at college.

"Dream on. *I* don't even have a car, Molly. How 'bout a bookstore gift certificate? You can buy more Sylvia Plath."

The offer was accepted and the meal resumed, with much happy munching of Claude and Naomi's homemade macaroons. We took up our Haggadahs once again and read on. When it came time to welcome the visit of the prophet Elijah, Talia seated herself at her synthesizer and began to sight-read the song that accompanies his welcome. We gathered around her and tried to sing along. It was a simple melody; we had it down in no time. Proud of our accomplishment, we began to get a bit carried away—as in *loud*—and were so vocal that we barely heard a knocking at the door.

"I'll get it," Molly volunteered. She opened the door and stood there, somewhere between shocked and bemused. "Ma?! Elijah's here."

"Of course he is, honey. It says right here in the text, 'A participant opens the door for Elijah.' " As a sidebar, seder participants are supposed to drink four cups of wine over the course of the ritual, so suffice it to say, now that the evening was winding down, I was more than somewhat loopy.

"No, Mom, I mean *really* Elijah. *Faith's* Elijah."

The entire room went silent. I had to admit, the timely appearance of Elijah was pretty eerie. When was the last time a prophet showed up on cue at *your* house?

"There's a man in our midst," Claude whispered.

"I'm interrupting. I'm so sorry," Elijah apologized. "Faith told me to come over at nine o'clock. She thought the festivities would be over by now. If you give me the key, sweetheart, I can wait upstairs."

"Sweetheart," Izzy murmured, as though the word was a juicy secret.

"If it's all right with Susan, I'd like to invite you in, Elijah," Faith said.

I waved him over to the table. "C'mon. Have a macaroon. And some wine. I guess . . ." I said, handing him the silver Elijah's Cup, "I guess this goblet has your name on it."

Faith linked her arm through Elijah's. "This is my 'why is this night different' news. I didn't want to say anything during the meal because I was afraid I'd depress people. After all, I've lived in this building a long time. I'm even older than those washing machines," she added, to much laughter. "Elijah asked me today if I would do him the honor of moving in with him. Now, I'm an old-fashioned girl, and at first I thought I deserved a ring with that proposal, but I can't see myself getting married again at this stage in my life. And besides, Susan is always encouraging us to take risks and try something new. I'm sure the landlord will be delirious when he learns that a rent-controlled apartment will be up for grabs, but I am looking forward to pottering around my new garden in Brooklyn Heights."

"You're moving to Brooklyn!" Meriel exclaimed. "We'll be neighbors almost."

"Yes . . . next year I'll almost be able to *walk* to the West Indian Day parade."

"Oh my goodness," I said, beginning to cry. "You really *are* moving on."

Faith handed me her handkerchief. "I'll visit often," she promised. I still have my opera subscription and I don't think the Met will be moving to Brooklyn anytime soon."

"I'm so happy for you," I sniffled. "But sad for me. It's always hard when a therapist has to say good-bye to a client. But it's even harder when she has to say good-bye to a treasured friend."

"You're making *me* cry," Elijah gently kidded. "I'm sure you'll agree, Susan, that I've got me one unusual lady."

"Unusual? Is that a compliment?" Faith wanted to know. "Elijah was planning to take me out for some champagne. Dashing out in the middle of a dinner party goes against everything I was raised to do, but I don't want to keep him waiting much longer . . ."

"We're staying to help clear the table, Faith," said Elijah decisively. "The champagne'll chill."

Everyone pitched in. But after such a joyous meal, the mood in the laundry room had turned bittersweet.

"This is going to be my hardest Passover ever," Molly said, going over to congratulate Faith. "Mom, you thought it would be hard to give up pizza and pasta for a week, but now we've got to give up Faith too."

Faith draped her violet-clad arm over my daughter's shoulder. "Molly, in this life, you'll learn that things change—sometimes for the better, and sometimes not—and people you care about come and go and grow and move away. Life is as mutable as the water that comprises the lion's share of our bodies."

"Okay, yeah, I get that," Molly nodded, "but it still doesn't change what we're talking about."

"Oh, yes it does," said the older woman, eager for the last word on the subject. "Just because things will be a bit different from now on, it doesn't mean you have to lose Faith!"

Progress Notes

Me: Well, I waved good-bye to the moving van and to Faith in her yellow taxi this morning. Alice is off to England to talk dirty in a series of electromagnetic dust-rag commercials. In a couple of months I'll rent a car to drive Molly up to college, and when I return home, it will just be me and Ian, my Broadway baby. Over the past several months, I've lost a few clients and a husband. I finally found a more honest and solid relationship with my daughter, only to "lose" her to a four-year (I hope!) educational sojourn in Vermont. Believe me, I can see the irony in it; but this "loss" is everyone's gain.

And even though I may no longer be seeing a couple of my laundry room clients, they have all become my friends.

What about Eli? I still lose sleep at night worrying over whether I had given everything I could have to our marriage. I second-guess myself constantly. Our separation, and possible divorce, has not been easy on me. In my mind I try to revisit as many days as I can of our twenty-plus years as a couple, looking for clues to see if there's something I might have done better. Or differently. Or all over again. There are plenty of times when I look to blame Eli.

But if I were my own client, I would remind myself rather pointedly that agonizing over what I coulda-shoulda-mighta done so that my marriage didn't end up in the glass-half-empty column is an exercise that is not only futile, but self-destructive. There's a vast difference between emotional self-flagellation and how I would counsel myself to healthily explore the situation: through rational analysis, assessment, and awareness of what happened, why it happened, and whether it could have been avoided. And if Eli decides that he wants to come back, or not—and at this point it's looking more like "not"—I will be able to handle the situation with strength and self-confidence.

After all, isn't that exactly what Mala Sonia said I'd do?

It's one of my credos, both personally and professionally, that you have to be willing to take risks if you want to get close to someone. To risk love of any kind is to risk the pain that comes of loss. And it's the experience of both that makes us truly human.

But here's an interesting question: if you've lost someone close to you, but you've given them your all—showed them and shared with them the most vulnerable parts of yourself as well as your more resilient and tenacious sides, and they've been just as open with you—haven't you also *won* as well?

I guess it all comes out in the wash.

Want More?

Turn the page to enter
Avon's Little Black Book —

the dish, the scoop and the
cherry on top from
LESLIE CARROLL

Balletomane Magazine
Shaw's Giselle Gave Me the Wilis

It's always a treat to see a fine performance of *Giselle* but I would encourage anyone within a hundred miles of Manhattan to jeté, don't walk, to see a stunning debut in the role. New York City Ballet's Talia Shaw, back in the rosin after a crippling injury several months ago, imbues the fragile title character with a range of emotions that this writer has not seen since she saw Fonteyn dance the role decades ago. Just because I'm an octogenarian doesn't mean I'm in my dotage; Shaw is the real thing. To his credit, City Ballet's artistic director Peter Martins has increased Shaw's repertoire gradually so that she has had time to grow into the great roles. And as the young country girl jilted by her lover, Shaw truly shines, her emotional connection to the doomed Giselle right on point, capturing both the joy and exuberance of the early scenes and the elegiac wistfulness of the denouement.

Her technique and control have matured over the years as well: sprightly and bouncy when she needs to be, with flawless allegro work; and strong and supple as a reed, with one of the surest and most disciplined arabesques I have seen in years. Perfectly partnered by the always-elegant Damian Woetzel as a truly tormented Albrecht, Talia Shaw's performance is an experience not to be missed and one surely guaranteed to elevate this relatively unknown, homegrown American ballerina into the pantheon of great Giselles.

Lenore Hetter

The Little Red Restaurant Guide

New York City

Great Eats for $25 and under

NO PROBLEM
113 DeKalb Avenue
Brooklyn NY
718–555–5924

FOOD	AMBIENCE	SERVICE	PRICE
28	19	25	$25

Review

"A Jamaican vacation right in your own back yard," any local will tell you that reservations are a must at this hot new Caribbean entry, with "Mama"—the incomparable Meriel Delacour—in the kitchen. At No Problem, you'll savor all the Jamaican staples—curried goat, jerk chicken, and the moistest black fruit cake this side of Kingston, served in a cheery decor by a friendly, laid-back staff that won't set your wallet back.

The New York Sun-Tribune
Alice Finnegan and Dan Carpenter

Alice Finnegan, daughter of Frank and Leah Finnegan of
Boca Raton, and Dan Carpenter, son of the late Ronald Carpenter and Helen Carpenter Tavares of Saratoga Springs, have
announced their engagement. A September wedding is
planned.

The bride-to-be, who will keep her name, is a professional
actress. She has performed Off-Broadway, most recently in
the long-running interactive comedy *Grandma Finnegan's
Wake,* and is currently represented internationally in television
and print advertising as the "Snatch Girl."

Mr. Carpenter is a self-described "Mister Fixit" with a specialty in antique furniture restoration. He is also a folk gui-
tarist. His first CD, cut this past June, is titled *If You Were My
Lady* and features Ms. Finnegan on some of the background
vocals.

The couple "met cute" in the elevator of Ms. Finnegan's
apartment building. "He was carrying one of those little black
bags and I thought he was a doctor, especially when he said
he was paying a house call. Turns out, he was going to repair
his niece's Victorian dollhouse!"

Stage Business
The Actors Resource

Harry Potter Magic Comes to Broadway

The Great White Way will be transformed into Hogwarts when the long-awaited musical version of the first Harry Potter classic, *Harry Potter and the Sorcerer's Stone,* chugs into the Shubert Theater in November. Rumors have been buzzing for months about Brian Vinero's witty lyrics and solid book, which honors the tried-and-true source material while adding its own special brand of magic. J. K. Rowling is said to be over the moon about the way her blockbuster novel is being retooled for the stage. The talented Adam Guettel, the man with the strongest musical theatre pedigree in America, has written the charming and oh-so-singable score. Young Ian Lederer, a Broadway veteran at the tender age of twelve, who really captured hearts when he performed the title role in the workshop versions of HP, is set to star. Let's hope he can nab that Tony Award before his voice changes! For all you potential Hermiones, Snapes, and Dumbledores out there, turn to the Casting section for the AEA casting notice and breakdown.

Simi Sheward

American Beauty
Top Ten College Freshmen (and Women!)

This month, *American Beauty* honors the best and brightest of this year's crop of exiting college freshmen: students who've made a difference in the lives of the people around them.

Nineteen-year-old Molly Lederer's novel, *Confessions of an Overachieving Underachiever,* which chronicles life in the trenches amid the insanely competitive world of New York's private high schools and the high-stakes college admissions race, will be published by Avon Trade next fall. She's also just signed a six-figure deal for the motion picture rights to the book, "The first of many, I hope," she cheerfully avers. Molly completed her first year at Bennington as an English major. "They didn't have a Creative Writing major anymore when I applied, but after me, they changed their curriculum again." True, the Vermont college, better known for its free-thinking "fruits and nuts kind of students," as Molly calls them, has decided to bring back the Creative Writing major.

"When word got out that one of our freshmen had a publishing contract—and then a movie deal—based on a manuscript that was nurtured by her professors here at Bennington, well, there was such a flurry of e-mails asking us about our Creative Writing major that we were ashamed to admit we'd discontinued it," said Bennington provost Akia Summers. "Thanks to Molly, we're back on track."

A note to prospective Bennington Creative Writing students: get those college admissions applications in early!

Molly Lederer will be *American Beauty*'s student guest editor in the August issue. What does she think of this exciting assignment? "It's all so Sylvia Plath!"

Lion Lines
In Praise of Older Women

Faith Nesbit has made a sizable donation to the Butler Library in the name of her late husband, Columbia grad (class of '51) Dr. Ben Nesbit. Dr. Nesbit was a pioneer in the field of gastroenterology, but had a passion for "just about everything under the sun," according to his widow. "Ben loved history, the classics, baseball, Javanese puppet theatre, Italian cuisine, seventeenth-century Flemish architecture . . . it was hard for me to keep up with him!" Mrs. Nesbit said that she had thought of earmarking the money for a specific area of interest, but she felt that it would be better spent on a diverse range of subjects. "I think Ben would have been very pleased with my decision. He's up there somewhere, smiling."

New York Journal of Jurisprudence
Newter & Spade Presses First Amendment Suit and Wins

Newter & Spade, in a rare pro bono representation, has struck a blow for First Amendment rights. Romance novelist Casey Rabinowitz, who writes under the pseudonym Ciara Romero, was appearing at a Nassau County Barnes & Noble as part of the book tour for her current release, *And then He Kissed Me There,* when two police officers interrupted her reading and arrested her for public lewdness. Rabinowitz spent seventy-two hours in lockup before she was arraigned. Amy Wither-spoon, on behalf of Newter & Spade, brought suit in the Eastern District of New York, claiming that the defendant was well within her First Amendment rights to read passages aloud from her own work, " 'however purple and lurid they might be to some auditors'."

Federal District Court Judge Shera Goldberg ruled for the defendant, awarding fifty thousand dollars for defamation and monetary damages on the counterclaims.

Full decision will be published tomorrow.

Urban Parent
A Valentine to Nontraditional Moms

Lesbian moms speak out on everything from overcoming prejudices to icing cupcakes at three A.M.

"The most important thing a parent can give a kid is TLC," says Naomi Sciorra, who with Claude Chan, her life partner, adopted Jin, a Chinese baby girl last year. Claude agrees. "There are so many children out there, particularly children of color, or girls in China, for instance, who have been deemed by their own cultures as less than desirable. How can any reasonable person not find that appalling? Where's their humanity?"

Sciorra is adamant in stating her view that a loving home is "obviously preferable" to life in an orphanage, no matter the nationality, religion, race, or sexual orientation of the parents. "Where is it written that a man plus a woman of the same ethnicity as their child equals the perfect family?"

Claude laughed. "Yeah, think of the number of people who grew up in so-called 'normal' or 'mainstream' homes who are in therapy!"

Having spent a good deal of time with Chan and Sciorra, I can safely assure the naysayers that Jin is one very happy—and very lucky—little girl.

Erica Barth

Psychology Tomorrow
Clients Who Air Their Dirty Linen in More Ways than One

Susan Lederer is a Manhattan psychotherapist. Nothing unusual about that, especially on the Upper West Side, where there are probably more analysts per square inch of real estate than there are parking meters. What makes Lederer's practice so uncommon is that she devotes a significant part of her week to conducting free private therapy sessions in her pre-war apartment building's laundry room. Her patients, fellow tenants (and all women, as of this writing) have really cottoned to the idea. "My clients find the atmosphere relaxed and informal—though I wish we could do something about those gray walls—and the various scents of detergent and fabric softener seem to have a beneficial side effect. One of my women calls our sessions 'aromapsychotherapy.'"

Lederer's clients credit her unorthodox method with any number of outstanding breakthroughs in their emotional and psychological health and well-being. "I would have been mortified to walk into some office filled with ferns and a receptionist who wonders what my neuroses are and all that," said Faith Nesbit, who now commutes from Brooklyn to her weekly sessions with Lederer. "What can I say? I missed her energy. Or maybe I'm still crazy; I guess some people would say that a seventy-three-year-old woman who hops the D train at dawn to go all the way into Manhattan to talk about herself for fifty minutes is somewhat off her rocker. Susan is a very warm and loving person. Never, ever judgmental. I don't even know if she realizes what a treasure she is."

LESLIE CARROLL

Ron Rinaldi

Native New Yorker **LESLIE CARROLL** is also a professional actress, dramatist, and journalist. In addition to her contemporary fiction, she writes historical fiction under the pen name Amanda Elyot. Visit Leslie on the web at *www.tlt.com/authors/lesliecarroll.htm.*

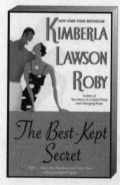